SHARKS, WHALES & DOLPHINS

A DK PUBLISHING BOOK

Project editors Marion Dent, Scott Steedman
Art editors Bob Gordon, Jill Plank, Jane Tetzlaff
Managing editor Gillian Denton
Managing art editor Julia Harris
Production Louise Barratt, Catherine Semark
Picture research Kathy Lockley,
Sarah Moule, Suzanne Williams
Consultants Dr. Peter Evans, Dr. Paul
Thompson, and Dr. Geoffrey Waller
Special thanks The University Marine Biological Station
(Scotland), Sea Life Centres (UK), Marineland (Antibes,
France), and Harderwijk Marine Mammal Park (Holland)

First American Edition, 1997
2 4 6 8 10 9 7 5 3 1

Published in the United States by
DK Publishing, Inc., 95 Madison Avenue
New York, New York 10016

Visit us on the World Wide Web at http://www.dk.com

Copyright © 1997 Dorling Kindersley Limited, London

ISBN 0-7894-2218-2

Reproduced in Singapore by Colourscan.
Printed in Singapore by Toppan.

Seal with layers
of fur to keep
it warm

Leaping killer
whale, or orca

EYEWITNESS ANTHOLOGIES

SHARKS, WHALES & DOLPHINS

Written by
DR. MIRANDA MACQUITY & VASSILI PAPASTAVROU

Photographed by
FRANK GREENAWAY

West Indian
manatee

Bottlenose dolphin

Model of a great
white shark

Male walrus

Elephant seal
skeleton

DK PUBLISHING, INC.

Contents

Starry smooth-hound

Introduction

This book has been designed to show the great diversity of life in the oceans and seas. The first section (pp. 6–43) concentrates on the various creatures that live near the surface of shallow water to deep within the sea and on the seabed. The second section (pp. 44–73) examines the lives of sharks from one so tiny it will fit into an adult's hand to the huge megamouth of which only six have been found to date. The third section (pp. 74–107) covers marine mammals, particulary whales, seals, and sea lions, dolphins and porpoises, walruses, and sea cows. The fourth and final section (pp. 108–125) looks at human exploration – of divers and submersibles, of fish harvests and ocean products – and why the oceans of the world are now in peril.

Flippers used in snorkeling and scuba diving

Blue-spotted ray

Juvenile dogfish

Barnacle-encrusted Roman jar

A tiger shark's jaw

Cross-section of a nautilus's shell

Common sun starfish

Oceans today

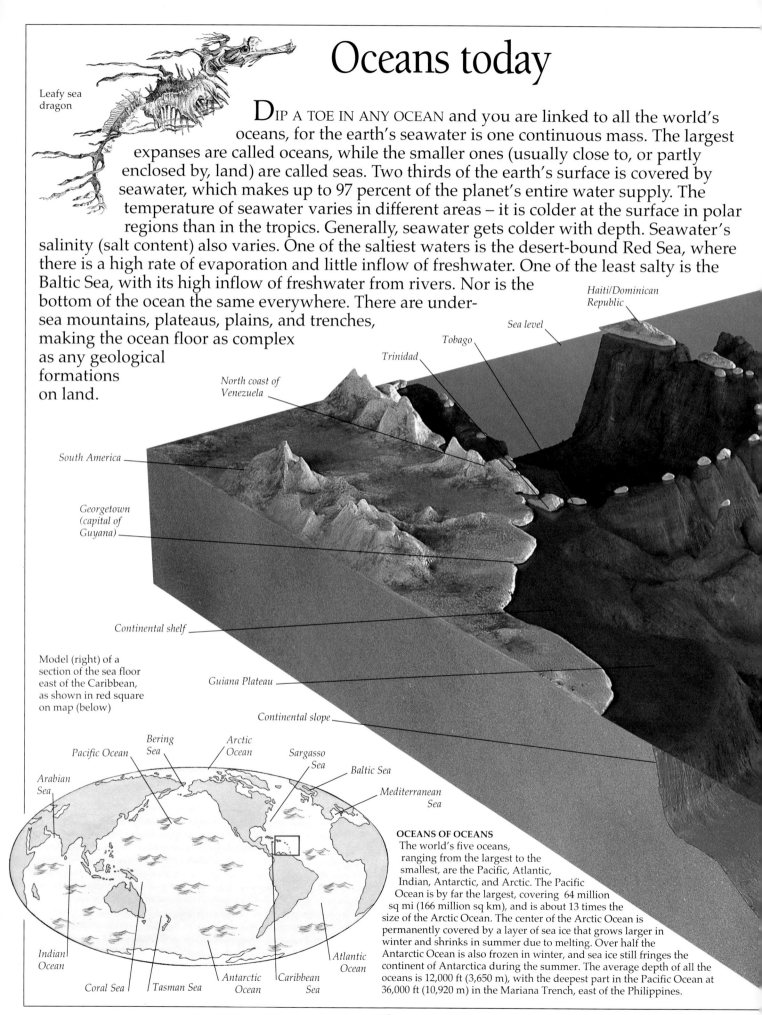

Leafy sea dragon

DIP A TOE IN ANY OCEAN and you are linked to all the world's oceans, for the earth's seawater is one continuous mass. The largest expanses are called oceans, while the smaller ones (usually close to, or partly enclosed by, land) are called seas. Two thirds of the earth's surface is covered by seawater, which makes up to 97 percent of the planet's entire water supply. The temperature of seawater varies in different areas – it is colder at the surface in polar regions than in the tropics. Generally, seawater gets colder with depth. Seawater's salinity (salt content) also varies. One of the saltiest waters is the desert-bound Red Sea, where there is a high rate of evaporation and little inflow of freshwater. One of the least salty is the Baltic Sea, with its high inflow of freshwater from rivers. Nor is the bottom of the ocean the same everywhere. There are undersea mountains, plateaus, plains, and trenches, making the ocean floor as complex as any geological formations on land.

Haiti/Dominican Republic

Sea level

Tobago

Trinidad

North coast of Venezuela

South America

Georgetown (capital of Guyana)

Continental shelf

Model (right) of a section of the sea floor east of the Caribbean, as shown in red square on map (below)

Guiana Plateau

Continental slope

Arctic Ocean

Bering Sea

Pacific Ocean

Sargasso Sea

Baltic Sea

Arabian Sea

Mediterranean Sea

Indian Ocean

Atlantic Ocean

Coral Sea

Tasman Sea

Antarctic Ocean

Caribbean Sea

OCEANS OF OCEANS
The world's five oceans, ranging from the largest to the smallest, are the Pacific, Atlantic, Indian, Antarctic, and Arctic. The Pacific Ocean is by far the largest, covering 64 million sq mi (166 million sq km), and is about 13 times the size of the Arctic Ocean. The center of the Arctic Ocean is permanently covered by a layer of sea ice that grows larger in winter and shrinks in summer due to melting. Over half the Antarctic Ocean is also frozen in winter, and sea ice still fringes the continent of Antarctica during the summer. The average depth of all the oceans is 12,000 ft (3,650 m), with the deepest part in the Pacific Ocean at 36,000 ft (10,920 m) in the Mariana Trench, east of the Philippines.

SEA OR LAKE?
The water in the Dead Sea is saltier than any ocean because the water that drains into it evaporates in the hot sun, leaving behind the salts. A body is more buoyant in such salty water, making it easier to float. The Dead Sea is a lake, not a sea, because it is completely surrounded by land. True seas are always connected to the ocean by a channel.

Floating on the
Dead Sea

GOD OF THE WATERS
Neptune, the Roman god of the sea, is usually shown riding a dolphin and carrying a trident (pronged spear). It was thought he controlled freshwater supplies, so offerings were made to him at the driest time of the year.

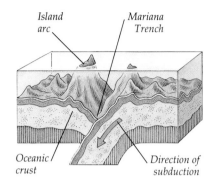

Island arc

Mariana Trench

Oceanic crust

Direction of subduction

Formation of Mariana Trench

DISAPPEARING ACT
The gigantic plates on the earth's crust move like a conveyor belt. As new areas of ocean floor form at spreading centers, old areas disappear into the molten heart of the planet. This diagram shows one oceanic plate being forced under another (subduction) in the Mariana Trench, creating an island arc.

Hatteras Abyssal Plain

Puerto Rico Trench

Nares Abyssal Plain

Mid-Atlantic Ridge

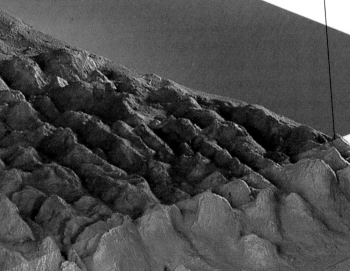

Kane fracture zone

Vema fracture zone

Demerara Abyssal Plain

THE OCEAN FLOOR
This model shows the features on the bottom of the Atlantic Ocean off the northeast coast of South America from Guyana to Venezuela. Off this coast is the continental shelf, a region of relatively shallow water about 660 ft (200 m) deep. Here the continental shelf is about 125 mi (200 km) wide, whereas that off the coast of northern Asia is as much as 1,000 mi (1,600 km) wide. At the outer edge of the continental shelf, the ocean floor drops away steeply to form the continental slope. Sediments eroded from the land and carried by rivers, such as the Orinoco, accumulate at the bottom of this continental slope. The ocean floor then opens out in virtually flat areas, known as abyssal plains, which are covered with a deep layer of soft sediments. The Puerto Rico Trench is formed where one of the earth's plates (the North American plate) is sliding past another (the Caribbean plate). An arc of volcanic islands have also been created where the North American plate is forced under the Caribbean plate. The fracture zones are offsets of the Mid-Atlantic Ridge.

Life in the oceans

FROM THE SEASHORE to the deepest depths, oceans are home to some of the most diverse life on earth. Animals live either on the seabed or in midwater, where they swim or float. Plants are only found in the sunlit zone, where there is enough light for growth. Animals are found at all depths of the oceans, though are most abundant in the sunlit zone, where food is plentiful. Not all free-swimming animals stay in one zone – the sperm whale dives to over 1,640 ft (500 m) to feed on squid, returning to the surface to breathe air. Some animals from cold, deep waters, such as the Greenland shark in the Atlantic, are also found in the cold surface waters of polar regions. Over 90 percent of all species dwell on the bottom. A single rock can be home to over ten major groups, such as corals, mollusks, and sponges. Most ocean animals and plants have their origins in the sea, but some, such as whales and sea grasses, are descended from ancestors that once lived on land.

Blood star

Common sun star

SHORE LIFE
Often found on the shore at low tide, starfish also live in deeper water. Sea life on the shore must either be tough enough to withstand drying out, or find shelter in rock pools. The toughest animals and plants live high on the shore. The least able to cope in air are found at the bottom.

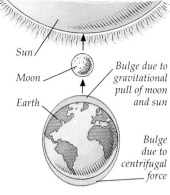

Sun
Moon
Earth
Bulge due to gravitational pull of moon and sun
Bulge due to centrifugal force

TIME AND TIDE
Anyone spending time at the beach or in an estuary will notice the tides. Tides are caused by the gravitational pull of the moon on the earth's mass of seawater. An equal and opposite bulge of water occurs on the side of the earth away from the moon, due to centrifugal force. As the earth spins on its axis, the bulges (high tides) usually occur twice a day in any one place. The highest and lowest tides occur when the moon and sun are in line, causing the greatest gravitational pull. These are the spring tides at new and full moon.

SQUISHY SQUID
Squid are among the most common animals living in the ocean. Like fish, they often swim around in schools for protection in numbers. Their torpedo-shaped bodies are streamlined so they can swim fast.

Inside squid's soft body is a horny, penlike shell

Tentacles reach out to grasp food

Deep-sea cat shark grows to only 20 in (50 cm) long

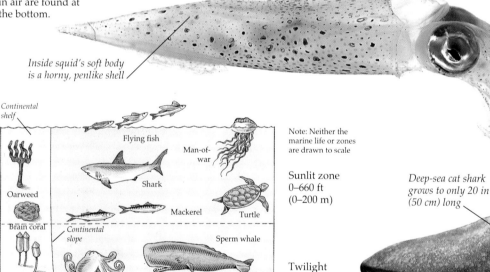

Continental shelf

Flying fish

Man-of-war

Oarweed

Shark

Mackerel

Turtle

Brain coral

Continental slope

Sperm whale

Sponges

Octopus

Hatchet fish

Sea pens

Rat-tail fish

Sea spider

Gulper eel

Anglerfish

Sea cucumbers

Brittle star

Abyssal plain

Flower-basket sponge

Tripod fish

Deep-sea anemone

Note: Neither the marine life or zones are drawn to scale

Sunlit zone
0–660 ft
(0–200 m)

Twilight zone
660–3,300 ft
(200–1,000 m)

Dark zone
3,300–13,200 ft
(1,000–4,000 m)

Abyss
13,200–19,800 ft
(4,000–6,000 m)

Trench
Over 19,800 ft
(6,000 m)

THE OCEAN'S ZONES
The ocean is divided up into broad zones, according to how far down sunlight penetrates and the water temperature. In the sunlit zone, there is plenty of light, much water movement, and seasonal changes in temperature. Beneath this is the twilight zone, the maximum depth to which light penetrates. Temperatures here decrease rapidly with depth to about 41°F (5°C). Deeper yet is the dark zone, where there is no light and temperatures drop to about 34–36°F (1–2°C). Still in darkness and even deeper is the abyss, while the deepest part of the ocean occurs in the trenches. There are also zones on the seabed. The shallowest zone ranges from the low-tide mark to the edge of the continental shelf. Below this are the zones of the continental slope and finally the abyssal plains.

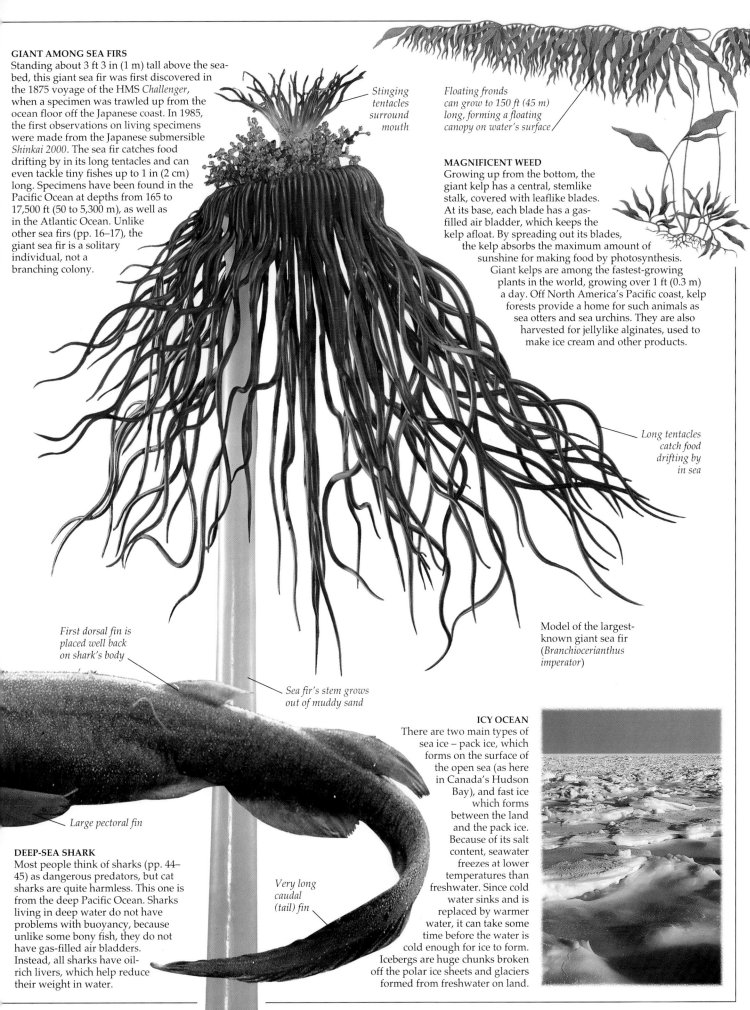

GIANT AMONG SEA FIRS
Standing about 3 ft 3 in (1 m) tall above the sea-bed, this giant sea fir was first discovered in the 1875 voyage of the HMS *Challenger*, when a specimen was trawled up from the ocean floor off the Japanese coast. In 1985, the first observations on living specimens were made from the Japanese submersible *Shinkai 2000*. The sea fir catches food drifting by in its long tentacles and can even tackle tiny fishes up to 1 in (2 cm) long. Specimens have been found in the Pacific Ocean at depths from 165 to 17,500 ft (50 to 5,300 m), as well as in the Atlantic Ocean. Unlike other sea firs (pp. 16–17), the giant sea fir is a solitary individual, not a branching colony.

*Stinging
tentacles
surround
mouth*

*Floating fronds
can grow to 150 ft (45 m)
long, forming a floating
canopy on water's surface*

MAGNIFICENT WEED
Growing up from the bottom, the giant kelp has a central, stemlike stalk, covered with leaflike blades. At its base, each blade has a gas-filled air bladder, which keeps the kelp afloat. By spreading out its blades, the kelp absorbs the maximum amount of sunshine for making food by photosynthesis. Giant kelps are among the fastest-growing plants in the world, growing over 1 ft (0.3 m) a day. Off North America's Pacific coast, kelp forests provide a home for such animals as sea otters and sea urchins. They are also harvested for jellylike alginates, used to make ice cream and other products.

*Long tentacles
catch food
drifting by
in sea*

*First dorsal fin is
placed well back
on shark's body*

*Sea fir's stem grows
out of muddy sand*

Model of the largest-known giant sea fir (*Branchiocerianthus imperator*)

Large pectoral fin

DEEP-SEA SHARK
Most people think of sharks (pp. 44–45) as dangerous predators, but cat sharks are quite harmless. This one is from the deep Pacific Ocean. Sharks living in deep water do not have problems with buoyancy, because unlike some bony fish, they do not have gas-filled air bladders. Instead, all sharks have oil-rich livers, which help reduce their weight in water.

*Very long
caudal
(tail) fin*

ICY OCEAN
There are two main types of sea ice – pack ice, which forms on the surface of the open sea (as here in Canada's Hudson Bay), and fast ice which forms between the land and the pack ice. Because of its salt content, seawater freezes at lower temperatures than freshwater. Since cold water sinks and is replaced by warmer water, it can take some time before the water is cold enough for ice to form. Icebergs are huge chunks broken off the polar ice sheets and glaciers formed from freshwater on land.

Sandy and muddy

IN SHALLOW COASTAL WATERS, from the lowest part of the shore to the edge of the continental shelf, sand and mud are washed from the land, creating vast stretches of sea floor that look like underwater deserts. Without rocks, there are no abundant growths of seaweeds to hide among, so animals that move above the sandy floor are exposed to predators. Many creatures protect themselves by burrowing in the soft seabed. Some worms hide inside their own tubes and feed by spreading out a fan of tentacles or by drawing water containing food particles into their tubes. Other worms, such as the sea mouse, move around in search of food. Flatfish (fish with eyes on one side of the head in the adult, like a flounder) are common on the sandy seabed, looking for any readily available food, such as peacock worms. All the animals shown here live in the coastal waters of the Atlantic Ocean.

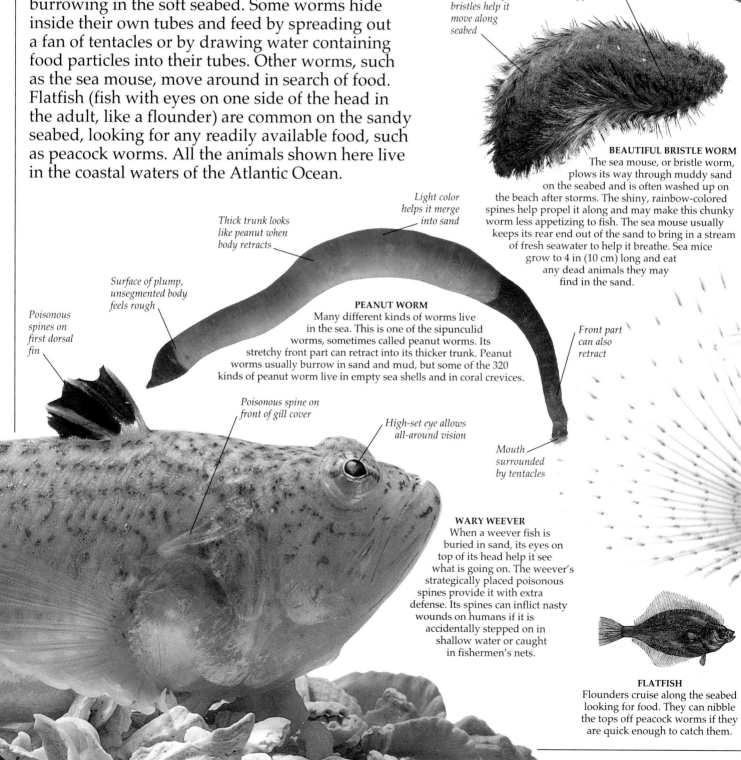

Tough papery tube protects soft worm inside

Worm can grow up to 16 in (40 cm) long

Bulky body covered by dense mat of fine hairs

Coarse, shiny bristles help it move along seabed

BEAUTIFUL BRISTLE WORM
The sea mouse, or bristle worm, plows its way through muddy sand on the seabed and is often washed up on the beach after storms. The shiny, rainbow-colored spines help propel it along and may make this chunky worm less appetizing to fish. The sea mouse usually keeps its rear end out of the sand to bring in a stream of fresh seawater to help it breathe. Sea mice grow to 4 in (10 cm) long and eat any dead animals they may find in the sand.

Light color helps it merge into sand

Thick trunk looks like peanut when body retracts

Surface of plump, unsegmented body feels rough

PEANUT WORM
Many different kinds of worms live in the sea. This is one of the sipunculid worms, sometimes called peanut worms. Its stretchy front part can retract into its thicker trunk. Peanut worms usually burrow in sand and mud, but some of the 320 kinds of peanut worm live in empty sea shells and in coral crevices.

Poisonous spines on first dorsal fin

Front part can also retract

Poisonous spine on front of gill cover

High-set eye allows all-around vision

Mouth surrounded by tentacles

WARY WEEVER
When a weever fish is buried in sand, its eyes on top of its head help it see what is going on. The weever's strategically placed poisonous spines provide it with extra defense. Its spines can inflict nasty wounds on humans if it is accidentally stepped on in shallow water or caught in fishermen's nets.

FLATFISH
Flounders cruise along the seabed looking for food. They can nibble the tops off peacock worms if they are quick enough to catch them.

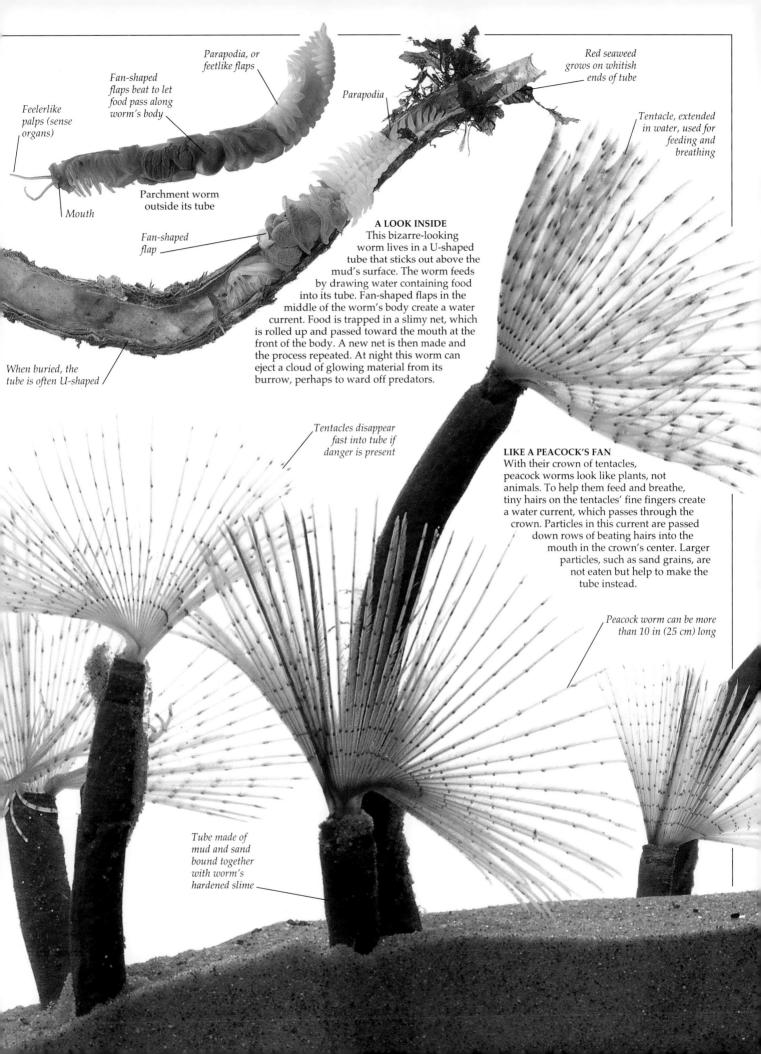

Feelerlike
palps (sense
organs)

Fan-shaped
flaps beat to let
food pass along
worm's body

Parapodia, or
feetlike flaps

Parapodia

Red seaweed
grows on whitish
ends of tube

Tentacle, extended
in water, used for
feeding and
breathing

Mouth

Parchment worm
outside its tube

Fan-shaped
flap

A LOOK INSIDE
This bizarre-looking
worm lives in a U-shaped
tube that sticks out above the
mud's surface. The worm feeds
by drawing water containing food
into its tube. Fan-shaped flaps in the
middle of the worm's body create a water
current. Food is trapped in a slimy net, which
is rolled up and passed toward the mouth at the
front of the body. A new net is then made and
the process repeated. At night this worm can
eject a cloud of glowing material from its
burrow, perhaps to ward off predators.

When buried, the
tube is often U-shaped

Tentacles disappear
fast into tube if
danger is present

LIKE A PEACOCK'S FAN
With their crown of tentacles,
peacock worms look like plants, not
animals. To help them feed and breathe,
tiny hairs on the tentacles' fine fingers create
a water current, which passes through the
crown. Particles in this current are passed
down rows of beating hairs into the
mouth in the crown's center. Larger
particles, such as sand grains, are
not eaten but help to make the
tube instead.

Peacock worm can be more
than 10 in (25 cm) long

Tube made of
mud and sand
bound together
with worm's
hardened slime

Soft seabed

SWIMMING OVER a soft seabed, using a mask and snorkel, it is possible to see only a few animals because most of them live buried in the sand. Look closely and you may see signs of this buried life, such as clams' siphons or a crab's feathery antennae, poking through the sand to help get clean supplies of oxygen-containing water. Some fish, like the eagle ray, visit the soft seabed to feed on burrowing clams. Other animals are found only where sea grasses grow on sandy bottoms. Sea grasses are not seaweeds but flowering plants. They are food for many animals, including the dugong – the only plant-eating mammal that truly lives in the sea.

Tough skin protects dugong

DOCILE DUGONG
Dugongs (pp. 106–107) live in shallow tropical waters, where they feed on sea grasses growing in the soft seabed. They often dig down into the sand to eat the food-rich roots of sea grasses. These gentle, shy animals are still hunted in some places.

This sea pen can grow to 8 in (20 cm) in height

ELEGANT PEN
Looking like an old-fashioned quill pen, this relative of the sea anemone (pp. 24–25) lives in the soft seabed. Rows of tiny polyps, or buds, on each side of its body are used to capture small animals drifting by for food. Sea pens glow in the dark if disturbed. Some sea pens grow on the bottom of the deep ocean.

SHELL BOAT
In Botticelli's *The Birth of Venus*, the Roman goddess rises from the water in a scallop shell. In real life, scallop shells found in the soft seabed are too heavy to float.

Anemone-like polyp unfurls when feeding

Long dorsal fin runs along almost whole length of body

RED BAND FISH
This fish usually lives in burrows in the soft seabed, down to depths of about 660 ft (200 m). It is also found swimming among sea grasses. Sometimes red band fish are found washed up on the beach after storms. Out of its burrow, the fish swims by passing waves down its body. It feeds on small animals drifting by.

Long anal fin

Red band fish may grow to 28 in (70 cm) in length

Stem of sea pen anchors in sandy seabed

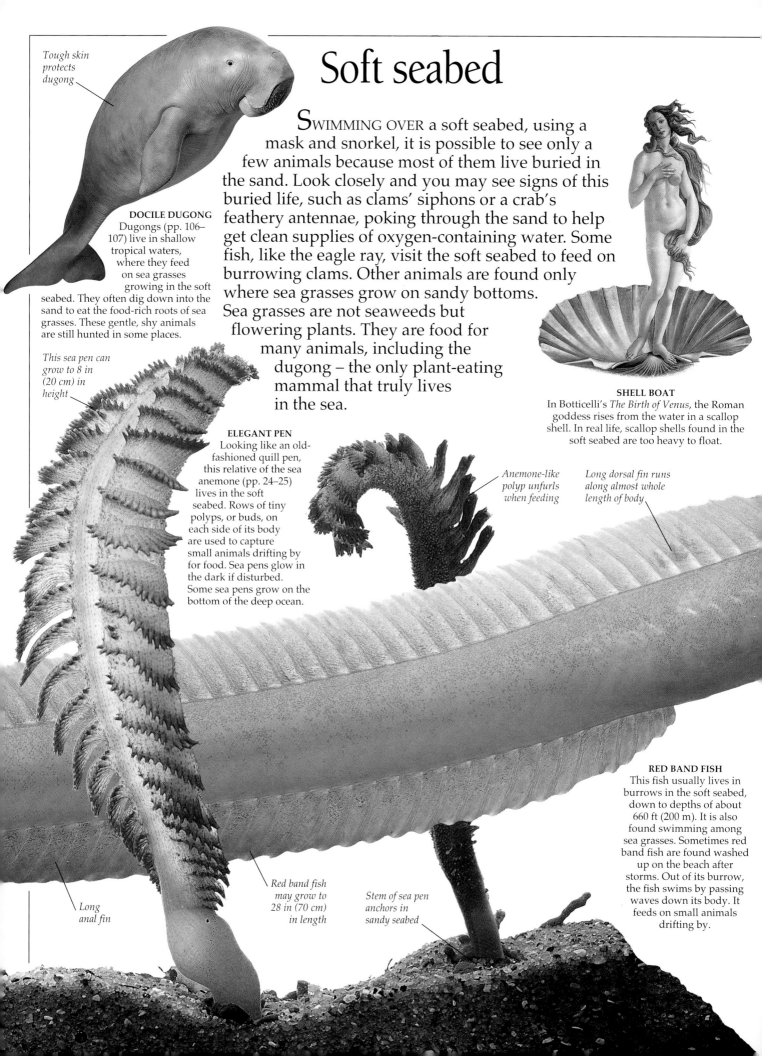

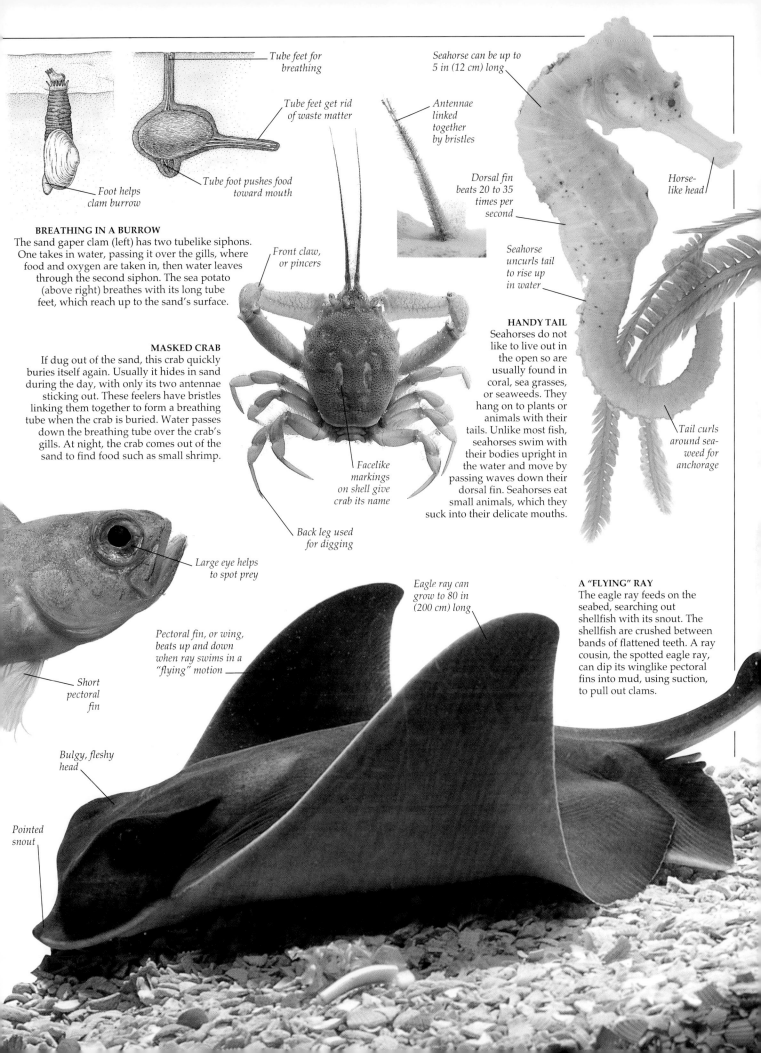

Tube feet for breathing

Tube feet get rid of waste matter

Foot helps clam burrow

Tube foot pushes food toward mouth

Seahorse can be up to 5 in (12 cm) long

Antennae linked together by bristles

Dorsal fin beats 20 to 35 times per second

Horse-like head

BREATHING IN A BURROW
The sand gaper clam (left) has two tubelike siphons. One takes in water, passing it over the gills, where food and oxygen are taken in, then water leaves through the second siphon. The sea potato (above right) breathes with its long tube feet, which reach up to the sand's surface.

Front claw, or pincers

Seahorse uncurls tail to rise up in water

MASKED CRAB
If dug out of the sand, this crab quickly buries itself again. Usually it hides in sand during the day, with only its two antennae sticking out. These feelers have bristles linking them together to form a breathing tube when the crab is buried. Water passes down the breathing tube over the crab's gills. At night, the crab comes out of the sand to find food such as small shrimp.

HANDY TAIL
Seahorses do not like to live out in the open so are usually found in coral, sea grasses, or seaweeds. They hang on to plants or animals with their tails. Unlike most fish, seahorses swim with their bodies upright in the water and move by passing waves down their dorsal fin. Seahorses eat small animals, which they suck into their delicate mouths.

Tail curls around sea-weed for anchorage

Facelike markings on shell give crab its name

Back leg used for digging

Large eye helps to spot prey

Eagle ray can grow to 80 in (200 cm) long

A "FLYING" RAY
The eagle ray feeds on the seabed, searching out shellfish with its snout. The shellfish are crushed between bands of flattened teeth. A ray cousin, the spotted eagle ray, can dip its winglike pectoral fins into mud, using suction, to pull out clams.

Pectoral fin, or wing, beats up and down when ray swims in a "flying" motion

Short pectoral fin

Bulgy, fleshy head

Pointed snout

Rocks underwater

ROCKY SEABEDS are found in coastal waters where currents sweep away any sand and mud. With the strong water movement, animals have to cling on to the rocks, find crevices to hide in, or take shelter among seaweeds. A few remarkable animals, such as the clamlike piddocks and some sea urchins, can bore into solid rock to make their homes. Sea urchins bore cavities in hard rock, while piddocks drill into softer rocks such as sandstone or chalk. Some creatures hide under smaller stones, but only if they are lodged in the soft seabed. When masses of loose pebbles roll around, animals and seaweeds can be crushed. However, some crustaceans, such as lobsters, can regain a lost limb crushed by a stone, and starfish can even regrow a missing arm. Some animals can survive at the seashore's edge, especially in rock pools, but many need to stay submerged.

Sea urchin boring into rocks

Piddock

ROCK BORERS
Some sea urchins use their spines and teeth beneath their shells to bore spaces in rock, while piddocks drill with the tips of their shells. Using its muscular foot, the piddock twists and turns to drill and hold on to its burrow. Both are found in shallow water and on the lower shore.

BEAUTIFUL BUTTERFLY
Blennies, small fish living in shallow water, often rest on the bottom and hide in crannies. They lay their eggs in sheltered places, such as abandoned bottles, and guard them from predators. Blennies feed on small creatures, such as mites, and live on rocky or stony ground to depths of 66 ft (20 m).

Dorsal fin has eyespot to frighten predators

Spiny shell helps deter predators

SPINY LOBSTER
European spiny lobsters, or crawfish, are reddish brown in life. With their small pincers, spiny lobsters are restricted to eating soft prey, such as worms or dead animals. They live among rocks, hiding in crevices during the day, but venturing out over the seabed at night to find food. Some kinds of spiny lobsters move in long lines, keeping in touch with the lobster in front with their antennae.

Delicate claw on tip of walking leg

European spiny lobster, also known as a crawfish

Leg used for walking

Tail can be flapped so lobster can swim backward

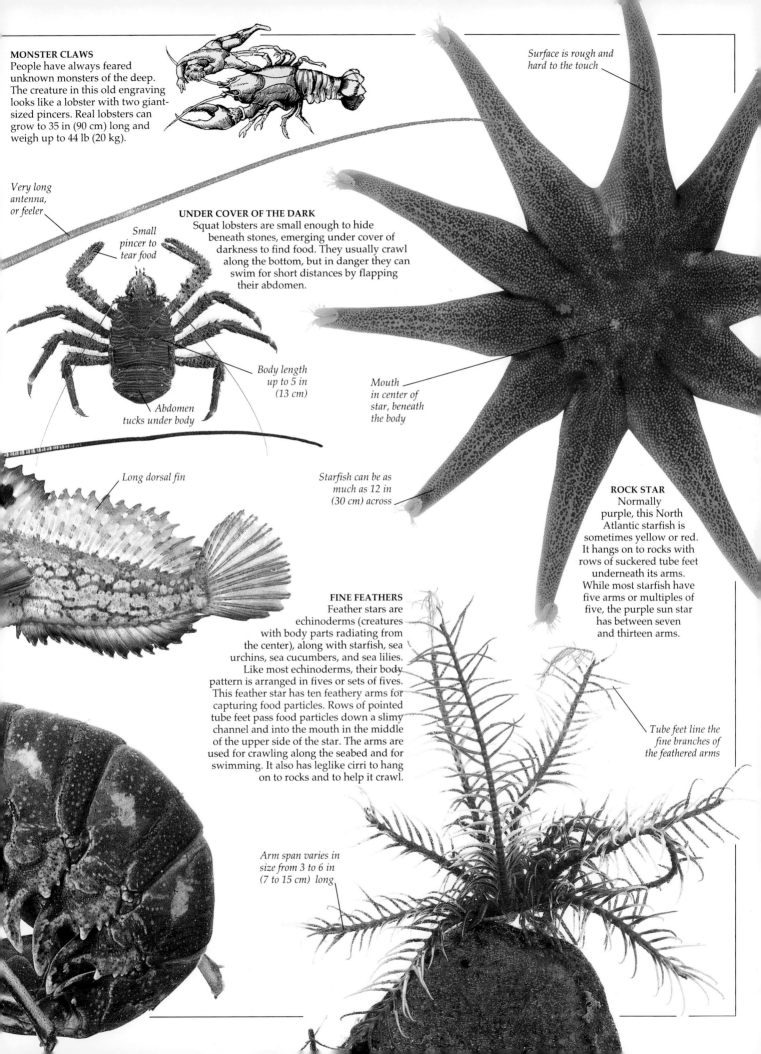

MONSTER CLAWS
People have always feared unknown monsters of the deep. The creature in this old engraving looks like a lobster with two giant-sized pincers. Real lobsters can grow to 35 in (90 cm) long and weigh up to 44 lb (20 kg).

Surface is rough and hard to the touch

Very long antenna, or feeler

Small pincer to tear food

UNDER COVER OF THE DARK
Squat lobsters are small enough to hide beneath stones, emerging under cover of darkness to find food. They usually crawl along the bottom, but in danger they can swim for short distances by flapping their abdomen.

Body length up to 5 in (13 cm)

Abdomen tucks under body

Mouth in center of star, beneath the body

Long dorsal fin

Starfish can be as much as 12 in (30 cm) across

ROCK STAR
Normally purple, this North Atlantic starfish is sometimes yellow or red. It hangs on to rocks with rows of suckered tube feet underneath its arms. While most starfish have five arms or multiples of five, the purple sun star has between seven and thirteen arms.

FINE FEATHERS
Feather stars are echinoderms (creatures with body parts radiating from the center), along with starfish, sea urchins, sea cucumbers, and sea lilies. Like most echinoderms, their body pattern is arranged in fives or sets of fives. This feather star has ten feathery arms for capturing food particles. Rows of pointed tube feet pass food particles down a slimy channel and into the mouth in the middle of the upper side of the star. The arms are used for crawling along the seabed and for swimming. It also has leglike cirri to hang on to rocks and to help it crawl.

Tube feet line the fine branches of the feathered arms

Arm span varies in size from 3 to 6 in (7 to 15 cm) long

On the rocks

In the shallow, cool waters above rocky seabeds, forests of large brown seaweeds called kelp provide a home, hunting ground, and resting place for many creatures. Along North America's Pacific coast, sea otters wrap themselves in kelp and snooze on the surface. At the kelp's base, its holdfast, or rootlike anchor, is home for many animals, such as crabs, and other seaweeds. Unlike the roots of land plants, kelp's holdfast is only an anchor – it does not absorb nutrients or water. Other animals live on the kelp's surface or grow directly onto the rocks, capturing food brought to them in the currents. Sea firs look like plants, but are animals belonging to the same group as sea anemones, jellyfish, and corals, and all have stinging tentacles. Mussels anchored to rocks are shelter for animals that live among, or within, their shells.

A type of brown seaweed (kelp) found in the Pacific Ocean

DELIGHTFUL MARINE MAMMAL
Sea otters swim and rest among the giant kelp fronds along North America's Pacific coast. They dive down to the seabed to pick up shellfish, smashing them open by banging them against a rock balanced on their chest.

ANCHORED ALGAE
Growing in shallow water, kelp is often battered by waves. Holdfasts of the large, tough, brown algae keep it firmly anchored by tightly gripping the rocks.

Holdfast of oarweed kelp

Holdfast must be strong, as some kinds of kelp can grow over 33 ft (10 m) long

PRETTY BABY
Young lumpsuckers are more beautiful than their dumpy parents, which cling on to rocks with suckerlike fins on their bellies. Adult lumpsuckers move into shallow water to breed, and the father guards the eggs.

Scaleless body is covered with small warty bumps

Juvenile lumpsucker

Each sturdy, blunt finger measures at least 1.25 in (3 cm) across

Fleshy fingers supported by tiny, hard splinters

White, anemone-like polyp captures food from fast-moving currents

DEAD-MAN'S FINGERS
When this soft coral is washed up on the shore, its rubbery, fleshy form lives up to its name! Growing on rocks, the colonies consist of many polyps (feeding heads) within a fleshy, orange or white base.

Gills

SEA MAT
The lacy-looking growth on the surface of this piece of kelp (left) is a bryozoan, or moss animal. These animals live in colonies where many individuals grow next to each other. Each little compartment houses one of these animals, which come out to feed, capturing food in their tiny tentacles. The colony grows, as individuals bud off new individuals. Other kinds of moss animal grow upward and look a little like seaweeds or corals. Between the sea mats, a blue-rayed limpet grazes on the kelp's surface.

SEA SLUG
Many sea slugs are meat eaters. This slug lives on the soft coral known as dead-man's fingers. Some sea slugs are able to eat the stinging tentacles of anemones and keep the stings for their own protection. Sea slug eggs hatch into swimming young, which then settle and turn into adults.

16

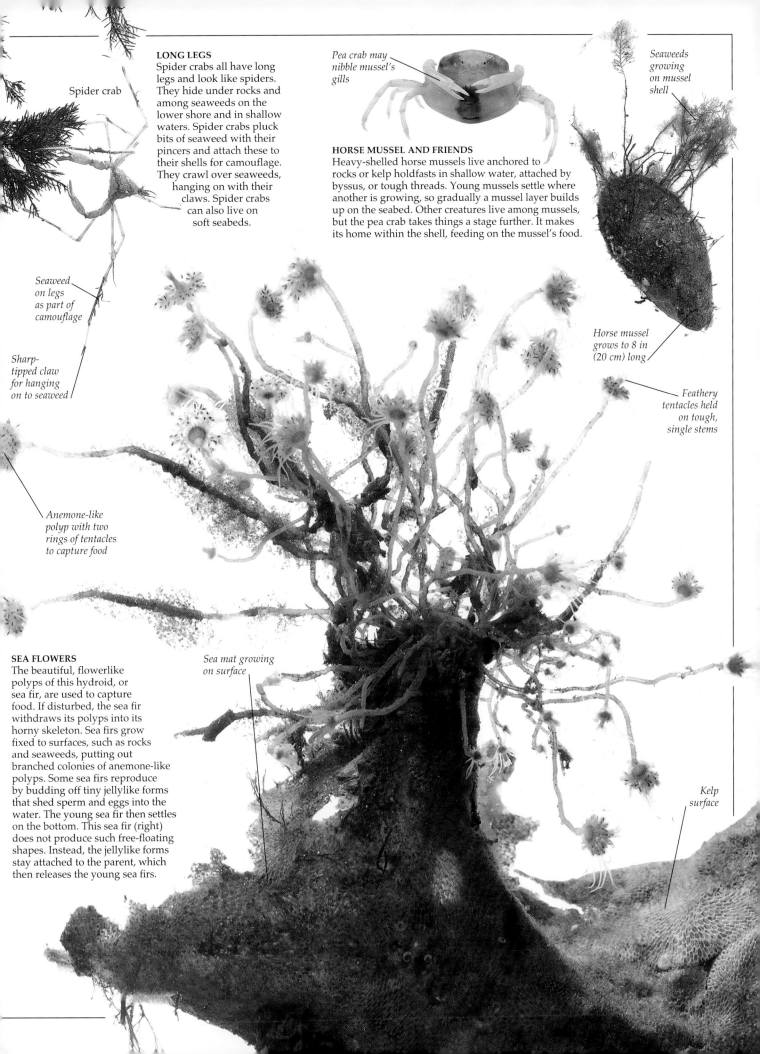

Spider crab

LONG LEGS
Spider crabs all have long legs and look like spiders. They hide under rocks and among seaweeds on the lower shore and in shallow waters. Spider crabs pluck bits of seaweed with their pincers and attach these to their shells for camouflage. They crawl over seaweeds, hanging on with their claws. Spider crabs can also live on soft seabeds.

Pea crab may nibble mussel's gills

Seaweeds growing on mussel shell

HORSE MUSSEL AND FRIENDS
Heavy-shelled horse mussels live anchored to rocks or kelp holdfasts in shallow water, attached by byssus, or tough threads. Young mussels settle where another is growing, so gradually a mussel layer builds up on the seabed. Other creatures live among mussels, but the pea crab takes things a stage further. It makes its home within the shell, feeding on the mussel's food.

Seaweed on legs as part of camouflage

Sharp-tipped claw for hanging on to seaweed

Horse mussel grows to 8 in (20 cm) long

Feathery tentacles held on tough, single stems

Anemone-like polyp with two rings of tentacles to capture food

SEA FLOWERS
The beautiful, flowerlike polyps of this hydroid, or sea fir, are used to capture food. If disturbed, the sea fir withdraws its polyps into its horny skeleton. Sea firs grow fixed to surfaces, such as rocks and seaweeds, putting out branched colonies of anemone-like polyps. Some sea firs reproduce by budding off tiny jellylike forms that shed sperm and eggs into the water. The young sea fir then settles on the bottom. This sea fir (right) does not produce such free-floating shapes. Instead, the jellylike forms stay attached to the parent, which then releases the young sea firs.

Sea mat growing on surface

Kelp surface

The coral kingdom

IN THE WARM, CRYSTAL-CLEAR WATERS of the tropics, coral reefs flourish, covering vast areas. Made of the skeletons of stony corals, coral reefs are cemented together by chalky algae. Most stony corals are colonies of many tiny, anemone-like individuals, called polyps. Each polyp makes its own hard limestone cup (skeleton), which protects its soft body. To make their skeletons, the coral polyps need the help of microscopic, single-celled algae that live inside them. The algae need sunlight to grow, which is why coral reefs are found only in sunny, surface waters. In return for giving the algae a home, corals get some food from them but also capture plankton with their tentacles. Only the upper layer of a reef is made of living corals, which build upon skeletons of dead polyps. Coral reefs are also home to soft corals and sea fans, which do not have stony skeletons. Related to sea anemones and jellyfish, corals grow in an exquisite variety of shapes (mushroom, daisy, staghorn) and some have colorful skeletons.

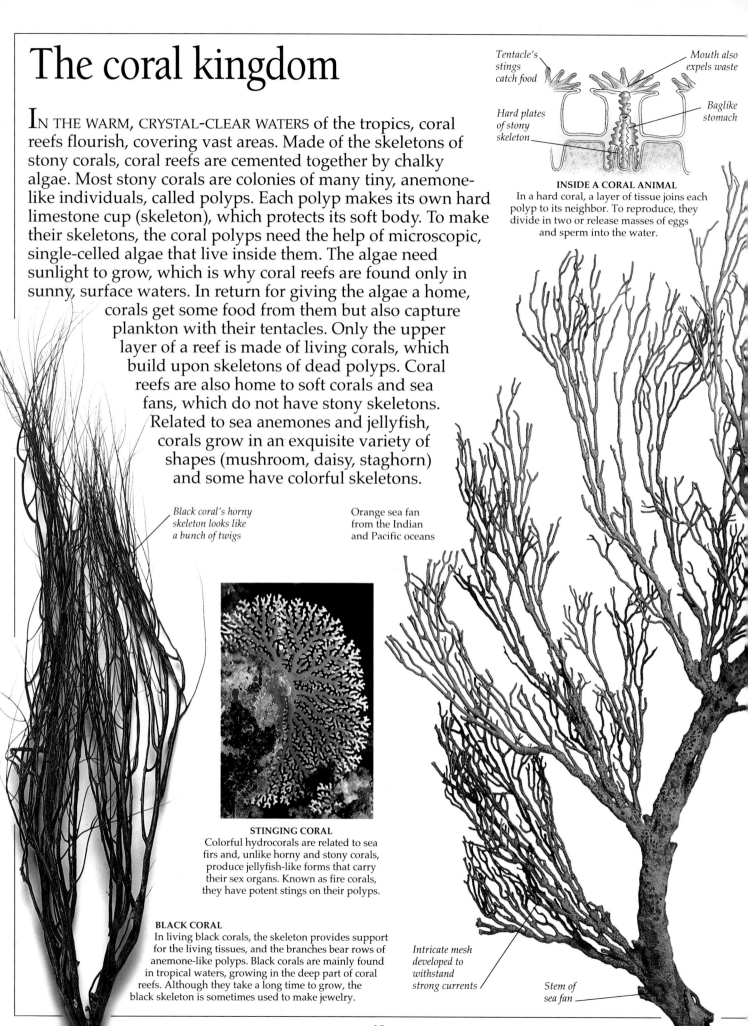

Tentacle's stings catch food

Mouth also expels waste

Hard plates of stony skeleton

Baglike stomach

INSIDE A CORAL ANIMAL
In a hard coral, a layer of tissue joins each polyp to its neighbor. To reproduce, they divide in two or release masses of eggs and sperm into the water.

Black coral's horny skeleton looks like a bunch of twigs

Orange sea fan from the Indian and Pacific oceans

STINGING CORAL
Colorful hydrocorals are related to sea firs and, unlike horny and stony corals, produce jellyfish-like forms that carry their sex organs. Known as fire corals, they have potent stings on their polyps.

BLACK CORAL
In living black corals, the skeleton provides support for the living tissues, and the branches bear rows of anemone-like polyps. Black corals are mainly found in tropical waters, growing in the deep part of coral reefs. Although they take a long time to grow, the black skeleton is sometimes used to make jewelry.

Intricate mesh developed to withstand strong currents

Stem of sea fan

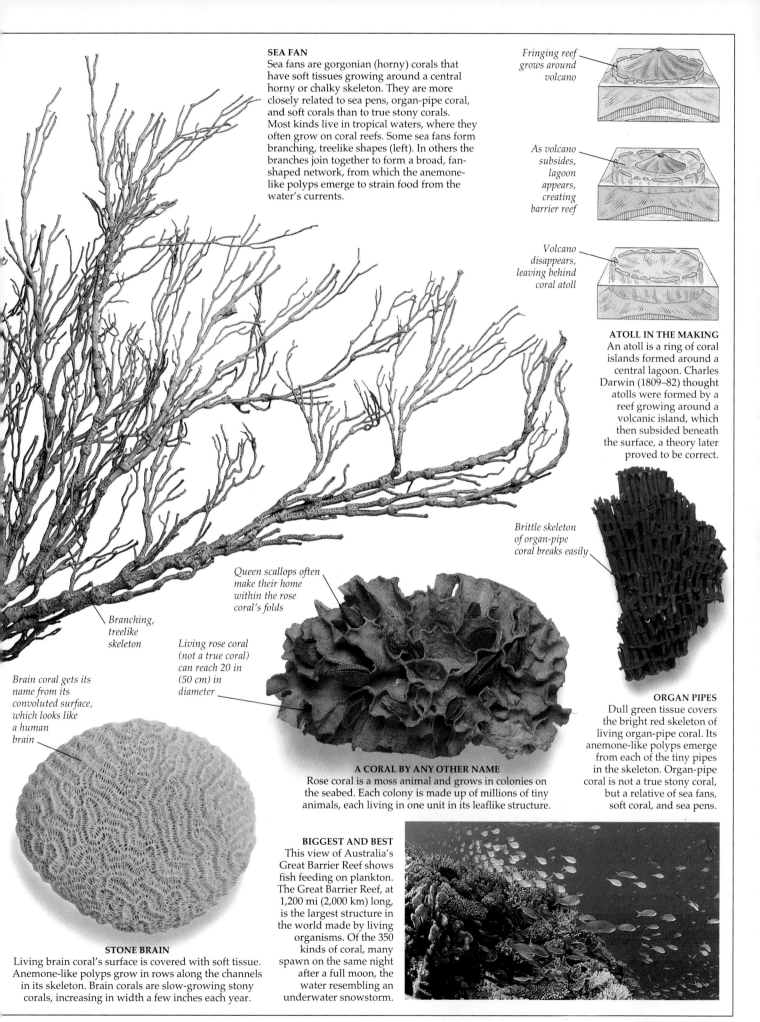

SEA FAN

Sea fans are gorgonian (horny) corals that have soft tissues growing around a central horny or chalky skeleton. They are more closely related to sea pens, organ-pipe coral, and soft corals than to true stony corals. Most kinds live in tropical waters, where they often grow on coral reefs. Some sea fans form branching, treelike shapes (left). In others the branches join together to form a broad, fan-shaped network, from which the anemone-like polyps emerge to strain food from the water's currents.

Fringing reef grows around volcano

As volcano subsides, lagoon appears, creating barrier reef

Volcano disappears, leaving behind coral atoll

ATOLL IN THE MAKING

An atoll is a ring of coral islands formed around a central lagoon. Charles Darwin (1809–82) thought atolls were formed by a reef growing around a volcanic island, which then subsided beneath the surface, a theory later proved to be correct.

Brittle skeleton of organ-pipe coral breaks easily

Branching, treelike skeleton

Queen scallops often make their home within the rose coral's folds

Brain coral gets its name from its convoluted surface, which looks like a human brain

Living rose coral (not a true coral) can reach 20 in (50 cm) in diameter

ORGAN PIPES

Dull green tissue covers the bright red skeleton of living organ-pipe coral. Its anemone-like polyps emerge from each of the tiny pipes in the skeleton. Organ-pipe coral is not a true stony coral, but a relative of sea fans, soft coral, and sea pens.

A CORAL BY ANY OTHER NAME

Rose coral is a moss animal and grows in colonies on the seabed. Each colony is made up of millions of tiny animals, each living in one unit in its leaflike structure.

STONE BRAIN

Living brain coral's surface is covered with soft tissue. Anemone-like polyps grow in rows along the channels in its skeleton. Brain corals are slow-growing stony corals, increasing in width a few inches each year.

BIGGEST AND BEST

This view of Australia's Great Barrier Reef shows fish feeding on plankton. The Great Barrier Reef, at 1,200 mi (2,000 km) long, is the largest structure in the world made by living organisms. Of the 350 kinds of coral, many spawn on the same night after a full moon, the water resembling an underwater snowstorm.

Life on a coral reef

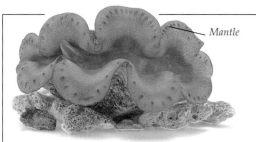

Mantle

A GIANT CLAM
The giant blue clam grows to about 1 ft (30 cm) long, but the largest giant clams may reach 3 ft 4 in (1 m). The colorful mantles exposed at the edge of their shells contain hordes of single-celled algae that make their own food by using the energy from sunlight. The clam gets some of its food by harvesting this growing crop of algae.

CORAL REEFS HAVE an amazing variety of marine life, from teeming multitudes of brightly colored fish to giant clams wedged into rocks. Every bit of space on the reef provides a hiding place or shelter for some animal or plant. At night, a host of amazing creatures emerge from coral caves and crevices to feed. All the living organisms on the reef depend for their survival on the stony corals, which recycle the scarce nutrients from the clear, blue, tropical waters. People as well as animals rely on coral reefs, for they protect coastlines and attract tourist money. Some island nations even live on coral atolls. Sadly, in spite of being one of the great natural wonders of the world, coral reefs are now under threat. Reefs are being broken up for building materials, damaged by snorkelers and divers touching or stepping on them, dynamited by fishermen, ripped up by curio collectors, covered by soil eroded by the destruction of rain forests, and polluted by sewage and oil spills.

Green color helps camouflage sea slug among seaweeds

Tentacles of sea anemone covered with stings to put off predators

Large eye for keeping a watch for danger

Layer of slimy mucus protects clown fish from anemone's stinging tentacles

Side fin used to steer and change direction

FRILLY LETTUCE
Sea slugs are related to sea snails but do not have shells. Many sea slugs living on coral reefs feed on corals, but the lettuce slug feeds on algae growing on the reef by sucking the sap from individual cells. Chloroplasts, the green part of plant cells, are then stored in the slug's digestive system, where they continue to trap energy from sunlight to make food. Many other reef sea slugs recycle the stings they eat from the coral's tentacles and are brightly colored to warn that they are dangerous.

Stripes break up clown fish's outline, so it is more difficult for predators to see the fish on the reef

LIVING IN HARMONY
Clown fish, which shelter in anemones, live on coral reefs in the Pacific and Indian oceans. Unlike other fish, clown fish are not stung by the anemones. They are protected by a layer of slimy mucus, and the anemone's stinging cells are not even triggered by the fish's presence. Clown fish seldom venture far from their anemone home for fear of attack by other fish. There are many types of clown fish, some living only with certain kinds of anemones.

DATE MUSSEL
Many different clams live on coral reefs. This date mussel makes its home by producing chemicals to wear a hole in the hard coral. Like most clams, the mussel feeds by collecting food particles from water passing through its gills.

Date mussel on a coral reef in the Red Sea

Narrow snout probes for sponges and other animals that grow on rocks

Bright colors help attract a mate

Plain yellow caudal (tail) fin

Adult emperor angelfish's colors and patterns act as signals to other angelfish

Adult

GROWING UP
Angelfish are common inhabitants of coral reefs. The young emperor angelfish looks quite different from the adult; possibly these colors protect it better. Once the adults pair up, they establish a territory on the reef where they can feed. Their colors and patterns help other emperors recognize them, and see that their patch of the reef is occupied.

Juvenile

Ring patterns may draw predator away from juvenile's more vulnerable head

Special glands in skin make slug taste bad to deter predators

Soft body has no shell to protect slug

Flat, slimy foot enables slug to crawl over slippery seaweed

Bright green color from eating algae

Lettuce slug breathes through its skin, which looks like the leaf of a plant

Special fat tentacles for smelling food

Crown-of-thorns starfish eating coral

NOTORIOUS STARFISH
The crown-of-thorns starfish devours the soft parts of a gorgonian coral. Like many other starfish, it feeds by turning its stomach inside out, producing enzymes that digest its prey. Plagues of these starfish attacked Australia's Great Barrier Reef in the 1960s and 1970s, killing many corals,

Tentacles can be pulled back inside body for protection

Tentacles around mouth used for feeding

Spines on tough skin detract predators

One of five rows of tube feet helps sea cucumber crawl

COLORFUL CUCUMBER
One of the most colorful kinds of sea cucumber lives on or close to reefs in the Indo-Pacific region. Sea cucumbers are echinoderms (pp. 14–15), like starfish, sea urchins, and sea lilies. The sea cucumber puts out its sticky tentacles to feed on small particles of food. Once the food has stuck to the mucus on the tentacle, it is placed inside the mouth and the food removed.

Sea meadows

THE MOST ABUNDANT PLANTS IN THE OCEAN are too small to be seen with the naked eye. Usually single-celled, these minute, floating plants are called phytoplankton. Like all plants, they need sunlight to grow, so are only found in the ocean's upper zones. With the right conditions, phytoplankton multiply quickly, within a few days, as each cell divides into two, and so on. To grow, phytoplankton need nutrients from the seawater and lots of sunlight. The most light occurs in the tropics but nutrients there, especially nitrogen and phosphorus, are often in short supply. Spectacular phytoplankton blooms are found in cooler waters where nutrients (dead plant and animal waste) are brought up from the bottom during storms, but also in both cool and warm waters where there are upwellings of nutrient-rich water. Phytoplankton are eaten by swarms of tiny, drifting animals, called zooplankton, which provide a feast for small fish, such as herring. Those in turn are eaten by larger fish, such as dogfish, which are eaten by still larger fish or other predators, such as dolphins. Some larger ocean animals (whale sharks and blue whales) feed directly on zooplankton.

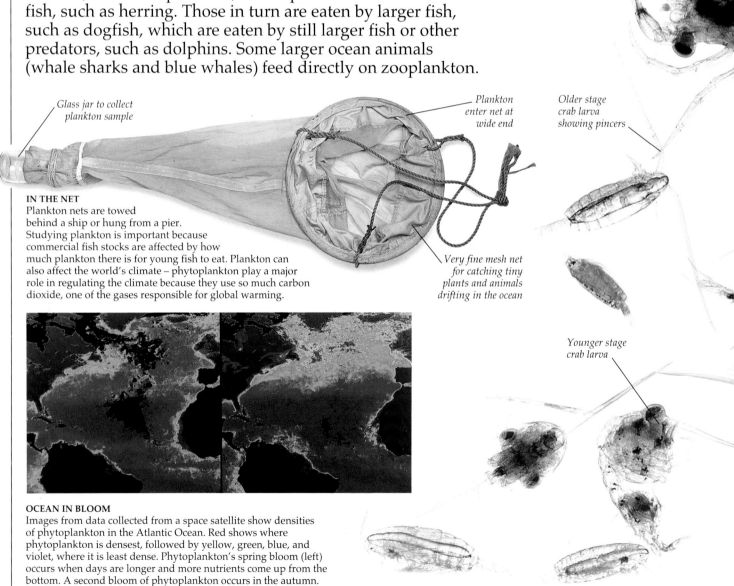

PLANT FOOD
This diatom is one of many phyto-plankton that drift in the ocean. Diatoms are the most common kinds of phytoplankton in cooler waters, but single-celled plants called dinoflagellates are common in tropical waters. Many diatoms are single cells, but this one consists of a chain of cells.

Glass jar to collect plankton sample

Plankton enter net at wide end

Older stage crab larva showing pincers

IN THE NET
Plankton nets are towed behind a ship or hung from a pier. Studying plankton is important because commercial fish stocks are affected by how much plankton there is for young fish to eat. Plankton can also affect the world's climate – phytoplankton play a major role in regulating the climate because they use so much carbon dioxide, one of the gases responsible for global warming.

Very fine mesh net for catching tiny plants and animals drifting in the ocean

Younger stage crab larva

OCEAN IN BLOOM
Images from data collected from a space satellite show densities of phytoplankton in the Atlantic Ocean. Red shows where phytoplankton is densest, followed by yellow, green, blue, and violet, where it is least dense. Phytoplankton's spring bloom (left) occurs when days are longer and more nutrients come up from the bottom. A second bloom of phytoplankton occurs in the autumn. When phytoplankton die, they sink to the seabed with gelatinous zooplankton remains, making sticky clumps called marine "snow."

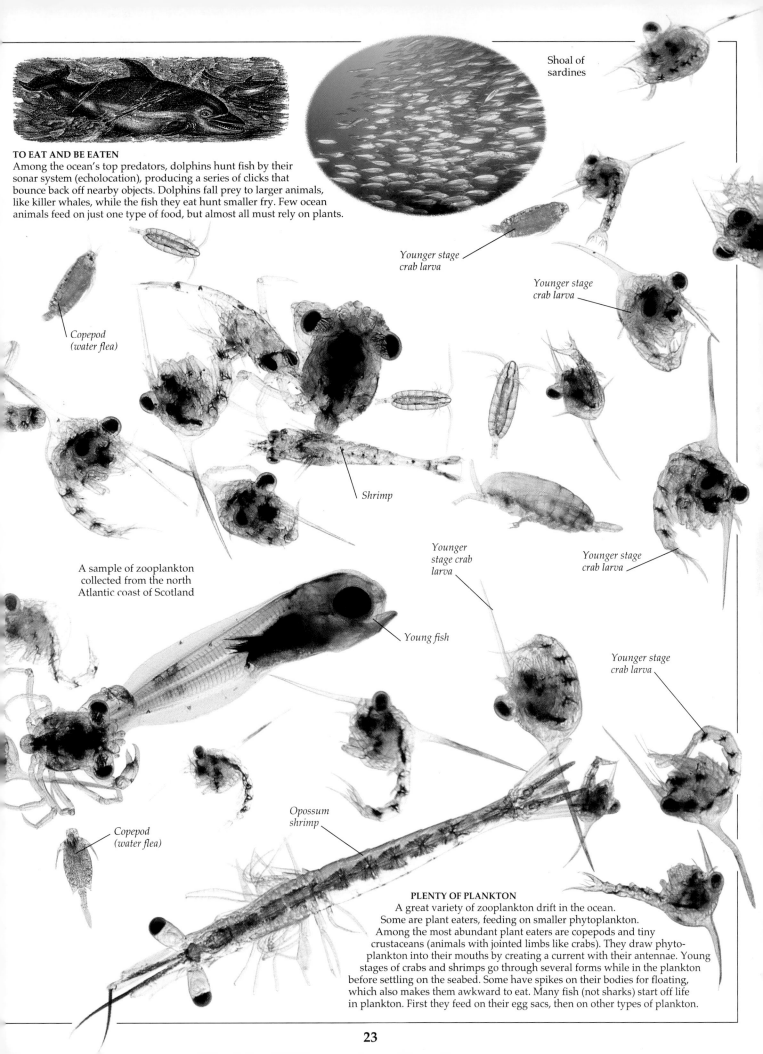

TO EAT AND BE EATEN
Among the ocean's top predators, dolphins hunt fish by their sonar system (echolocation), producing a series of clicks that bounce back off nearby objects. Dolphins fall prey to larger animals, like killer whales, while the fish they eat hunt smaller fry. Few ocean animals feed on just one type of food, but almost all must rely on plants.

Shoal of sardines

Younger stage crab larva

Younger stage crab larva

Copepod (water flea)

Shrimp

A sample of zooplankton collected from the north Atlantic coast of Scotland

Younger stage crab larva

Younger stage crab larva

Young fish

Younger stage crab larva

Copepod (water flea)

Opossum shrimp

PLENTY OF PLANKTON
A great variety of zooplankton drift in the ocean. Some are plant eaters, feeding on smaller phytoplankton. Among the most abundant plant eaters are copepods and tiny crustaceans (animals with jointed limbs like crabs). They draw phytoplankton into their mouths by creating a current with their antennae. Young stages of crabs and shrimps go through several forms while in the plankton before settling on the seabed. Some have spikes on their bodies for floating, which also makes them awkward to eat. Many fish (not sharks) start off life in plankton. First they feed on their egg sacs, then on other types of plankton.

Predators and prey

SOME OCEAN ANIMALS are herbivores (plant eaters), from fish nibbling seaweeds on coral reefs to dugongs chewing sea grasses. There are also many carnivores (meat eaters) in the ocean. Some, such as blue sharks and barracuda, are swift hunters, while others, such as anglerfish and sea anemones, set traps for their prey and wait with snapping jaws or stinging tentacles. Many animals, from the humble sea fan to the giant baleen whale, filter food out of the water. Sea birds find their meals in the ocean by diving for a beakful of prey. Other ocean animals are omnivores – they eat both plants and animals.

COOPERATIVE FEEDING
Humpback whales herd schools of fish by letting out a stream of bubbles as they swim around it. With their mouths open wide to gulp in food and water, whales keep the fish but expel water through sievelike baleen plates in their mouths.

Tiny prey caught in mucus

CAUGHT BY SLIME
Unlike the many jellyfish that trap prey with their stinging tentacles, common jellyfish catch small plankton (drifting animals) in sticky mucus (slime) produced by its bell. The four fleshy arms beneath the bell collect up the food-laden slime, and tiny, hairlike cilia channel it into the mouth.

FANG FACE
The wolffish has strong, fanglike teeth for crunching through the hard shells of crabs, sea urchins, and mussels. As the front set are worn down each year, they are replaced by a new set growing in behind. Wolffish live in cool, deep, northern waters, where they lurk in rocky holes.

Dorsal fin runs along entire length of body

Crooked, yellow, fanglike teeth

Shorter pectoral fin

Tough, wrinkled skin helps protect wolffish living near the seabed

*Spines to
protect
urchin*

GRAZING AWAY
The European common sea urchin grazes on seaweeds and animals that grow on the surface of seaweeds, such as sea mats. The urchin uses the set of rasping teeth, called "Aristotle's lantern," on the underside of its shell, which are operated by a complex set of jaws inside. The grazing activities of urchins can control how much seaweed grows in an area. If too many urchins are collected for food or tourist souvenirs, a rocky reef can become overgrown by seaweed.

Pelican
diving

*Brown
pelican
catches
fish in
pouch-
like beak*

*Tube feet used to
walk slowly along
the seabed*

*Sea urchin's mouth
surrounded by five
rasping teeth*

FISH FEED
Like all pelicans, the brown pelican has a big beak with a large flap of skin, or pouch, to capture a variety of fish. Once they have spotted their prey, they dive into the water, but are too bulky to dive far below the surface. Only brown pelicans dive for their prey. When the pelican surfaces, water is drained from the pouch and the fish swallowed.

Tiny teeth of a
basking shark

TO BITE OR NOT TO BITE
A tiger shark's tooth is like a multipurpose tool, with a sharp point for piercing prey and a serrated bladelike edge for slicing. This shark can eat almost anything, from hard-shelled turtles to soft-bodied seals and sea birds. The rows of a basking shark's tiny teeth are not used, since this shark filters food out of the water with a sieve of gill rakers.

Tiger
shark's
tooth

TENTACLE TRAPS
The flowerlike dahlia anemones are deadly traps for unwary shrimps and small fish that stray too close to their stinging tentacles. When the prey brush past, hundreds of nematocysts (stinging cells) are triggered and fire their stings. These stings ensnare and weaken prey. The tentacles pass the stricken prey toward the mouth in the center of the anemone – the entrance to the baglike stomach, where the prey is digested.

*Stinging
tentacle*

*Any undigested
pieces of food are
ejected through
the mouth*

*Suckerlike disk lets dahlia anemone
attach to any hard surface*

Homes and hiding

STAYING HIDDEN is one of the best means of defense – if a predator cannot see you, it cannot eat you! Many sea animals shelter among seaweeds, in rocky crevices, or under the sand. Matching the colors and even the texture of the background also helps sea creatures remain undetected. The sargassum fish even look like bits of seaweed. Hard shells are useful protection, at least from weak-jawed predators. Sea snails and clams make their own shells that cover the body. Crabs and lobsters have outer shells like suits of armor, covering the body and each jointed limb. The hermit crab is unusual because only the front part of the body and the legs are covered by a hard shell. Its abdomen is soft, so a hermit crab uses the empty shell of a sea snail to protect itself.

BLENDING IN
Cuttlefish have different-colored pigments and rapidly change color to escape predators. Their eyes perceive the color of their surroundings, and nerve signals are sent by the brain to tiny bags of pigment in the skin. When these pigment bags contract, the cuttlefish's color becomes lighter.

Cuttlefish becomes darker when pigment bags expand

WHAT A WEED!
This fish lives among floating clumps of sargassum seaweed, where frilly growths on its head, body, and fins help it avoid being seen by predators, making a realistic disguise. Many different animals live in sargassum seaweed, which drifts in large quantities in the Sargasso Sea of the North Atlantic.

Hermit crab leaving old whelk shell

Anemone

When out of its shell, crab is vulnerable to predators

Investigating its new home by checking size with its claws

Hermit crab can be persuaded to move into a Perspex shell so its movements can be viewed

ALL CHANGE
Like all crustaceans, a hermit crab grows by shedding its hard, outer skeleton. The hermit crab does this in the safety of its snail shell home. As it grows, however, it must find a larger shell to move into. Before leaving its old shell, it will test the size of a new home. If it is not large enough or is cracked, the hermit crab looks for another shell. When the hermit crab has found one that is just right, it carefully pulls its body out of its old shell, tucking it quickly into the new shell. As the hermit crab grows larger, it moves into large whelk shells and lives submerged on the seabed in shallow water.

Leg with pointed claws to get a grip on seabed when walking

Antenna

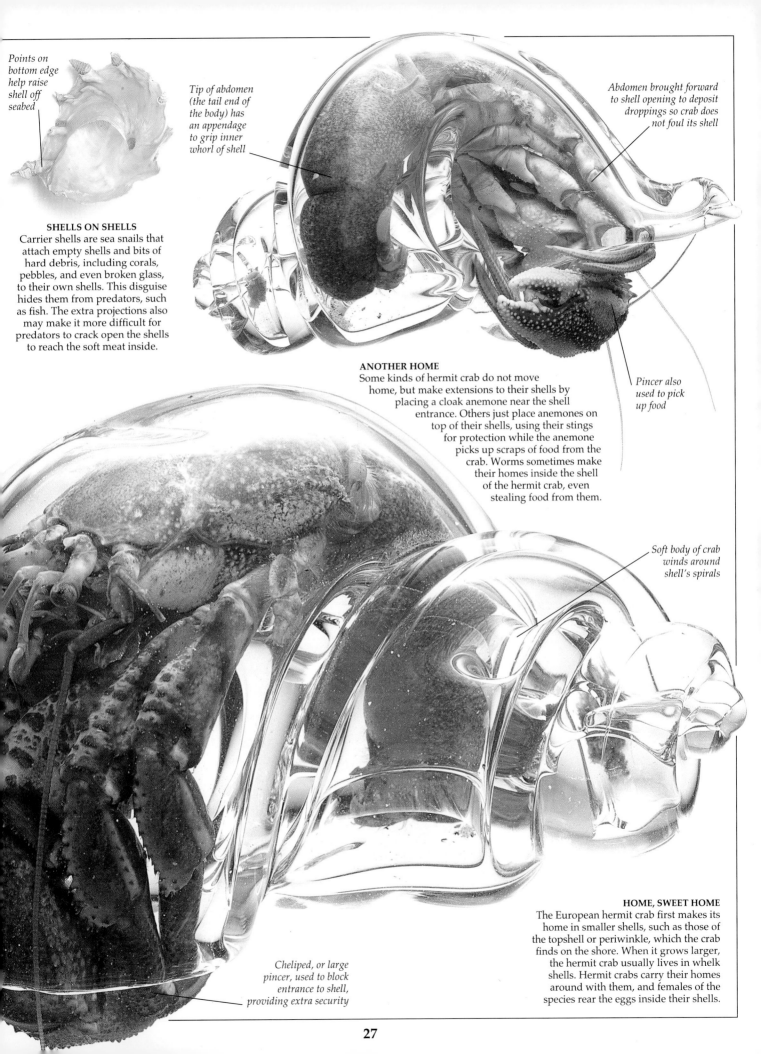

Points on bottom edge help raise shell off seabed

Tip of abdomen (the tail end of the body) has an appendage to grip inner whorl of shell

Abdomen brought forward to shell opening to deposit droppings so crab does not foul its shell

SHELLS ON SHELLS
Carrier shells are sea snails that attach empty shells and bits of hard debris, including corals, pebbles, and even broken glass, to their own shells. This disguise hides them from predators, such as fish. The extra projections also may make it more difficult for predators to crack open the shells to reach the soft meat inside.

Pincer also used to pick up food

ANOTHER HOME
Some kinds of hermit crab do not move home, but make extensions to their shells by placing a cloak anemone near the shell entrance. Others just place anemones on top of their shells, using their stings for protection while the anemone picks up scraps of food from the crab. Worms sometimes make their homes inside the shell of the hermit crab, even stealing food from them.

Soft body of crab winds around shell's spirals

Cheliped, or large pincer, used to block entrance to shell, providing extra security

HOME, SWEET HOME
The European hermit crab first makes its home in smaller shells, such as those of the topshell or periwinkle, which the crab finds on the shore. When it grows larger, the hermit crab usually lives in whelk shells. Hermit crabs carry their homes around with them, and females of the species rear the eggs inside their shells.

Attack and defense

MANY SEA CREATURES have special tactics for defending themselves from predators or attacking prey. Some produce venom (poison) to defend themselves and often advertise their danger with distinctive markings. Lionfish's stripes alert their enemies to their venomous spines, but being easy to see, they have to surprise their prey as they hunt in the open or ambush them from behind clumps of coral. Stonefish are also armed with venomous spines, blending perfectly with their background when waiting on a reef for prey to swim by. Octopi change color to match that of their background. If attacked, the blue-ringed octopus produces blue spots to warn that its bite is poisonous. Disappearing in a cloud of ink is another useful trick used by octopi, squid, and cuttlefish. Most clams withdraw their delicate soft parts into their shells, but the gaping file shell's tentacles are a deterrent – producing an irritating sticky fluid. But no defense method is foolproof. Even the most venomous jellyfish can be eaten by carnivorous turtles that are immune to their stings.

DEADLY STONEFISH
The stonefish is one of the deadliest creatures in the ocean. A stonefish's venom, which is projected through the sharp spines on its back, causes such intense pain that a person stepping on one may go into shock and die.

Ink cloud forming around cuttlefish

Long, dorsal spine with venom glands in grooves

INK SCREEN
Cephalopods, which include cuttlefish, squid, and octopi, produce a cloud of ink when threatened, to confuse an enemy and allow time for escape. The ink, produced in a gland linked to the gut, is ejected in a blast of water from a tubelike funnel near its head.

Horny projection above eye

Maerl (a chalky, red seaweed) grows in a thick mass along the stony seabed

Three venomous anal spines

KEEP CLEAR
The striped body of a lionfish warns predators that it is dangerous. A predator trying to bite a lionfish may be impaled by one or more of its poisonous spines. If it survives, the predator will remember the danger and leave the lionfish alone in future. Lionfish can swim openly, looking for smaller prey with little risk of attack. They live in tropical waters from the Indian to the Pacific oceans. In spite of being poisonous, they are popular aquarium fish because of their beauty.

Stripes warn predators that lionfish is dangerous

BLUE FOR DANGER
If this octopus becomes irritated, or when it is feeding, blue-ringed spots appear on its skin, warning of its poisonous bite. Although this octopus is similar in size to a person's hand, its bite can sometimes be fatal. Blue-ringed octopi live in shallow waters around Australia and some Pacific Ocean islands.

Two venomous spines on tail can pierce the swimmer's skin and inject its venom

Stingray's sting is sharp and serrated so it can easily pierce the skin

Painting of sea monsters, c. 1880s

Pectoral fin used for swimming

STING IN THE TAIL
This blue-spotted ray lives in the warm waters of both the Indian and Pacific oceans as well as the Red Sea, where it is often found lurking on the sandy seabed. If stepped on, shooting pains occur in the foot for over an hour, though the pain gradually wears off.

SOMETHING SCARY
Early sailors knew that some creatures living in the sea were dangerous and could kill people. Tales about these sea monsters, though common, often became greatly exaggerated. Monster stories were also invented to account for ships that foundered due to dangerous sea conditions.

VICIOUS JELLYFISH
Jellyfish are well known for their nasty stings, but none are nastier than those of the box jellyfish, or sea wasp. They often swim near the coasts of northern Australia and southeast Asia. Its stings produce horrible welts on anyone who comes in contact with their trailing tentacles. A badly stung person can die in four minutes.

When shell is closed, there is still a gap between the shell's two halves

Tentacles stick out when shell "gapes"

SHAGGY SHELLS
These gaping file shells cannot withdraw their masses of orange tentacles inside the two halves of their shell for protection, so the tentacles produce a sour-tasting, sticky substance to deter predators. If tentacles are nibbled off, they can regrow. Gaping file shells make their homes in seaweed, putting out byssus threads for anchorage. They can also make "nests" among horse mussels and oarweeds. If dislodged from their homes, they can move by expelling water from their shell and using their tentacles like oars.

Shell is up to 1 in (2.54 cm) long

The jet set

ONE WAY TO GET AROUND QUICKLY in water is by jet propulsion. Squid, octopi, and some mollusks (like clams) do this by squirting water from the body cavity. Jet propulsion can be used just for swimming, but it also helps mollusks escape from predators. Squid are best at jet propulsion – their bodies are permanently streamlined to reduce drag (resistance to water). Some kinds of scallops also use jet propulsion and are among the few clams that can swim. Most clams (mollusks with shells in two halves) can only bury themselves in the sand, or are anchored to the seabed. The common octopus lives on the rocky seabed in the coastal waters of the Atlantic Ocean and the Mediterranean and Caribbean seas. If attacked, it can jet off.

TENTACLE TALES
A Norwegian story tells of the Kraken, a giant sea monster that wrapped its arms around ships before sinking them. The legend may be based on the mysterious giant squid, which live in deep waters. Dead individuals sometimes are washed up on the shore, but no one has ever seen them swimming in the depths.

JET PROPULSION
The engines powering jet planes produce jets of air to fly in much the same way that octopi, squid, and cuttlefish produce jets of water to propel themselves through the water.

Funnel

Long arms to grasp prey

FLEXIBLE FUNNEL
Sticking out from the edge of the octopus's baglike body is its funnel. The funnel can bend to aim the jet of water backward or forward, and so control the direction in which the octopus heads off.

1 ON THE BOTTOM
The common octopus hides during the day in its rocky lair, coming out at night to look for such food as crustaceans. The octopus slowly approaches its prey, then pounces, wrapping it between the webbing at the base of its arms.

Powerful suckers grip the rock, so octopus can pull itself along

Sucker is sensitive to touch and taste

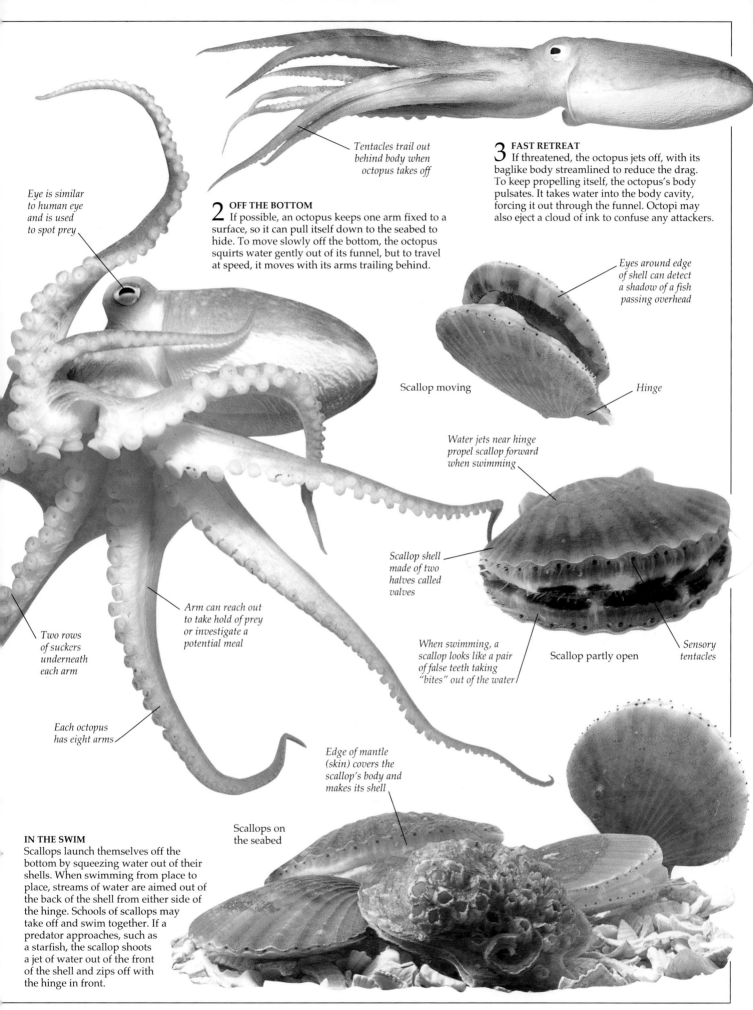

*Tentacles trail out
behind body when
octopus takes off*

*Eye is similar
to human eye
and is used
to spot prey*

2 OFF THE BOTTOM
If possible, an octopus keeps one arm fixed to a surface, so it can pull itself down to the seabed to hide. To move slowly off the bottom, the octopus squirts water gently out of its funnel, but to travel at speed, it moves with its arms trailing behind.

3 FAST RETREAT
If threatened, the octopus jets off, with its baglike body streamlined to reduce the drag. To keep propelling itself, the octopus's body pulsates. It takes water into the body cavity, forcing it out through the funnel. Octopi may also eject a cloud of ink to confuse any attackers.

*Eyes around edge
of shell can detect
a shadow of a fish
passing overhead*

Scallop moving

Hinge

*Water jets near hinge
propel scallop forward
when swimming*

*Scallop shell
made of two
halves called
valves*

*Arm can reach out
to take hold of prey
or investigate a
potential meal*

*Two rows
of suckers
underneath
each arm*

*When swimming, a
scallop looks like a pair
of false teeth taking
"bites" out of the water*

Scallop partly open

*Sensory
tentacles*

*Each octopus
has eight arms*

*Edge of mantle
(skin) covers the
scallop's body and
makes its shell*

IN THE SWIM
Scallops launch themselves off the bottom by squeezing water out of their shells. When swimming from place to place, streams of water are aimed out of the back of the shell from either side of the hinge. Schools of scallops may take off and swim together. If a predator approaches, such as a starfish, the scallop shoots a jet of water out of the front of the shell and zips off with the hinge in front.

Scallops on
the seabed

Moving along

FLYING FISH
Gathering speed underwater, flying fish leap clear of the surface to escape predators, then glide for over 30 seconds by spreading out the side fins.

AT SCHOOL
Fish often swim together in a school (like these blue-striped snappers), where a single fish has less chance of being attacked by a predator than when swimming on its own. The moving mass of individuals may confuse a predator; also, there are more pairs of eyes on the lookout for an attacker.

E VERY SWIMMER KNOWS that it is harder to move an arm or a leg through seawater than through air. This is because seawater is much denser than air. To be a fast swimmer like a dolphin, tuna, or sailfish, it helps to have a streamlined shape, like a torpedo, to reduce drag, or resistance to water. A smooth skin and few projections from the body also allow an animal to move through water more easily. The density of seawater does have an advantage in that it helps to support the weight of an animal's body. The heaviest animal that ever lived on earth is the blue whale, which weighs up to 150 tons. Some heavy-shelled creatures, like the chambered nautilus, have gas-filled floats to stop them from sinking. Some ocean animals, such as dolphins and flying fish, get up enough speed underwater to leap briefly into the air, but not all ocean animals are good swimmers. Many can only swim slowly, some drift along in the currents, crawl along the bottom, burrow in the sand, or stay put, anchored to the seabed.

IN THE SWING
During the day, many electric rays prefer to stay hidden on the sandy bottom, relying on their electric organs for defense, but they do swim if disturbed and at night when searching for prey. There are over 30 kinds of electric ray, mostly living in warm waters. Most other rays have spindly tails (unlike the electric ray's broad tail), and move through water using their pectoral fins. Waves pass from the front to the back of the pectoral fins, which, in larger rays like mantas, become so exaggerated that the fins actually beat up and down.

Electric ray's smooth skin can be either dark green or red-brown in color

Spiracle (a one-way valve) takes in water, which is pumped out through gill slits underneath

Electric rays can grow to 6 ft (1.8 m) and weigh as much as 110 lb (50 kg)

Pelvic fin

Swimming sequence of an electric ray, *Torpedo nobiliana*

DIVING DEEP
True seals move through water by beating their back flippers and tail from side to side and using their front flippers to steer. Their nostrils are closed to prevent water entering the airways. Harbor seals (right) can dive to 300 ft (90 m), but the champion seal diver is the Antarctic's Weddell seal, diving to 2,000 ft (600 m). Seals do not get the bends (pp. 110–111), because they breathe out before diving and, unlike humans, do not breathe compressed air. When underwater, seals use oxygen stored in the blood.

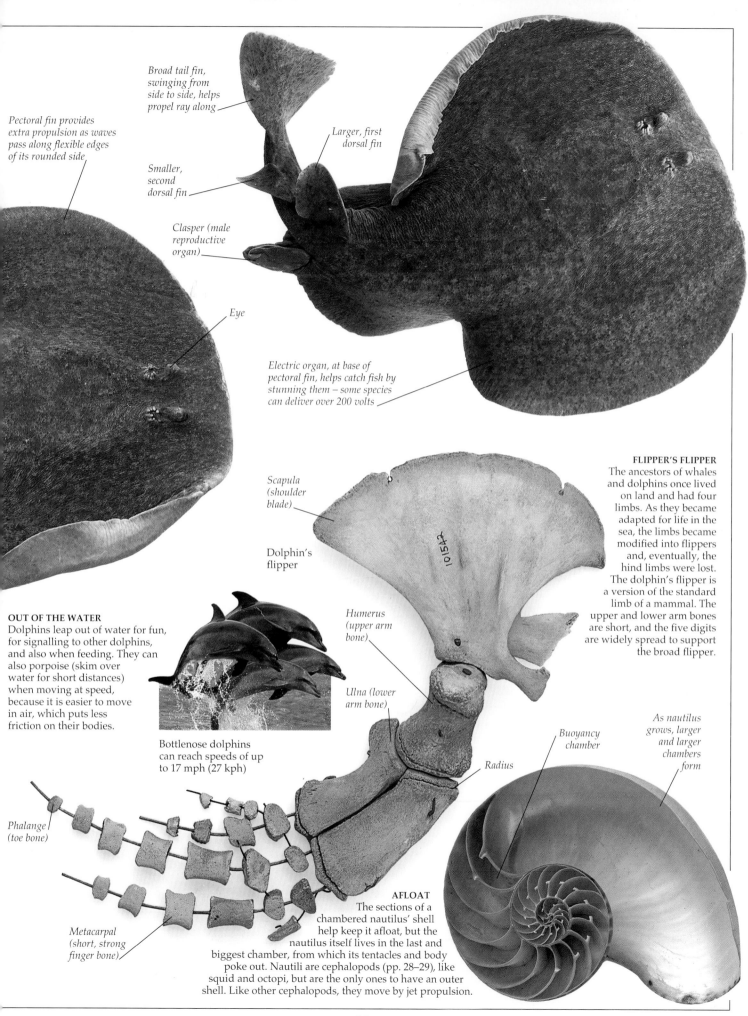

Broad tail fin, swinging from side to side, helps propel ray along

Pectoral fin provides extra propulsion as waves pass along flexible edges of its rounded side

Larger, first dorsal fin

Smaller, second dorsal fin

Clasper (male reproductive organ)

Eye

Electric organ, at base of pectoral fin, helps catch fish by stunning them – some species can deliver over 200 volts

FLIPPER'S FLIPPER
The ancestors of whales and dolphins once lived on land and had four limbs. As they became adapted for life in the sea, the limbs became modified into flippers and, eventually, the hind limbs were lost. The dolphin's flipper is a version of the standard limb of a mammal. The upper and lower arm bones are short, and the five digits are widely spread to support the broad flipper.

Scapula (shoulder blade)

Dolphin's flipper

Humerus (upper arm bone)

OUT OF THE WATER
Dolphins leap out of water for fun, for signalling to other dolphins, and also when feeding. They can also porpoise (skim over water for short distances) when moving at speed, because it is easier to move in air, which puts less friction on their bodies.

Ulna (lower arm bone)

Bottlenose dolphins can reach speeds of up to 17 mph (27 kph)

Buoyancy chamber

As nautilus grows, larger and larger chambers form

Radius

Phalange (toe bone)

Metacarpal (short, strong finger bone)

AFLOAT
The sections of a chambered nautilus' shell help keep it afloat, but the nautilus itself lives in the last and biggest chamber, from which its tentacles and body poke out. Nautili are cephalopods (pp. 28–29), like squid and octopi, but are the only ones to have an outer shell. Like other cephalopods, they move by jet propulsion.

Ocean travelers

To MAKE THE MOST of the vast expanses of water, some sea animals travel great distances, crisscrossing the oceans to find the best places to feed and breed. Whales such as the humpback are well known for feeding in the cold, food-rich waters of the far north or south, traveling to the warm waters of the tropics to breed and give birth. Many long-distance voyagers, such as turtles, seals, and sea birds, feed out at sea, but come ashore to breed. Freshwater eels are unusual because they go to the ocean to breed, then their young travel back to rivers, where they grow to maturity. Salmon do the reverse, growing up in the ocean and returning to rivers to breed (pp. 118–119). Ocean travelers often make use of currents to speed them on their way. Even animals that cannot swim can travel far and wide by hitching a ride on another animal or by drifting along on a piece of wood.

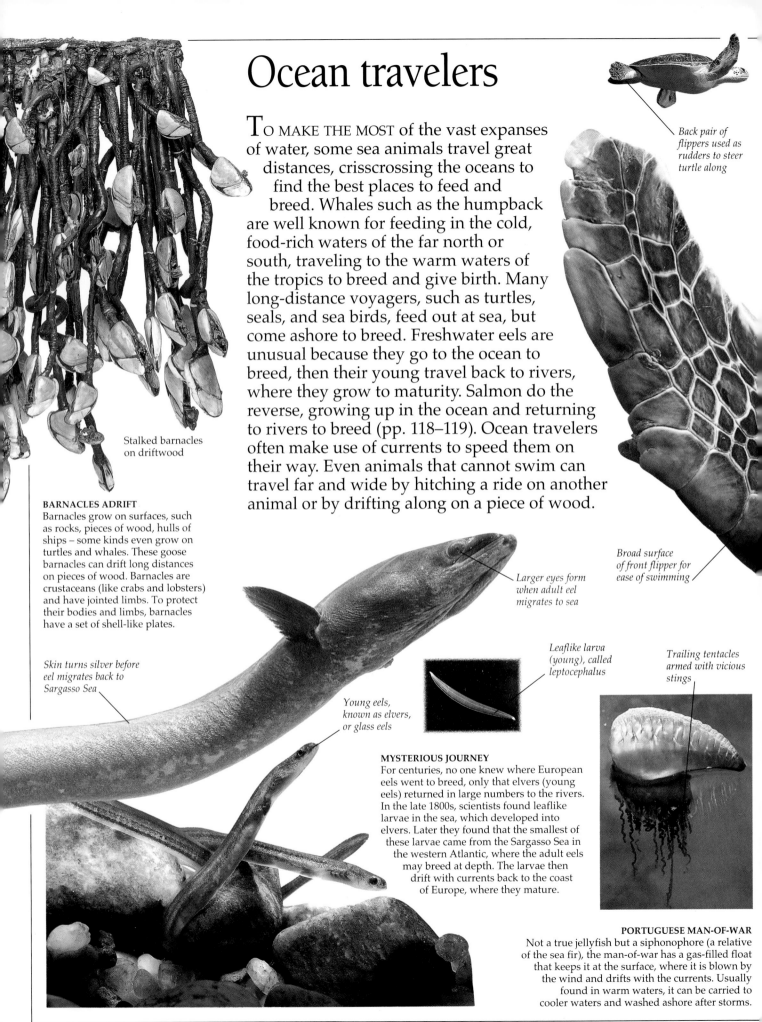

Back pair of flippers used as rudders to steer turtle along

Broad surface of front flipper for ease of swimming

Stalked barnacles on driftwood

BARNACLES ADRIFT
Barnacles grow on surfaces, such as rocks, pieces of wood, hulls of ships – some kinds even grow on turtles and whales. These goose barnacles can drift long distances on pieces of wood. Barnacles are crustaceans (like crabs and lobsters) and have jointed limbs. To protect their bodies and limbs, barnacles have a set of shell-like plates.

Skin turns silver before eel migrates back to Sargasso Sea

Larger eyes form when adult eel migrates to sea

Leaflike larva (young), called leptocephalus

Trailing tentacles armed with vicious stings

Young eels, known as elvers, or glass eels

MYSTERIOUS JOURNEY
For centuries, no one knew where European eels went to breed, only that elvers (young eels) returned in large numbers to the rivers. In the late 1800s, scientists found leaflike larvae in the sea, which developed into elvers. Later they found that the smallest of these larvae came from the Sargasso Sea in the western Atlantic, where the adult eels may breed at depth. The larvae then drift with currents back to the coast of Europe, where they mature.

PORTUGUESE MAN-OF-WAR
Not a true jellyfish but a siphonophore (a relative of the sea fir), the man-of-war has a gas-filled float that keeps it at the surface, where it is blown by the wind and drifts with the currents. Usually found in warm waters, it can be carried to cooler waters and washed ashore after storms.

Swimming sequence of a green turtle

Turtle shell is streamlined for gliding through water

UNDERWATER FLIER

Green turtles live in the warm waters of the Atlantic, Pacific, and Indian oceans. Like all turtles, they come ashore to lay their eggs. First the females mate in shallow water with the waiting males. Later, under cover of darkness, the females crawl up the beach to lay their eggs in the sand before heading back to the water. They may return several times in one breeding season to lay further batches of eggs. Some green turtles are known to travel several hundred miles or more to reach their breeding beaches where they hatched themselves. Green turtles feed on sea grasses and seaweeds.

Front pair of flippers help turtle to "fly" through water

Turtles are air breathers, so must come to surface to breathe through their nostrils

Green turtle (*Chelonia mydas*) is on the endangered species list

TURTLE TRIP

In the Japanese legend, Urashima Taro rides into the kingdom of the sea on a turtle. After spending some time in the depths, he begs the sea goddess to let him go home. She allows this, but gives him a box that he must never open. On his return he finds his home has changed and no one knows him. Hoping for some comfort, he opens the box, but the spell is broken. He becomes a very old man because he has spent not three years – but 300 – in the sea.

The twilight zone

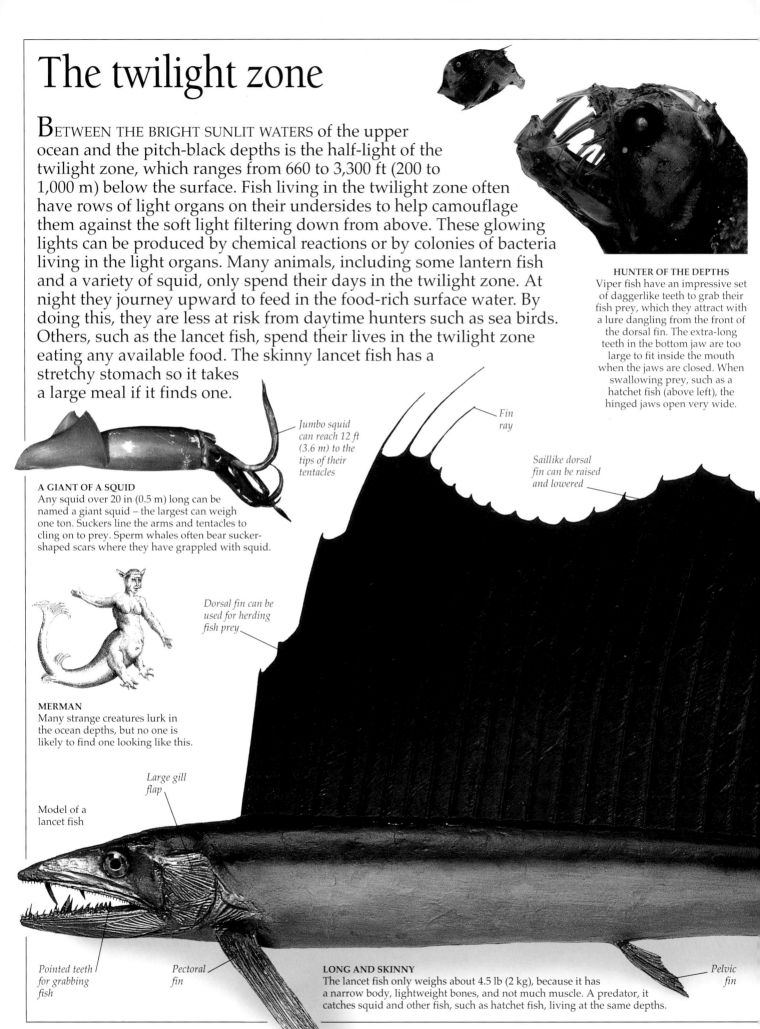

BETWEEN THE BRIGHT SUNLIT WATERS of the upper ocean and the pitch-black depths is the half-light of the twilight zone, which ranges from 660 to 3,300 ft (200 to 1,000 m) below the surface. Fish living in the twilight zone often have rows of light organs on their undersides to help camouflage them against the soft light filtering down from above. These glowing lights can be produced by chemical reactions or by colonies of bacteria living in the light organs. Many animals, including some lantern fish and a variety of squid, only spend their days in the twilight zone. At night they journey upward to feed in the food-rich surface water. By doing this, they are less at risk from daytime hunters such as sea birds. Others, such as the lancet fish, spend their lives in the twilight zone eating any available food. The skinny lancet fish has a stretchy stomach so it takes a large meal if it finds one.

HUNTER OF THE DEPTHS
Viper fish have an impressive set of daggerlike teeth to grab their fish prey, which they attract with a lure dangling from the front of the dorsal fin. The extra-long teeth in the bottom jaw are too large to fit inside the mouth when the jaws are closed. When swallowing prey, such as a hatchet fish (above left), the hinged jaws open very wide.

Jumbo squid can reach 12 ft (3.6 m) to the tips of their tentacles

Fin ray

Saillike dorsal fin can be raised and lowered

A GIANT OF A SQUID
Any squid over 20 in (0.5 m) long can be named a giant squid – the largest can weigh one ton. Suckers line the arms and tentacles to cling on to prey. Sperm whales often bear sucker-shaped scars where they have grappled with squid.

Dorsal fin can be used for herding fish prey

MERMAN
Many strange creatures lurk in the ocean depths, but no one is likely to find one looking like this.

Large gill flap

Model of a lancet fish

Pointed teeth for grabbing fish

Pectoral fin

LONG AND SKINNY
The lancet fish only weighs about 4.5 lb (2 kg), because it has a narrow body, lightweight bones, and not much muscle. A predator, it catches squid and other fish, such as hatchet fish, living at the same depths.

Pelvic fin

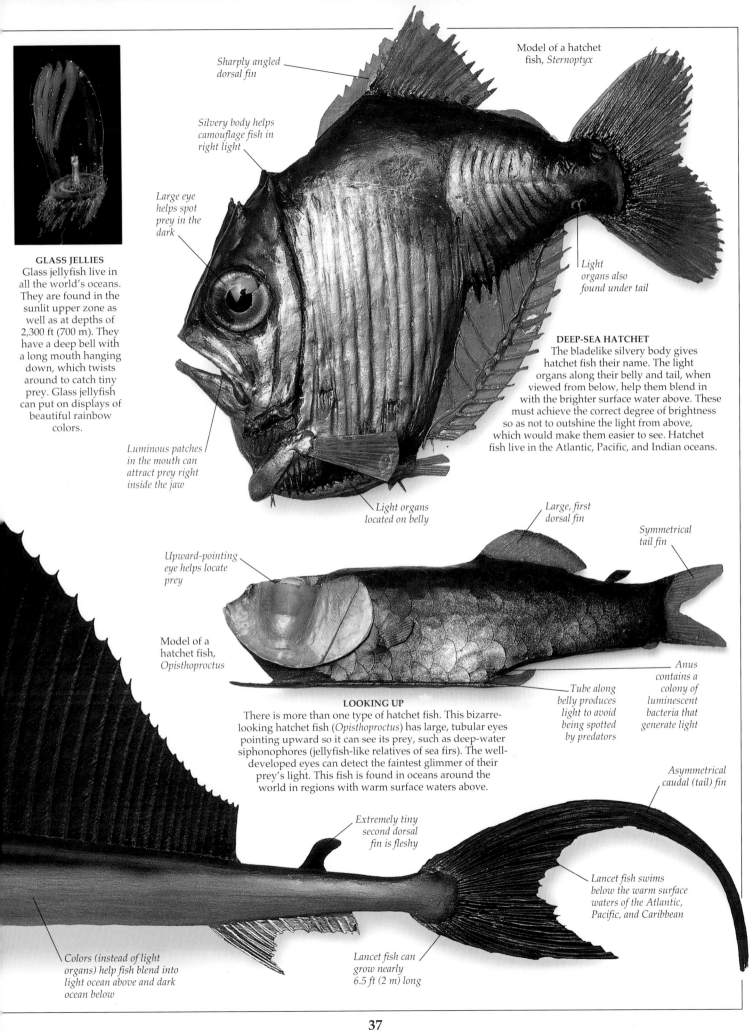

Sharply angled
dorsal fin

Model of a hatchet
fish, *Sternoptyx*

Silvery body helps
camouflage fish in
right light

Large eye
helps spot
prey in the
dark

Light
organs also
found under tail

GLASS JELLIES
Glass jellyfish live in
all the world's oceans.
They are found in the
sunlit upper zone as
well as at depths of
2,300 ft (700 m). They
have a deep bell with
a long mouth hanging
down, which twists
around to catch tiny
prey. Glass jellyfish
can put on displays of
beautiful rainbow
colors.

DEEP-SEA HATCHET
The bladelike silvery body gives
hatchet fish their name. The light
organs along their belly and tail, when
viewed from below, help them blend in
with the brighter surface water above. These
must achieve the correct degree of brightness
so as not to outshine the light from above,
which would make them easier to see. Hatchet
fish live in the Atlantic, Pacific, and Indian oceans.

Luminous patches
in the mouth can
attract prey right
inside the jaw

Light organs
located on belly

Large, first
dorsal fin

Symmetrical
tail fin

Upward-pointing
eye helps locate
prey

Model of a
hatchet fish,
Opisthoproctus

Anus
contains a
colony of
luminescent
bacteria that
generate light

LOOKING UP
There is more than one type of hatchet fish. This bizarre-
looking hatchet fish (*Opisthoproctus*) has large, tubular eyes
pointing upward so it can see its prey, such as deep-water
siphonophores (jellyfish-like relatives of sea firs). The well-
developed eyes can detect the faintest glimmer of their
prey's light. This fish is found in oceans around the
world in regions with warm surface waters above.

Tube along
belly produces
light to avoid
being spotted
by predators

Asymmetrical
caudal (tail) fin

Extremely tiny
second dorsal
fin is fleshy

Lancet fish swims
below the warm surface
waters of the Atlantic,
Pacific, and Caribbean

Colors (instead of light
organs) help fish blend into
light ocean above and dark
ocean below

Lancet fish can
grow nearly
6.5 ft (2 m) long

The darkest depths

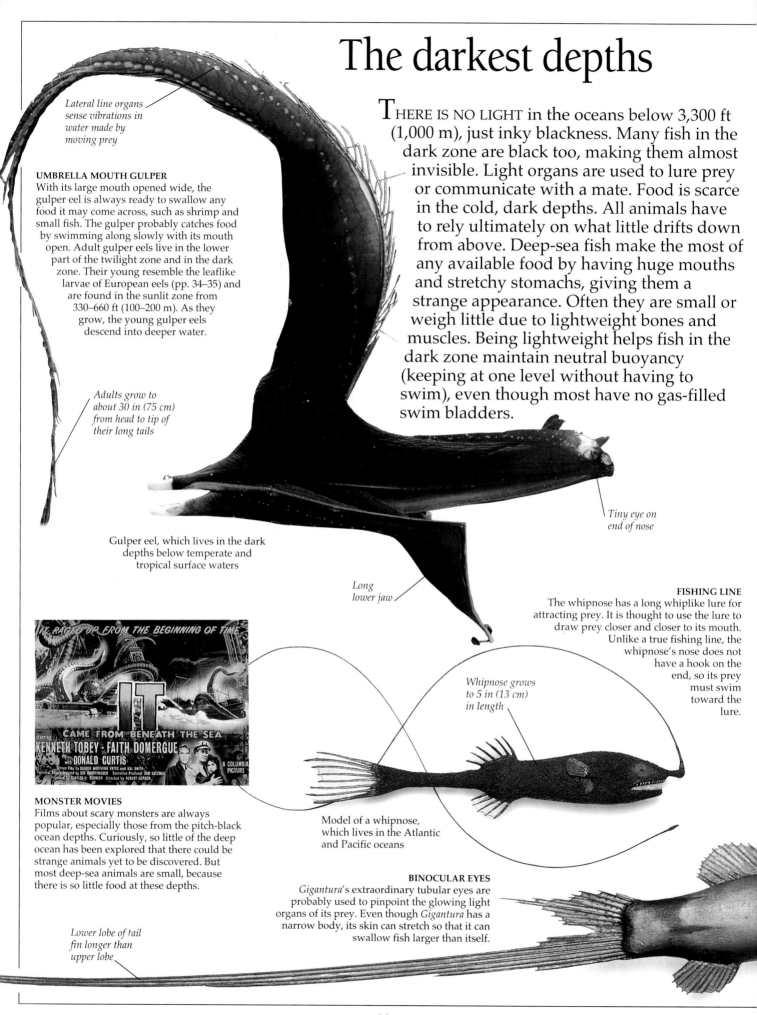

THERE IS NO LIGHT in the oceans below 3,300 ft (1,000 m), just inky blackness. Many fish in the dark zone are black too, making them almost invisible. Light organs are used to lure prey or communicate with a mate. Food is scarce in the cold, dark depths. All animals have to rely ultimately on what little drifts down from above. Deep-sea fish make the most of any available food by having huge mouths and stretchy stomachs, giving them a strange appearance. Often they are small or weigh little due to lightweight bones and muscles. Being lightweight helps fish in the dark zone maintain neutral buoyancy (keeping at one level without having to swim), even though most have no gas-filled swim bladders.

Lateral line organs sense vibrations in water made by moving prey

UMBRELLA MOUTH GULPER
With its large mouth opened wide, the gulper eel is always ready to swallow any food it may come across, such as shrimp and small fish. The gulper probably catches food by swimming along slowly with its mouth open. Adult gulper eels live in the lower part of the twilight zone and in the dark zone. Their young resemble the leaflike larvae of European eels (pp. 34–35) and are found in the sunlit zone from 330–660 ft (100–200 m). As they grow, the young gulper eels descend into deeper water.

Adults grow to about 30 in (75 cm) from head to tip of their long tails

Tiny eye on end of nose

Gulper eel, which lives in the dark depths below temperate and tropical surface waters

Long lower jaw

FISHING LINE
The whipnose has a long whiplike lure for attracting prey. It is thought to use the lure to draw prey closer and closer to its mouth. Unlike a true fishing line, the whipnose's nose does not have a hook on the end, so its prey must swim toward the lure.

Whipnose grows to 5 in (13 cm) in length

MONSTER MOVIES
Films about scary monsters are always popular, especially those from the pitch-black ocean depths. Curiously, so little of the deep ocean has been explored that there could be strange animals yet to be discovered. But most deep-sea animals are small, because there is so little food at these depths.

Model of a whipnose, which lives in the Atlantic and Pacific oceans

BINOCULAR EYES
Gigantura's extraordinary tubular eyes are probably used to pinpoint the glowing light organs of its prey. Even though *Gigantura* has a narrow body, its skin can stretch so that it can swallow fish larger than itself.

Lower lobe of tail fin longer than upper lobe

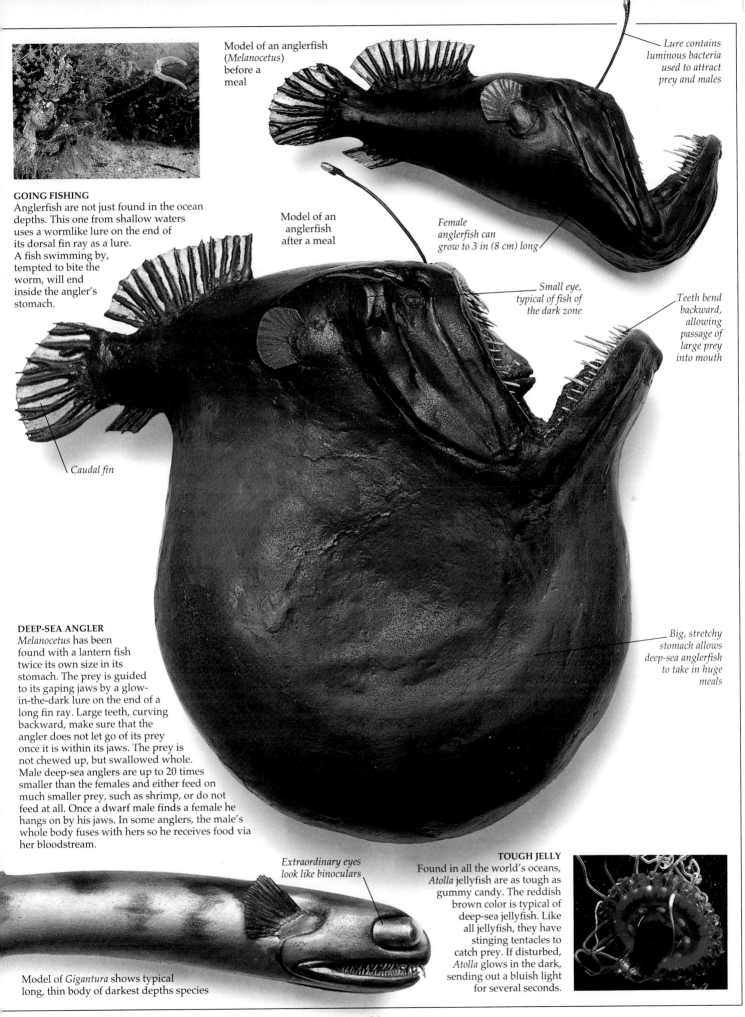

Model of an anglerfish
(*Melanocetus*)
before a
meal

Lure contains
luminous bacteria
used to attract
prey and males

GOING FISHING
Anglerfish are not just found in the ocean
depths. This one from shallow waters
uses a wormlike lure on the end of
its dorsal fin ray as a lure.
A fish swimming by,
tempted to bite the
worm, will end
inside the angler's
stomach.

Model of an
anglerfish
after a meal

Female
anglerfish can
grow to 3 in (8 cm) long

Small eye,
typical of fish of
the dark zone

Teeth bend
backward,
allowing
passage
of large prey
into mouth

Caudal fin

DEEP-SEA ANGLER
Melanocetus has been
found with a lantern fish
twice its own size in its
stomach. The prey is guided
to its gaping jaws by a glow-
in-the-dark lure on the end of a
long fin ray. Large teeth, curving
backward, make sure that the
angler does not let go of its prey
once it is within its jaws. The prey is
not chewed up, but swallowed whole.
Male deep-sea anglers are up to 20 times
smaller than the females and either feed on
much smaller prey, such as shrimp, or do not
feed at all. Once a dwarf male finds a female he
hangs on by his jaws. In some anglers, the male's
whole body fuses with hers so he receives food via
her bloodstream.

Big, stretchy
stomach allows
deep-sea anglerfish
to take in huge
meals

Extraordinary eyes
look like binoculars

TOUGH JELLY
Found in all the world's oceans,
Atolla jellyfish are as tough as
gummy candy. The reddish
brown color is typical of
deep-sea jellyfish. Like
all jellyfish, they have
stinging tentacles to
catch prey. If disturbed,
Atolla glows in the dark,
sending out a bluish light
for several seconds.

Model of *Gigantura* shows typical
long, thin body of darkest depths species

Dried remains of sea anemones

On the bottom

THE BOTTOM OF THE DEEP OCEAN is not an easy place to live. There is little food and it is dark and cold. Much of the seabed is covered with soft clays or mudlike oozes made of skeletons of tiny sea animals and plants. The ooze on the vast open plains of the abyss can reach several hundred yards thick. Animals walking along the bottom have long legs to avoid stirring it up. Some grow anchored to the seabed and have long stems to keep their feeding structures clear of the ooze. Food particles can be filtered out of the water, for example, by the feathery arms of sea lilies or through the many pores in sponges. Some animals, such as sea cucumbers, manage to feed on the seabed by extracting food particles from the ooze. Food particles are the remains of dead animals (and their droppings) and plants that have sunk down from above. Occasionally a larger carcass reaches the bottom uneaten – a real bonanza for any mobile bottom dwellers, which home in on it from all around. Because food is scarce and temperatures so low, most animals living in the deep ocean take a long time to grow.

Underwater cables were laid across the Atlantic Ocean to relay telegraphic messages, c. 1870

GLASSY STRANDS
This sponge grows anchored to the soft seabed by its stem of glass strands. Sea anemones often grow on their stems. When a glass-rope sponge dies, the cup-shaped part disappears and all that is left is the stem stuck in the seabed.

NOT A TRUE SPIDER
Sea spiders look like land spiders, but belong to a separate group called pycnogonids. Some deep-sea spiders have a leg span of 2 ft (60 cm) across, so can stride along without stirring up clouds of particles. They can also swim, launching off the seabed, bringing their legs toward their bodies, then sinking down again.

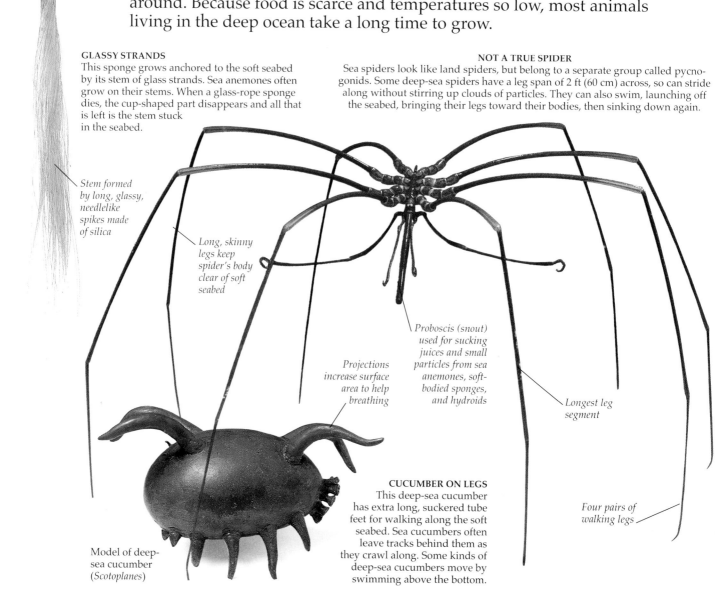

Stem formed by long, glassy, needlelike spikes made of silica

Long, skinny legs keep spider's body clear of soft seabed

Projections increase surface area to help breathing

Proboscis (snout) used for sucking juices and small particles from sea anemones, soft-bodied sponges, and hydroids

Longest leg segment

CUCUMBER ON LEGS
This deep-sea cucumber has extra long, suckered tube feet for walking along the soft seabed. Sea cucumbers often leave tracks behind them as they crawl along. Some kinds of deep-sea cucumbers move by swimming above the bottom.

Four pairs of walking legs

Model of deep-sea cucumber (Scotoplanes)

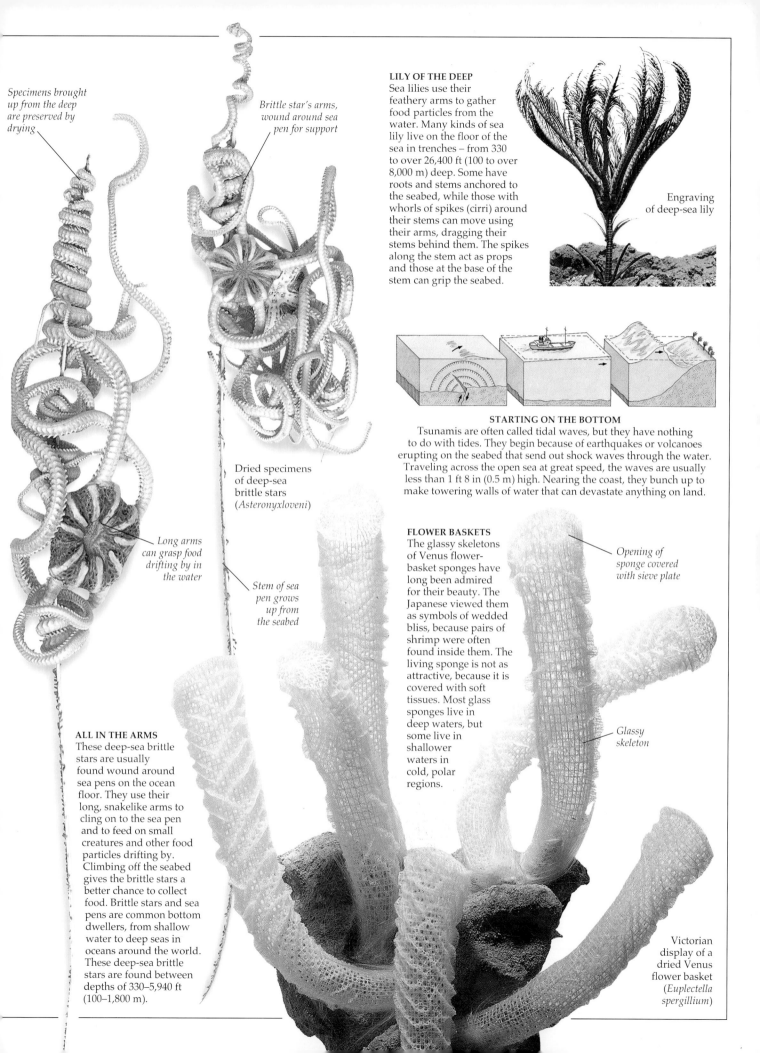

Specimens brought up from the deep are preserved by drying

Brittle star's arms, wound around sea pen for support

LILY OF THE DEEP
Sea lilies use their feathery arms to gather food particles from the water. Many kinds of sea lily live on the floor of the sea in trenches – from 330 to over 26,400 ft (100 to over 8,000 m) deep. Some have roots and stems anchored to the seabed, while those with whorls of spikes (cirri) around their stems can move using their arms, dragging their stems behind them. The spikes along the stem act as props and those at the base of the stem can grip the seabed.

Engraving of deep-sea lily

Dried specimens of deep-sea brittle stars (*Asteronyxloveni*)

Long arms can grasp food drifting by in the water

Stem of sea pen grows up from the seabed

STARTING ON THE BOTTOM
Tsunamis are often called tidal waves, but they have nothing to do with tides. They begin because of earthquakes or volcanoes erupting on the seabed that send out shock waves through the water. Traveling across the open sea at great speed, the waves are usually less than 1 ft 8 in (0.5 m) high. Nearing the coast, they bunch up to make towering walls of water that can devastate anything on land.

FLOWER BASKETS
The glassy skeletons of Venus flower-basket sponges have long been admired for their beauty. The Japanese viewed them as symbols of wedded bliss, because pairs of shrimp were often found inside them. The living sponge is not as attractive, because it is covered with soft tissues. Most glass sponges live in deep waters, but some live in shallower waters in cold, polar regions.

Opening of sponge covered with sieve plate

Glassy skeleton

ALL IN THE ARMS
These deep-sea brittle stars are usually found wound around sea pens on the ocean floor. They use their long, snakelike arms to cling on to the sea pen and to feed on small creatures and other food particles drifting by. Climbing off the seabed gives the brittle stars a better chance to collect food. Brittle stars and sea pens are common bottom dwellers, from shallow water to deep seas in oceans around the world. These deep-sea brittle stars are found between depths of 330–5,940 ft (100–1,800 m).

Victorian display of a dried Venus flower basket (*Euplectella spergillium*)

Vents and smokers

IN PARTS OF THE OCEAN FLOOR, there are cracks in the crust from which extremely hot, mineral-rich water gushes. These vents (hot springs) exist at the spreading centers where the gigantic plates that make up the earth's crust are moving apart. Cold seawater sinks deep into cracks, where it heats up and collects quantities of dissolved minerals. At temperatures of up to 750°F (400°C), hot water spews out, depositing some minerals to form black smokers, or chimneys. Hot water produced by vents helps bacterial growth, which creates food from the hydrogen sulfide in the water. Extraordinary animals crowd around the cracks and rely on these microbes for food. Scientists using submersibles (pp. 112–113) in the late 1970s discovered the first vent communities in the Pacific. Since then, vents have been discovered in other spreading centers in the Pacific and the Mid-Atlantic Ridge.

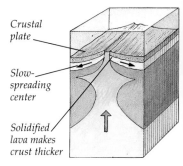

Crustal plate

Slow-spreading center

Solidified lava makes crust thicker

GROWING OCEAN
New areas of ocean floor are continually being created at spreading centers between two crustal plates. When lava (hot, molten rock) emerges from within the crust, it cools and solidifies, adding material to the edge of each adjoining plate. Old areas of ocean floor are destroyed as one plate slides under another. Lava from volcanic eruptions at spreading centers can kill off communities of vent animals.

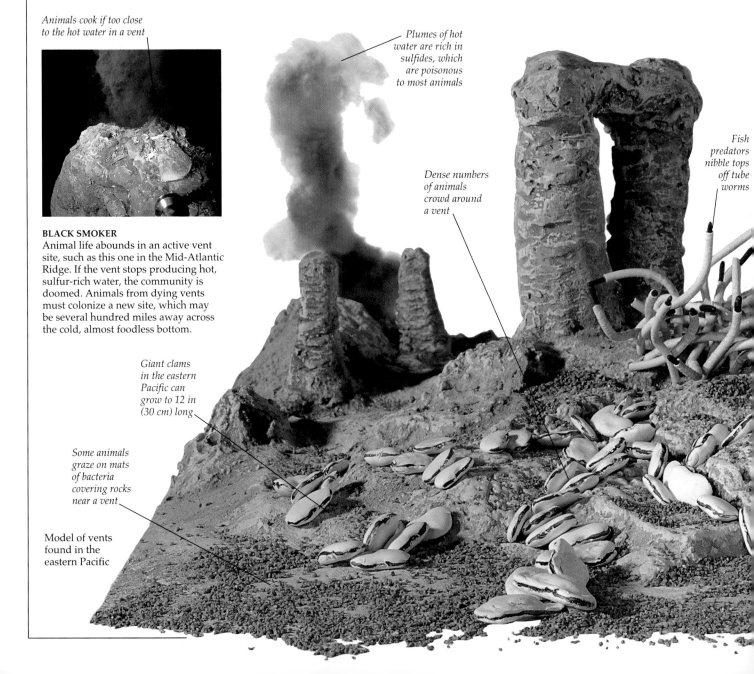

Animals cook if too close to the hot water in a vent

Plumes of hot water are rich in sulfides, which are poisonous to most animals

Dense numbers of animals crowd around a vent

Fish predators nibble tops off tube worms

BLACK SMOKER
Animal life abounds in an active vent site, such as this one in the Mid-Atlantic Ridge. If the vent stops producing hot, sulfur-rich water, the community is doomed. Animals from dying vents must colonize a new site, which may be several hundred miles away across the cold, almost foodless bottom.

Giant clams in the eastern Pacific can grow to 12 in (30 cm) long

Some animals graze on mats of bacteria covering rocks near a vent

Model of vents found in the eastern Pacific

Deep-sea fish photographed from Alvin *near a vent on the Mid-Atlantic Ridge*

Alvin by the support ship, Atlantis II

Black smoker chimney can reach 33 ft (10 m) high

Chimney made from mineral deposits

CHAMPION SUBMERSIBLE
The U.S. submersible *Alvin* took the first scientists down to observe marine life near the Galápagos vents in the east Pacific in the 1970s. Since then, *Alvin* has completed many dives to vents around the world, to depths of 12,500 ft (3,800 m). Other submersibles that have dived on vent sites include the French *Nautile* (pp. 116–117) and the Russians *Mir I* and *II*.

VENT COMMUNITIES
This model shows the vent communities in the eastern Pacific, where giant clams and tube worms are the most distinctive animals. Vents in other parts of the world have different kinds of animals, such as the hairy snails from the Mariana Trench and eyeless shrimps from vents along the Mid-Atlantic Ridge.

Tube worm can grow to 10 ft (3 m) long

Giant tube worm has bacteria inside its body that provide the worm with food

What is a shark?

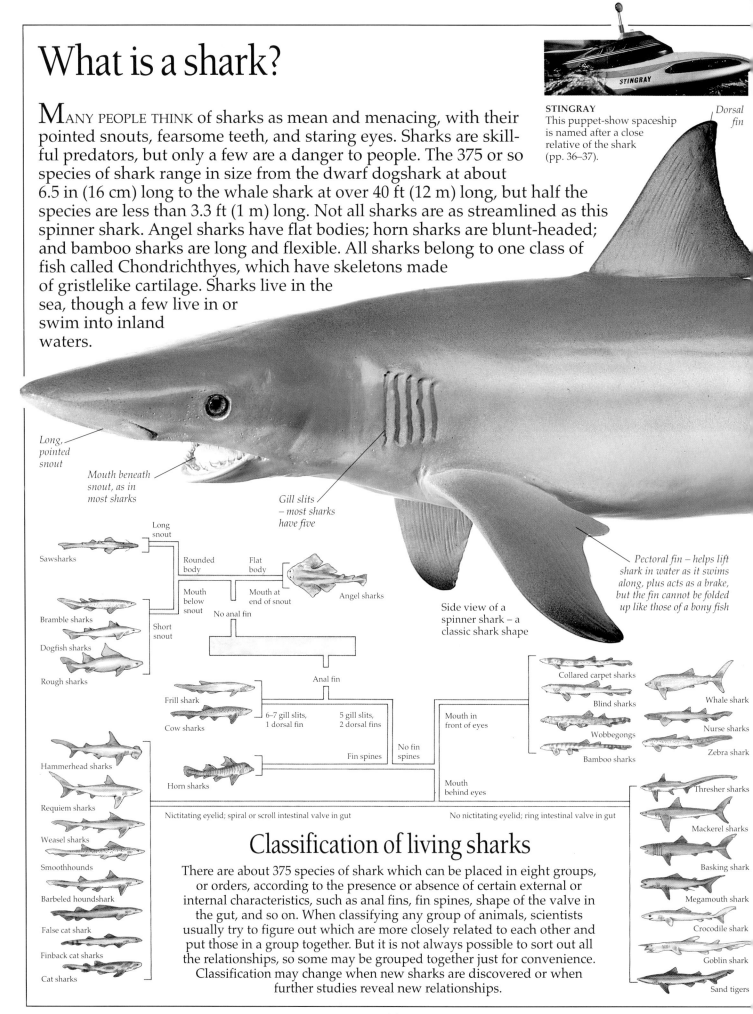

Many people think of sharks as mean and menacing, with their pointed snouts, fearsome teeth, and staring eyes. Sharks are skillful predators, but only a few are a danger to people. The 375 or so species of shark range in size from the dwarf dogshark at about 6.5 in (16 cm) long to the whale shark at over 40 ft (12 m) long, but half the species are less than 3.3 ft (1 m) long. Not all sharks are as streamlined as this spinner shark. Angel sharks have flat bodies; horn sharks are blunt-headed; and bamboo sharks are long and flexible. All sharks belong to one class of fish called Chondrichthyes, which have skeletons made of gristlelike cartilage. Sharks live in the sea, though a few live in or swim into inland waters.

STINGRAY
This puppet-show spaceship is named after a close relative of the shark (pp. 36–37).

Dorsal fin

Long, pointed snout

Mouth beneath snout, as in most sharks

Gill slits – most sharks have five

Pectoral fin – helps lift shark in water as it swims along, plus acts as a brake, but the fin cannot be folded up like those of a bony fish

Side view of a spinner shark – a classic shark shape

Sawsharks

Long snout

Rounded body

Flat body

Mouth below snout

Mouth at end of snout

Angel sharks

No anal fin

Bramble sharks

Dogfish sharks

Short snout

Rough sharks

Frill shark

Cow sharks

Anal fin

6–7 gill slits, 1 dorsal fin

5 gill slits, 2 dorsal fins

Mouth in front of eyes

Collared carpet sharks

Blind sharks

Whale shark

Wobbegongs

Nurse sharks

Bamboo sharks

Zebra shark

Hammerhead sharks

Requiem sharks

Weasel sharks

Smoothhounds

Barbeled houndshark

False cat shark

Finback cat sharks

Cat sharks

Horn sharks

Fin spines

No fin spines

Mouth behind eyes

Thresher sharks

Mackerel sharks

Basking shark

Megamouth shark

Crocodile shark

Goblin shark

Sand tigers

Nictitating eyelid; spiral or scroll intestinal valve in gut

No nictitating eyelid; ring intestinal valve in gut

Classification of living sharks

There are about 375 species of shark which can be placed in eight groups, or orders, according to the presence or absence of certain external or internal characteristics, such as anal fins, fin spines, shape of the valve in the gut, and so on. When classifying any group of animals, scientists usually try to figure out which are more closely related to each other and put those in a group together. But it is not always possible to sort out all the relationships, so some may be grouped together just for convenience. Classification may change when new sharks are discovered or when further studies reveal new relationships.

THOUSANDS OF TEETH

Sharks never run out of teeth. When the front ones become worn or break, they are replaced by new ones in the row behind (right). Some sharks shed one or two teeth at a time, while others, like spiny dogfish and cookiecutters (pp. 72–73), replace a whole row at a time. As the shark grows, its new teeth are larger than the ones replaced. During its life, a shark will produce thousands of teeth. Each new tooth forms in the shark's gums and rotates forward until it eventually drops out. Sharks' teeth are embedded in their gums and are not directly attached to their jaws, like those of bony fish.

Jaws and teeth of sand tiger shark

Skin of bramble shark

SCALES

Most bony fish have scales covering their skin. Their scales are not replaced – they increase in size as the fish grows.

Fish scale

ROUGH SKIN

Sharks are covered in small, toothlike denticles, which give the skin a rough feel if stroked the wrong way. Bramble sharks (above) have large denticles scattered sparsely over the skin instead of in a continuous cover as in other sharks. As sharks grow, the denticles are shed and replaced by slightly larger ones, in the same way the teeth are replaced. The structure of a denticle is the same as a shark's tooth.

SHARK VS. FISH

Sharks, rays, skates, and chimeras are cartilaginous fish belonging to the class Chondrichthyes. Their skeletons are rubbery, unlike those of bony fish, which are more rigid. Most bony fish have ray-fins, like the bib (left). The most notable differences between sharks and bony fish are that bony fish have a gill cover, or operculum, instead of gill slits, and scales instead of denticles. Bony fish also have a swim bladder, or gas-filled sac, which helps them control their buoyancy.

Caudal fin

Pelvic fin – acts as a stabilizer to prevent shark from rolling

Anal fin

SPINNING IN CIRCLES

The spinner shark is named for its habit of spinning around on its axis, which it does to confuse its fish prey as it hunts in a school of fish. Spinner sharks grow to 8 ft (2.5 m) long and live in the warm coastal and deeper waters of the Atlantic, Indian, and western Pacific oceans.

Third dorsal fin

Second dorsal fin

First dorsal fin

Side view of a bib

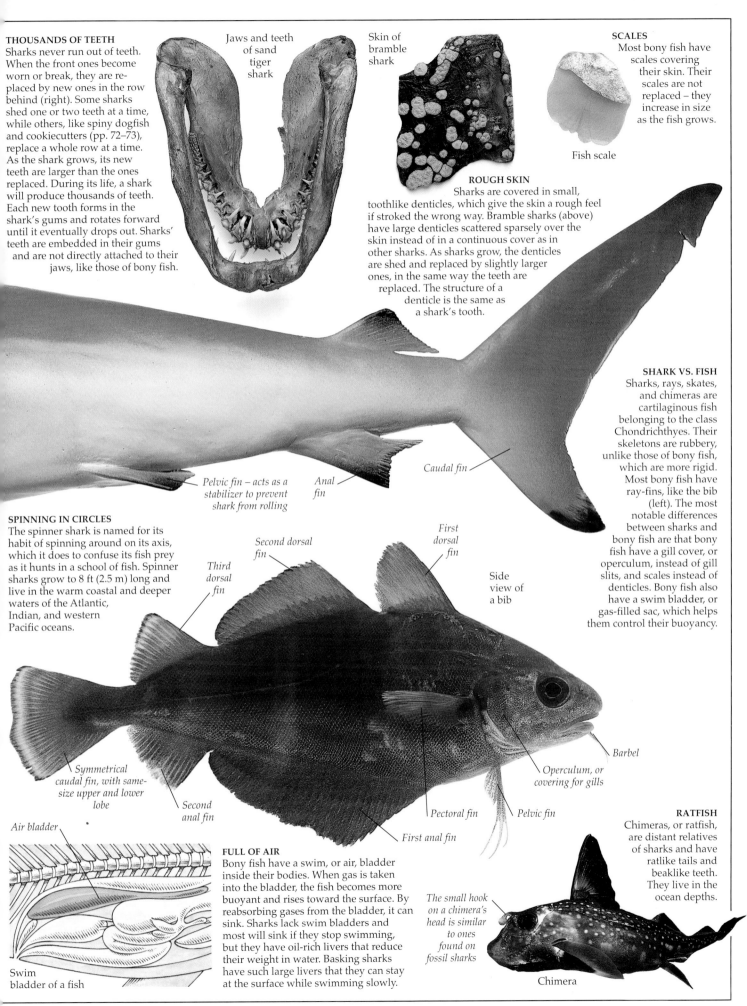

Symmetrical caudal fin, with same-size upper and lower lobe

Second anal fin

Barbel

Operculum, or covering for gills

Pectoral fin

Pelvic fin

First anal fin

Air bladder

FULL OF AIR

Bony fish have a swim, or air, bladder inside their bodies. When gas is taken into the bladder, the fish becomes more buoyant and rises toward the surface. By reabsorbing gases from the bladder, it can sink. Sharks lack swim bladders and most will sink if they stop swimming, but they have oil-rich livers that reduce their weight in water. Basking sharks have such large livers that they can stay at the surface while swimming slowly.

Swim bladder of a fish

The small hook on a chimera's head is similar to ones found on fossil sharks

RATFISH

Chimeras, or ratfish, are distant relatives of sharks and have ratlike tails and beaklike teeth. They live in the ocean depths.

Chimera

45

Inside a shark

Packaged neatly inside this spinner shark's body are all the organs that keep it alive. To breathe, sharks have gills that absorb oxygen from the water and release carbon dioxide back into it. These gases are transported to and from the gills by the blood. The heart pumps the blood around the body, delivering oxygen and nutrients while taking away carbon dioxide and other wastes. To get energy for all their activities, including growth and repair, sharks need to eat. Food passes from the mouth into the digestive system, which is like a large tube. From the mouth the food goes down the gullet into the stomach, where digestion begins, and then into the intestine where digested food is absorbed. Indigestible wastes collect in the rectum to be passed out of the body. Digested food is further processed in the large liver. Kidneys remove wastes from the blood and regulate blood concentration. Large muscles in the body wall keep the shark swimming, and the skeleton and skin provide support. The brain coordinates the shark's actions with signals or instructions passed back and forth along the spinal cord. Finally, sharks, like all animals, cannot live forever and must reproduce to carry on the species. Female sharks have ovaries that produce eggs, and males produce sperm from their testes. When sperm meets egg, a new life begins.

DANGER BELOW
Sharks have been known to attack people coming down into water, as this Australian parachutist will soon discover.

Paired kidneys regulate waste products to keep the concentration of body fluids just above that of seawater, or sharks will dehydrate

Segmented swimming muscles contract alternately, sending a wave motion from head to tail

Model of female spinner shark, showing internal anatomy

Vent between claspers for disposing of body wastes

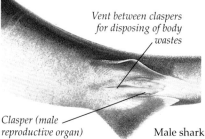

Clasper (male reproductive organ)

Male shark

Female shark (claspers absent)

Cloaca (opening for reproduction, and vent for waste disposal)

MALE OR FEMALE
All male sharks have a pair of claspers that are formed from the inner edge of their pelvic fins. During mating, one of the claspers is rotated forward and inserted into the female's body opening, or cloaca. Sperm is pumped down a groove in the clasper into the female, so fertilization of her eggs takes place inside her body.

Rectal gland (third kidney) passes excess salt out of the body through the vent

Scroll valve in intestine, or gut; some sharks have spiral or ring valves

Left lobe of large liver

Caudal fin

ALL IN THE TAIL
Sharks have a vertebral column, or backbone, that extends into the upper lobe of their caudal fin, or tail. This type of caudal fin is called a heterocercal tail, as opposed to those in most bony fish, where the upper lobe does not contain an extension of the upper vertebral column. Cartilaginous rods and dermal filaments help to strengthen the shark's tail.

Vertebral column

Cartilaginous rod

Dermal filament

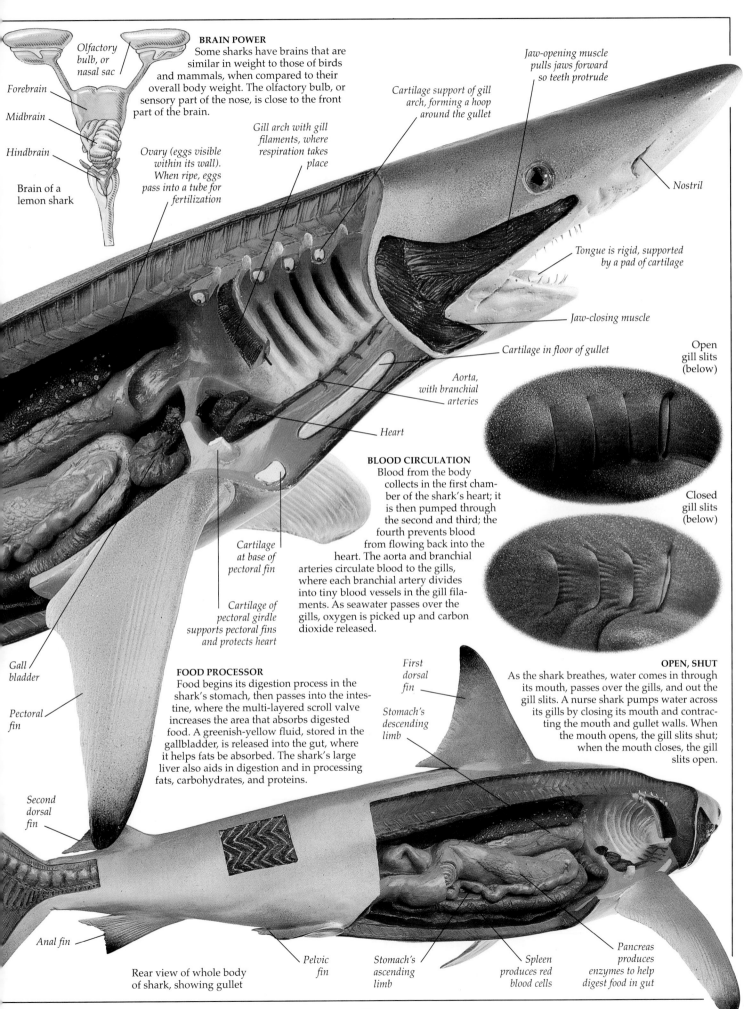

BRAIN POWER
Some sharks have brains that are similar in weight to those of birds and mammals, when compared to their overall body weight. The olfactory bulb, or sensory part of the nose, is close to the front part of the brain.

Olfactory bulb, or nasal sac

Forebrain

Midbrain

Hindbrain

Brain of a lemon shark

Ovary (eggs visible within its wall). When ripe, eggs pass into a tube for fertilization

Gill arch with gill filaments, where respiration takes place

Cartilage support of gill arch, forming a hoop around the gullet

Jaw-opening muscle pulls jaws forward so teeth protrude

Nostril

Tongue is rigid, supported by a pad of cartilage

Jaw-closing muscle

Cartilage in floor of gullet

Aorta, with branchial arteries

Heart

Open gill slits (below)

Closed gill slits (below)

BLOOD CIRCULATION
Blood from the body collects in the first chamber of the shark's heart; it is then pumped through the second and third; the fourth prevents blood from flowing back into the heart. The aorta and branchial arteries circulate blood to the gills, where each branchial artery divides into tiny blood vessels in the gill filaments. As seawater passes over the gills, oxygen is picked up and carbon dioxide released.

Cartilage at base of pectoral fin

Cartilage of pectoral girdle supports pectoral fins and protects heart

Gall bladder

Pectoral fin

FOOD PROCESSOR
Food begins its digestion process in the shark's stomach, then passes into the intestine, where the multi-layered scroll valve increases the area that absorbs digested food. A greenish-yellow fluid, stored in the gallbladder, is released into the gut, where it helps fats be absorbed. The shark's large liver also aids in digestion and in processing fats, carbohydrates, and proteins.

First dorsal fin

Stomach's descending limb

OPEN, SHUT
As the shark breathes, water comes in through its mouth, passes over the gills, and out the gill slits. A nurse shark pumps water across its gills by closing its mouth and contracting the mouth and gullet walls. When the mouth opens, the gill slits shut; when the mouth closes, the gill slits open.

Second dorsal fin

Anal fin

Rear view of whole body of shark, showing gullet

Pelvic fin

Stomach's ascending limb

Spleen produces red blood cells

Pancreas produces enzymes to help digest food in gut

47

Amazing grace

THE THREE GRACES
According to Greek mythology, these three daughters of Zeus were the goddesses of grace and beauty.

SHARKS ARE GRACEFUL swimmers. They propel themselves through the water by beating their tails from side to side. The pectoral fins are held out from the body, and as water flows over them, lift is generated to keep the shark from sinking. Further lift is produced by the upper lobe of the tail, which tends to push the head down, so that the shark can swim level. Shark fins are not nearly as flexible as those of bony fish, but small changes to the angle at which the fins are held control whether the shark goes up, down, left, or right. Pectoral fins are also used for braking. Some sharks that live on the seabed, such as angel sharks (pp. 68–69) and epaulette sharks, can use their pectoral fins to crawl along the bottom. Unlike bony fish, sharks cannot move their pectoral fins like paddles so are unable to swim backward or hover in the water. They also lack a swim bladder, which acts as a buoyancy aid in bony fish. However, sharks do have an oil-rich liver (pp. 46–47), which helps reduce their weight in water.

TAIL END
Undulations, or S-shaped waves, pass down a shark's body as it moves forward (above). The tail bends more than the rest of the body, producing a forward thrust.

STARRY SMOOTHHOUND
The denticles on a shark's skin align in the direction of travel, helping to reduce drag. These denticles may trap a film of water, which would help sharks move more easily through the water.

CRUISING
With pectoral fins held straight out from its sides, the starry smoothhound (right) keeps swimming at the same level. The two dorsal fins keep the shark from rolling, and its tail gives a forward thrust.

One-year-old
leopard shark,
15 in (38 cm) long

SEE HOW IT BENDS
Leopard sharks (above) have flexible
bodies, so they can turn around
in small spaces. Like their close
relatives, the smoothhounds, leopard
sharks spend much of their time cruising
close to the bottom and also resting on the seabed.

A LITTLE LIFT GOES A LONG WAY
The large pectoral fins of the starry smoothhound (left) are similar
to an airplane's wings, because they provide lift to keep the shark from
sinking. When tilted they can also act as brakes, like the flaps on the
wings of an airplane, which are raised on landing. Submarines have
horizontal fins, called hydrofoils, which lift them upward like those
of a shark. Just like a hydrofoil, the leading (or front) edge of a shark's
pectoral fin is rounded and the trailing (or rear) edge is thin, so water
flows over it more easily. The pointed snout and tapered body are
streamlined and give little resistance to the water.

FULL STEAM AHEAD
A great white shark
(above) usually cruises
at about 1.8 mph
(3 kph). Its bulky body
hardly moves at all,
while its tail beats from
side to side. When
closing in on a kill, the
great white puts on an
impressive burst of
speed of up to 15 mph
(25 kph).

BIG SURPRISE!
Great whites can bend
their bodies but are
not nearly as flexible
as smaller sharks.
They have to surprise
their prey rather than
out-maneuver them.

49

Continued on next page

Continued from previous page

Tails and more tails

The shape of a shark's tail suits its way of life. Many sharks have tail fins with an upper lobe that is larger than the lower; as the tail swings from side to side, this larger lobe produces lift, which tends to push the head down. This is compensated for by lift from the pectoral fins, which keeps the shark from sinking to the bottom. In fast sharks, like the mako and great white, these two lobes are almost equal in size. Lift may also come from the base of the tail, which in the mako has small, horizontal keels (ridges). The extra height of these more symmetrically shaped tails gives a more powerful thrust. Slow bottom-dwellers, like the nurse shark, have less powerful tails, and their swimming motion is more eel-like, with obvious waves passing down to their tails.

BONNETHEAD'S TAIL
Bonnetheads are small hammer-heads (pp. 70–71), which grow to about 5 ft (1.5 m) in length. Like all sharks', the bonnethead's tail's upper lobe contains an extension of the vertebral column and is usually larger than the lower lobe. The upper lobe is at an angle and is above the shark's midline (imagine a line drawn through the shark from the tip of its snout to the end of its body).

Tail of a bonnethead shark

THRESHER'S TAIL
The upper lobe of the tail of a thresher shark (left) is as long as its body. From 5–8 ft (1.5–2.5 m) in length, the tails of the three different types of thresher are by far the longest of any shark. A thresher uses its tail to stun its prey. It can also inflict nasty injuries on anglers when the sharks are hauled on board.

Tail of a thresher shark

Keel

Tail view of a model of a great white shark (pp. 62–63)

GREAT WHITE'S TAIL
The upper and lower lobes of a great white's tail fin are almost equal in size. They lie high above, and low below, the shark's midline respectively. The keel helps the big shark to turn. The first dorsal fin is rigid and prevents the shark from rolling. Also, a great white can jump out of the water.

HEAVENLY TAKEOFF

To lift its huge body off the seabed, the angel shark beats its tail back and forth while tipping its large pectoral and pelvic fins for maximum lift. Once off the seabed, angels propel themselves forward by sculling with their tails, but they do not undulate, or wave, their pectoral fins like rays.

MIDAIR MAKO

Makos (pp. 60–61) are probably the fastest sharks in the sea, reaching speeds estimated to be 20 mph (32 kph) for a few moments. When caught on an angler's line, they leap clear of the surface in an effort to escape (above). Their tails are the same shape as another fast fish, the tuna, and like tunas they have keels along the base of their tails, which may give them more maneuverability, and perhaps provide some lift. They are active predators, pursuing mainly fish.

SWELL TAIL

Smaller than nurse sharks, at 3.3 ft (1 m) long, swell sharks (right) are sluggish animals, spending the day resting on the seabed and at night swimming close to the bottom. Their tails are set barely above their midlines.

HORN SHARK'S TAIL

The lower lobe of the horn shark's tail (pp. 44–45) is more developed than the swell shark's. The tail of this 3.3-ft (1-m) shark is also at a low angle to its midline, and it is a slow swimmer.

Lower lobe of angel shark's tail fin (pp. 68–69) is longer than upper lobe

TAIL OF A NURSE SHARK

Nurse sharks, at 10 ft (3 m) long, are rather slow swimmers and use their tails (right) for cruising near the bottom.

Making sense

SHARKS HAVE THE SAME FIVE SENSES as people – they can see, hear, smell, taste, and touch. There is also a sixth sense that allows sharks to detect weak electrical signals generated by their prey. This electro-sense may also help them to navigate on their journeys in the sea. The underwater world is very different from our own. Light levels decrease with depth, and colors fade to blues. Sound travels five times faster and farther. Odors are dissolved in water, not wafted in the air. Sharks can detect vibrations made by animals moving through the water, giving them the sense called "distant touch." It is hard to find out exactly how a shark perceives its world, but studies on their behavior and how sense organs work give some idea about what it is like to be a shark.

Blue shark's nictitating eyelid

Pore

Nostril

METAL DETECTOR
Sweeping a metal detector back and forth to find buried metal objects is like the way hammerheads (pp. 70–71) hunt for fish hiding in the sand.

GOING TO ITS HEAD
Like us, a shark's major sense organs are on its head. Seen on this blue shark are the eye, nostril, and sensory pores, which detect weak electrical signals. The eye is partly covered by a third eyelid, called a nictitating (or blinking) eyelid; it protects the eye when the shark attacks prey or nears unfamiliar objects. As the shark swims along, water flows through the nostril beneath the tip of the snout, bringing a constant stream of odors.

FEEDING FRENZY
When sharks are feeding on bait, they may become overexcited and snap wildly at their food. They may bite each other and even tear one another apart.

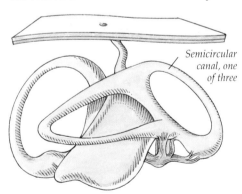

Semicircular canal, one of three

THE INNER EAR
Sharks do not have external ear flaps, but have ears inside their heads on either side of the brain case. Three semicircular canals placed at right angles to each other are like those found in the ears of all vertebrates. These canals help a shark figure out which way it has turned in the water. Receptors in the inner ear, like those in the lateral line on the skin, pick up sounds traveling through the water. Each ear has a small duct which leads to a pore on the top of the shark's head.

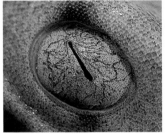

Epaulette's slit-shaped pupil

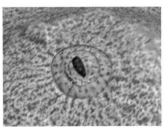

Angel shark's pupil

Horn shark's pupil

Dogfish with closed pupil

Reef shark with vertical pupil

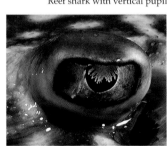

Ray with light-blocking screen

ALL KINDS OF EYES
According to how much light there is, the iris in a shark's eyes contracts or expands to alter the size of the pupil. The tapetum lucidum, a layer of cells at the back of the eye, reflects light back onto the retina, where images are focused, making maximum use of any available light. This helps sharks to see in dim light. Cats also have a tapetum, which is why their eyes reflect lights shined at them. On bright, sunny days a shark can shield its tapetum with a layer of pigment. Like a human retina, a shark retina has two types of cells – rods work in dim light and are sensitive to light changes; cones resolve details and probably allow sharks to see in color.

DISTANT TOUCH
Sharks have a lateral-line system running down each side of the body and onto the head. The lines are small canals with tiny pores beneath which are cells with minute hairs. Scattered over the body are similar hair cells called pit organs, which like the lateral lines pick up vibrations.

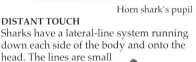

Lateral line

Starry smoothhound showing lateral line

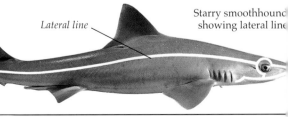

EYES ON STALKS
Hammerheads' eyes are on the end of their head projections, giving them a good view as they swing their heads back and forth. The nostrils are widely spaced on the front of the head, helping them detect where an odor is coming from. The head projections are packed with ampullae of Lorenzini, which detect electrical signals from hidden fish.

Compass

Imaginary magnet

North-south axis

Earth's magnetic field

COMPASS SENSE
Some sharks migrate hundreds of miles and seem to know where they are going, in what to us is a featureless ocean. Scientists think sharks have compass sense to guide them. In a real compass, a magnetic needle swings around to align itself to the earth's magnetic field. The earth's magnetic field (above) is created by its core, which acts like a giant magnet. Sharks seem able to swim in one direction by sensing changes in their own electrical fields in relation to the earth's magnetic field. Corrections have to be made for speed and direction of ocean currents, which may sweep the shark off course. Sharks may also be able to navigate by detecting magnetic patterns on the seabed.

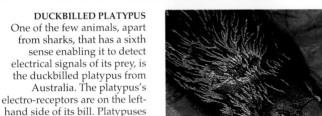

DUCKBILLED PLATYPUS
One of the few animals, apart from sharks, that has a sixth sense enabling it to detect electrical signals of its prey, is the duckbilled platypus from Australia. The platypus's electro-receptors are on the left-hand side of its bill. Platypuses live in streams, where they hunt for insects and other small creatures on the river bottom.

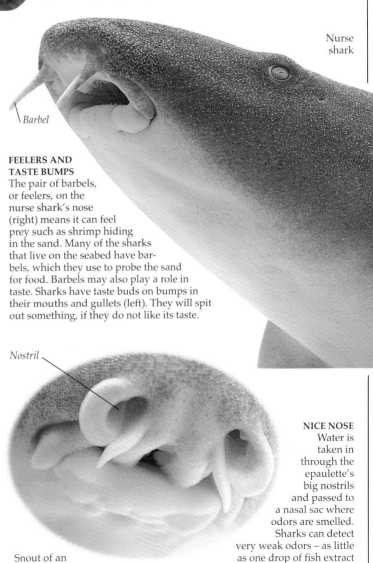

Nurse shark

Barbel

FEELERS AND TASTE BUMPS
The pair of barbels, or feelers, on the nurse shark's nose (right) means it can feel prey such as shrimp hiding in the sand. Many of the sharks that live on the seabed have barbels, which they use to probe the sand for food. Barbels may also play a role in taste. Sharks have taste buds on bumps in their mouths and gullets (left). They will spit out something, if they do not like its taste.

Nostril

NICE NOSE
Water is taken in through the epaulette's big nostrils and passed to a nasal sac where odors are smelled. Sharks can detect very weak odors – as little as one drop of fish extract diluted over a million times.

SPOTTY NOSE
The spots in front of the nostrils on this sand tiger's snout are sensory pores called ampullae of Lorenzini. The deep pores are full of jelly and connect at their base to nerves; they detect weak electrical signals produced by a prey's muscles and bodily processes. Sometimes sharks are confused by electrical signals given off by metal, so they will bite shark cages.

Snout of an epaulette shark

Reproduction and laying eggs

FOR SOME SHARKS, finding a mate means a long swim, because males and females often live in different parts of the ocean. When they meet, the male chases the female, biting her to encourage her to mate. He inserts one of his claspers (extensions of his pelvic fin) into her cloaca, or body opening (pp. 46–47). Seawater already drawn into a sac in the male's body is then squirted into a groove in his clasper. This water flushes sperm into her cloaca. In this way, the sperm fertilizes the female's eggs inside her body. In contrast, in bony fish, fertilization occurs outside the body, with sperm and eggs being shed into the water. Some female sharks can store sperm until they are ready to reproduce, so fertilization may not happen immediately. Most sharks give birth to live young (pp. 56–57), but some reproduce by laying eggs. The fertilized eggs are encased in a leathery shell and deposited by the female on the seabed, where the embryos, or developing shark pups, grow until they are ready to hatch. These sharks are oviparous, which means their young hatch from an egg laid outside the mother – just like birds and bony fish.

SPIRAL EGG
A horn shark wedges its spiral-shaped egg case into rocks, protecting it from predators.

CAT'S EGG
The cat shark's egg case is firmly anchored onto anything growing on the seabed. Shark eggs are large and well protected; because of this they stand a better chance of survival than the masses of small eggs laid by bony fish.

MERMAIDS
Mermaids are mythical sea creatures with a woman's body and a fish's tail. Since ancient times, sailors have made up stories about mermaids. The empty egg cases of dogfish and rays that wash up on the seashore are called mermaids' purses.

CATCH ME IF YOU CAN
This male whitetip reef shark is pursuing a female in the hope that she will mate with him. He may be attracted by her smell.

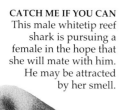

LOVE BITES
When a male whitetip reef shark gets close to a female (right), he bites her to arouse her interest. He will also grab her pectoral fin in his jaws to keep her close to him during mating. Very little is known of the mating habits of other large sharks.

THICK SKIN
Some female sharks, like this blue shark, have much thicker skin than males, which prevents serious injury during courtship. Most "love bites" are only skin deep and heal in a few weeks.

MATING SHARKS
People rarely see sharks mating in the wild, or even in aquariums. From a few observations, it seems that larger sharks mate side to side. Whitetip reef sharks (left) mate side to side and may pivot on their heads. The male of smaller sharks, such as dogfish (or cat sharks), is more flexible and wraps himself around the female when mating.

Tendril

DOGFISH EGGS
Every year female small spotted cat sharks, also known as lesser spotted dogfish, lay about 20 eggs in seaweed. The developing dogfish lie safe inside their egg cases. At first the egg cases are soft, but soon they harden in the seawater. The tendrils at the corners of the egg capsules anchor them to seaweed to prevent them being swept away by currents. Embryos take about eight to nine months to develop before they are ready to hatch. During this time each embryo gets its nourishment from its large yolk sac.

Dogfish embryo

Yolk sac

Pair of dogfish egg cases

Pair of ten-day-old dogfish

Cream-colored underside

DOGFISH PUPS
These young dogfish are only ten days old. They are only 4 in (10 cm) long, and they look like small versions of their parents. Shark pups are generally much larger and more developed than young of bony fish. Soon after hatching, the young dogfish start to feed on small creatures like shrimp. It will be ten years before they reach maturity and start to breed. When fully grown, dogfish are about 3 ft (1 m) long.

1 ONE-MONTH-OLD SWELL SHARK EMBRYO
Swell sharks live on the eastern side of the Pacific Ocean in shallow coastal waters. They are called swell sharks because when threatened they wedge themselves into a rocky crevice by gulping in mouthfuls of water. If taken out of the water, a swell shark can still swell up by taking in air. The female lays two eggs at a time, depositing them among clumps of seaweed. Each egg is protected by a leathery case. One month after it was laid, the fertilized egg has developed into a tiny embryo. The large egg sac is full of yolk, which nourishes the growing embryo.

Coloring consists of light and dark brown bands, with dark spots on shark's top side

2 EMBRYO AT THREE MONTHS
The embryo has grown much larger and already has eyes and a tail. The yolk sac is connected to the embryo's belly by a cord, and oxygen in the surrounding seawater passes through the leathery egg case so that the embryo is able to breathe.

3 SEVEN-MONTH-OLD EMBRYO
By now the embryo looks much more like a baby shark. It has a complete set of fins and is able to wriggle around inside the egg case. The two rows of spines on the baby's back will help give it a grip on the egg case as it pushes its way out. The baby shark, or pup, will hatch as soon as it has used up the rest of the yolk sac.

Two-month-old swell shark pup

4 TWO-MONTH-OLD PUP
After ten months, the young swell shark (6 in, 15 cm long) has hatched from the egg case. This is a most vulnerable moment in its young life because it is so small and there are many predators. Its mottled color pattern makes it hard to see when it is hiding on the seabed. It can also wedge itself into a hiding place by swelling up.

Live young

T̲HE MAJORITY OF SHARKS give birth to live young instead of laying eggs. Most of these sharks are ovoviviparous: that is, the embryo develops in a large, yolky egg kept inside the female's oviduct, or womblike cavity. The embryos hatch while still inside the mother, develop yet further, and then are born "again" as live baby sharks. In some ovoviviparous sharks, the first pups that develop eat any unfertilized eggs – plus their less developed brothers and sisters – in the mother's oviduct. In sand tiger sharks, for example, only one of the young cannibals survives in each side of the "womb." In viviparous (born live) sharks, such as lemon, blue, and bull sharks, each fertilized egg develops inside a separate compartment in the mother's oviduct. The unborn pup is fed via a placenta. As in humans and other mammals, the placenta acts like a sieve, allowing food and oxygen to pass from mother to baby, and waste materials from baby back to mother, through the connecting umbilical cord.

MOTHER AND BABY
Human babies need to be looked after for many years, but shark pups are not so lucky. They must fend for themselves as soon as they are born.

1

A LEMON SHARK IS BORN
(1) The tip of the pup's tail is just visible poking out of its mother's opening, or cloaca (pp. 46–47). Pregnant lemon sharks come into shallow coastal lagoons that are sheltered from the waves, to give birth. Scientists studying sharks at Bimini in the Bahamas sometimes catch female sharks for their research. (2) Here, the female has begun to give birth. (3) The scientist is acting like a midwife, and is helping the passage of the pup out of the mother's birth canal.

2

3

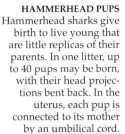

HAMMERHEAD PUPS
Hammerhead sharks give birth to live young that are little replicas of their parents. In one litter, up to 40 pups may be born, with their head projections bent back. In the uterus, each pup is connected to its mother by an umbilical cord.

BABY AFRICAN ELEPHANT
A baby elephant takes 22 months to develop inside its mother's womb, which is the longest gestation period of any mammal. The long pregnancy is not surprising, since a baby elephant weighs over 220 lb (100 kg) at birth. Some sharks have a nine-month gestation period, just like humans, though the spiny dogfish matches the elephant in taking 18 to 24 months to be born.

SPINY BABIES GO EASY ON THEIR MOTHERS
Giving birth is hard for any mother. Fortunately for a hedgehog mother, the spines of her babies do not poke out until after birth. The sharp spines on the dorsal fins of newborn spiny dogfish have protective coverings.

BIGEYE THRESHER PUPS
As bigeye thresher pups develop inside the uterus, they feed on bundles of un-fertilized eggs. The pups have long tails – just like their parents.

4

(4) The lemon shark pup, one of up to 17 pups, is still attached to its mother by the umbilical cord. She is nearly 10 ft (3 m) long, but her pups are only 24 in (60 cm) long. (5) The pup will rest for a while on the sea-bed, then swim away, breaking the umbilical cord. (6) Now the pup faces life on its own. It must seek the cover of mangrove roots and hide from predators, such as larger sharks and barracudas. For many years it will stay in a small nursery area in the shallows of the lagoon, near where it was born. Then it will make exploratory trips out of the lagoon to the coral reefs and will gradually spend more time farther out to sea.

6

5

Teeth and diet

SHARKS CONTINUALLY lose their teeth. When the front ones wear out, they are replaced by new ones growing in another row behind them. An individual shark goes through thousands of teeth in a lifetime. Most animals, like elephants and seals, cannot replace their teeth, and die when the teeth wear out. As the shark grows, its new teeth are larger than the ones they replace. Sharks' teeth come in many shapes according to what kind of food they eat. Teeth like small spikes are used for gripping small prey. Serrated teeth are used for cutting. Long, curved teeth can hold slippery fish. Blunt teeth crunch up shellfish. A few species of shark, like basking and whale sharks, have tiny teeth compared to their great size. They do not use their teeth to feed; they filter food out of the water instead. Some sharks produce different shaped teeth as they grow older.

Tiny teeth of basking shark

Gill rakers

MOUTH WIDE OPEN
Basking sharks swim along with their mouths open to catch shrimp and other small creatures called plankton that drift in the sea. The food is trapped on rows of bristles called gill rakers as the water flows through the mouth and out through the gill slits. The gill rakers are shed each year during the winter months when there is little food around. A new set of rakers grows in the spring, and then the basking sharks can start to feed again.

EPAULETTE EATING
Epaulette sharks live on coral reefs in the southwest Pacific Ocean around Australia and Papua New Guinea. They grow to about 3.3 ft (1 m) long and can crawl along the bottom using their pectoral fins. These sharks search among the shallows and tidepools for small fish, crabs, shrimps, and other small creatures to eat.

Epaulette eating

SMILE PLEASE
Swell sharks (top right) from the eastern Pacific Ocean have big mouths for their 3.3-ft (1-m) length. Armed with rows of tiny teeth, these sharks eat bony fish that rest on the seabed. Only the Port Jackson's rows of small front teeth (bottom right) are visible when its mouth is open. At the back of its jaws are strong, flat teeth for crushing shelled prey.

CRUNCHY DIET
Port Jackson sharks have small, pointed front teeth to grab their prey. The strong, flat back teeth crunch hard-shelled crabs, mussels (right), and sea urchins (below right).

Section through a Port Jackson's jaws

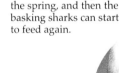

Mouth of swell shark

Mouth of Port Jackson

TIGER MOUTH
Tiger sharks cruise the warm waters of the world around islands and coasts of continents and often move in-shore at night to feed.

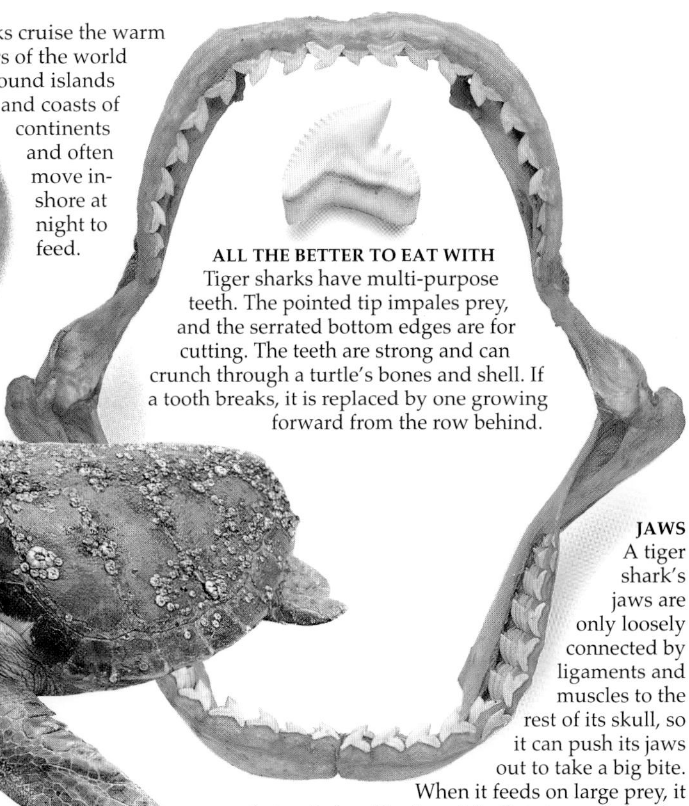

ALL THE BETTER TO EAT WITH
Tiger sharks have multi-purpose teeth. The pointed tip impales prey, and the serrated bottom edges are for cutting. The teeth are strong and can crunch through a turtle's bones and shell. If a tooth breaks, it is replaced by one growing forward from the row behind.

DAILY MENU
Tiger sharks eat all kinds of food from squishy jellyfish to tough-shelled turtles. They are not put off by the jellyfish's stings or even by venom from sea snakes. Even sea birds are not safe as tiger sharks will grab them from the surface of the sea. Carcasses of land animals washed into the sea, such as chickens, dogs, horses, and cows, are also eaten. Even tin cans, coal, and plastic bags have been found in tiger sharks' stomachs, and occasionally they will attack people.

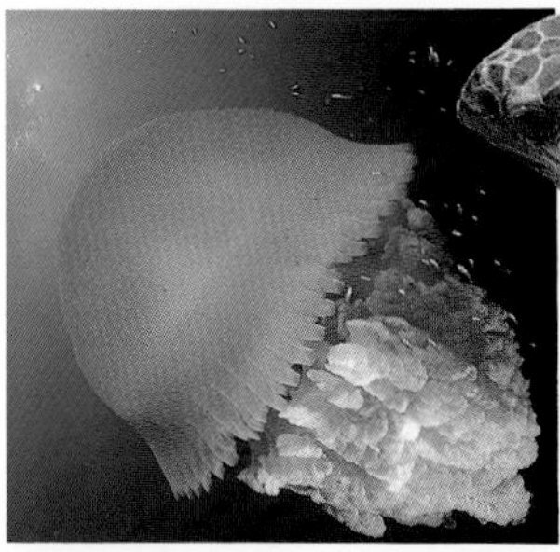

Sea turtle

Jellyfish

JAWS
A tiger shark's jaws are only loosely connected by ligaments and muscles to the rest of its skull, so it can push its jaws out to take a big bite. When it feeds on large prey, it shakes its head back and forth to tear off chunks.

DISH OF THE DAY
Sand tigers eat a variety of bony fish (left), as well as lobsters, small sharks, and rays.

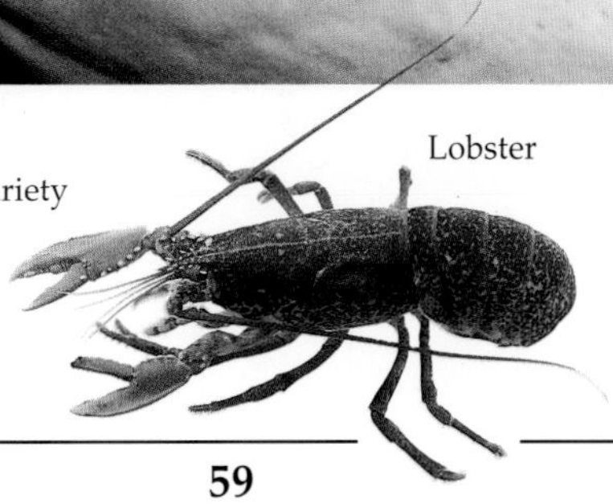

Goatfish

Lobster

RAGGED-TOOTH SHARK
Sand tigers, called ragged-tooth sharks in South Africa and gray nurse sharks in Australia, reach 10 ft (3 m) in length. Their long, curved teeth get progressively smaller from the front to the sides of the jaw and are ideal for snaring fish or squid. They look fierce but will attack only if provoked.

CLAWS

This 0.75-in-long (19-mm) copepod digs its sharp claws into a basking shark's skin. It feeds on skin secretions and blood. Basking sharks, infested by these and other parasites, become irritated. Reports tell of sharks leaping clear of the water to get rid of them.

Claw
Antenna
Head
Thoracic plate, or body section
Abdomen

BARNACLES ABOARD

This strange-looking lump is a barnacle, related to the ones found on the seashore. In the sea, the larvae, or young, of this barnacle attach themselves to dorsal fins of spurdogs or dogfish. The root, or stalk, of this 1-in-long (26-mm) barnacle has rootlets that absorb nutrients from the shark.

Soft shell
Root
Rootlet for absorbing food from shark

Friend or foe?

LIKE MOST ANIMALS, sharks have a variety of small friends and enemies that choose to live on, in, or near them. Small fish called remoras often hitch rides on sharks using suckers on their heads. Remoras help sharks stay healthy by eating the tiny shellfish called copepods that often infest sharks' fins and gills. Sometimes remoras hitch rides on the bow waves produced by a shark swimming though the water. Other kinds of fish, called pilot fish, also swim with sharks and ride their bow waves. Pilot fish probably feed off scraps left over after a shark's meal. Copepods, tapeworms, and other parasites live on or within sharks, feeding off their skin, blood, or digested food. Parasites may cause a shark discomfort, but they will rarely kill it.

CLEAN TEETH
Other animals have friends too. A bird cleans a crocodile's teeth and finds something tasty to eat.

Female

Male

CLING ONS
These small (0.5 in, 13 mm) crustaceans, or copepods, have adhesive pads to stick onto sharks' fins. They feed on skin secretions.

STREAMERS
Copepods are clinging onto the dorsal fins of this mako shark (above) and have egg cases streaming out behind them. Each case contains a stack of disk-shaped eggs. When the eggs are released, they hatch into tiny young, or larvae. These larvae drift about in the sea, passing through several stages of development before attaching themselves to a passing shark.

STICKING TOGETHER
Shark suckers, or remoras (left), live in the world's tropical oceans. Each has a ridged sucker on the top of its head that it uses to attach itself to sharks and rays. While hitching a ride, remoras often do their hosts a favor by nibbling off skin parasites. They may also steal scraps when the shark has a meal, and even feed on the placenta when a shark gives birth (pp. 56–57) to pups (above).

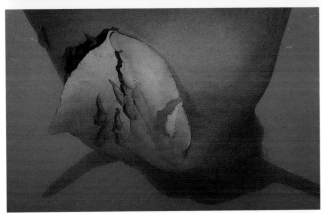

MOBILE HOME
Whale sharks (top) are so big that they provide living space for large numbers of remoras. Some remoras congregate around the mouth, even swimming inside the mouth cavity and gills, where they may feed on parasites; others nestle around the cloaca on a female shark (above). Remoras get free transportation from their giant hosts, by either attaching themselves or riding the shark's bow wave.

WORMS AND MORE WORMS
Hundreds of 1-ft (30-cm) tapeworms may live in a shark's gut, where they absorb food. Segments full of eggs from their tail ends are passed into the sea; the eggs hatch when eaten by a copepod. The young worm is passed to a bony fish when the fish eats the copepod. If a shark eats the fish, the cycle begins again.

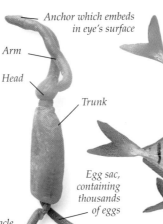

Tentacle
Head

Body

Anchor which embeds in eye's surface
Arm
Head
Trunk
Egg sac, containing thousands of eggs

EYE SPY
This strange copepod hangs by its long arms to a Greenland shark's eye. At 1.2 in long (31 mm), the parasite makes it hard for a 20-ft (6-m) shark to see. It feeds on the eye's surface tissues, but once there, it cannot let go.

PILOT FISH
Young golden trevally from the Pacific Ocean swim with larger fish, including sharks. Though they are called pilot fish, they do not guide sharks and other large fish to sources of food. They just like to school with larger fish. They may also be protected from other fish that do not like to be close to sharks. Pilot fish are much too agile to be eaten themselves.

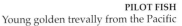

NAVIGATING
A large ship is guided into harbor by pilot boats, but sharks navigate on their own (pp. 52–53).

The great white shark

A POWERFUL PREDATOR, the great white inspires fear. This awesome shark grows to over 20 ft (6 m) long and weighs more than 2.4 tons (2.2 tonnes). It is the largest of the predatory sharks, capable of eating seals whole. The great white became famous in the *Jaws* movies, where it appears as a bloodthirsty creature intent on killing people. Attacks on people are rare and possibly occur when a shark mistakes a person for its usual prey, the seal. Despite its fame, little is known about the great white. Scientists have yet to discover where mating and birth occur, or what the shark's age is when it reproduces or dies. No one knows how many great whites there are, but in some areas they may be on the decline.

FRENCH LANDING
This old engraving of a great white landed on France's Mediterranean coast shows how a century ago people were also fascinated by sharks. Unless they were lucky enough to see sharks firsthand, artists had to rely on descriptions to make their drawings, since there were no photographs. There are several inaccuracies in this engraving – the artist has given the great white gill covers, like bony fish, as well as gill slits, and the tail of a thresher.

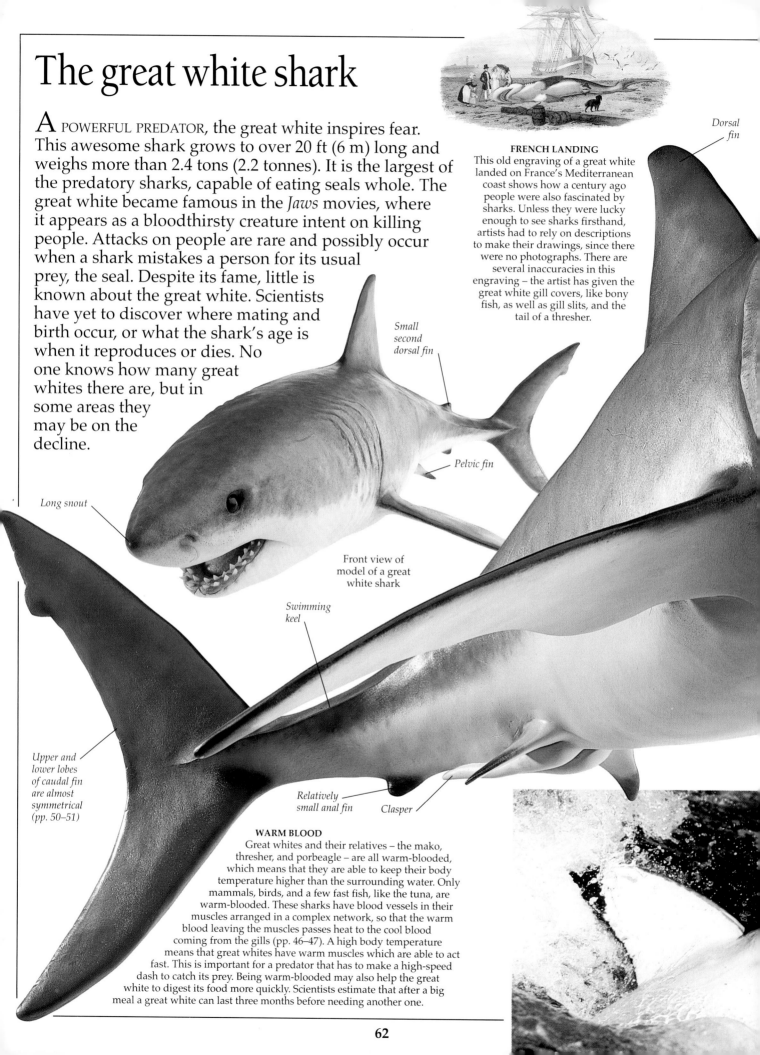

Dorsal fin

Small second dorsal fin

Pelvic fin

Long snout

Front view of model of a great white shark

Swimming keel

Upper and lower lobes of caudal fin are almost symmetrical (pp. 50–51)

Relatively small anal fin

Clasper

WARM BLOOD
Great whites and their relatives – the mako, thresher, and porbeagle – are all warm-blooded, which means that they are able to keep their body temperature higher than the surrounding water. Only mammals, birds, and a few fast fish, like the tuna, are warm-blooded. These sharks have blood vessels in their muscles arranged in a complex network, so that the warm blood leaving the muscles passes heat to the cool blood coming from the gills (pp. 46–47). A high body temperature means that great whites have warm muscles which are able to act fast. This is important for a predator that has to make a high-speed dash to catch its prey. Being warm-blooded may also help the great white to digest its food more quickly. Scientists estimate that after a big meal a great white can last three months before needing another one.

Pore, marking position of ampullae of Lorenzini – sensory organs for detecting prey's electric field (pp. 52–53)

Long gill slit – one of five

Sharp, serrated (notched) teeth

WHITE DEATH
A great white's coloring makes it difficult to see in the water, so it is able to sneak up on its victims. When seen from below, a shark's white undersides blend in with a bright sky's reflection at the water's surface. This magnificent shark is sometimes called "white pointer," referring to its pointed snout which makes it more streamlined. Great whites often have scratches and scars on their snouts, which may be the result of their prey fighting back. They are also sometimes bitten by larger members of their own kind that move in to take food away from them.

Full-length side view of model of a male great white shark

Pectoral fin

TAKING THE BAIT
Scientists, filmmakers, and photographers use chum (a mixture of blood and rotting fish) and other bait to attract great whites. Great whites are among the few sharks that stick their heads out of the water before, and sometimes during, attacks on prey. As the shark takes the bait, its eyes roll back in their sockets revealing the white surface of the eyeball. This protects the more vital front part of the eye from being scratched, which may happen if the shark is attacking live prey, such as a seal armed with claws and teeth.

TAGGING A GREAT WHITE
Dr. John McCosker, an American shark scientist, tags a great white off the Australian coast (top). Sonic tags have revealed that a great white can cruise at 1.8 mph (3 kph), traveling about 120 miles (200 km) in three days (above).

Gentle giants

HUMPBACK WHALES
Whale sharks are named after those other ocean giants – the whales – which are not fish but mammals.

Whale sharks are the largest fish in the world, reaching at least 40 ft (12 m) long and weighing 13 tons (13.2 tonnes), about as large as an adult gray whale. These docile sharks are harmless and will allow scuba divers to hitch rides by hanging onto their fins; the only danger is in getting scraped by the shark's rough skin, or accidentally knocked by the huge tail as it swings back and forth. These giant fish cruise at 2 mph (3 kph). They live in tropical and subtropical waters, and they feed by filtering food out of the water. Because they feed near the surface, where there is a good supply of food to support their large bulk, they occasionally run into ships. Scientists believe that whale sharks may either lay enormous 14-in (30-cm) long eggs or give birth to live young, hatched from eggs inside their bodies.

AT THE DENTIST
People use their teeth to chew food. If their teeth are removed, they need to replace them with false ones.

NOT MUCH OF A BITE
Whale sharks do not bite or chew food, so they do not need their teeth, which are no bigger than a match head.

Distribution of whale sharks

A GREAT GULP
Despite their huge size, whale sharks feed on plankton (tiny animals that drift in the sea), small fish, and squid. Other large fish, such as basking sharks (pp. 66–67), manta rays, and baleen whales (pp. 78–79), also feed by filtering food out of the water. Whale sharks scoop up water into their huge mouths, and as it passes over their gills and out through their gill slits, food is captured in filters. These filters are made up of a mesh of tissues supported by cartilaginous rods. Whale sharks occasionally eat larger fish such as mackerel and tuna, which are swallowed as they scoop up schools of smaller fish. They can feed in a vertical position, even sticking their heads out of the water and sinking down to draw large fish into their mouths.

White-spotted bamboo sharks grow to about 37 in (95 cm) long

Anal fin

Brown-banded bamboo sharks grow to just over 3.3 ft (1 m) long

Nurse sharks grow to 10 ft (3 m) long

Barbel

Epaulette sharks grow to just over 3.3 ft (1 m) long

ONE BIG HAPPY FAMILY
Although they are much smaller, these four sharks (white-spotted and brown-banded bamboos, nurse, and epaulette) all belong to the same group as the whale shark. The main features they have in common are the presence of an anal fin and the position of their mouths well in front of their eyes. They also have two barbels on the tips of their snouts that help them find food. Unlike the whale shark, these much smaller sharks all live on the seabed.

Basking beauties

WITH THEIR HUGE MOUTHS wide open, basking sharks cruise the ocean like giant mobile sieves, filtering countless tiny creatures from the water. This shark is the second largest fish in the world, after the whale shark (pp. 64–65); it grows to about 33 ft (10 m) long and weighs over 3.6 tons (4 tonnes). Basking sharks often swim at the surface on sunny days with their dorsal fins, and perhaps their snouts or tails out of the water. They are probably more attracted by the concentration of food at the surface than by the sunshine. Unfortunately, when the sharks are at the surface, they make easy targets for fishermen who harpoon them for the oil in their large livers, which may be a quarter of their body weight. These sharks are also killed because of the damage they do to salmon nets. Naturalists are concerned that too many are being killed; little is yet known about these fish – how they reproduce, how they migrate, and how many are left in the wild.

SHARK FISHING
At Achill Island off Ireland's northwest coast, basking sharks were once netted in a bay, then speared with a lance, and dragged ashore. Fishing stopped when the numbers of sharks coming into the bay declined.

Eye

Nostril

Gill arch – water passes through the arch and then through a sieve of gill rakers before flowing over the gills and out through the gill slits

OILY MOUTHS
Oil from sharks' livers has been used in cosmetics like lipsticks.

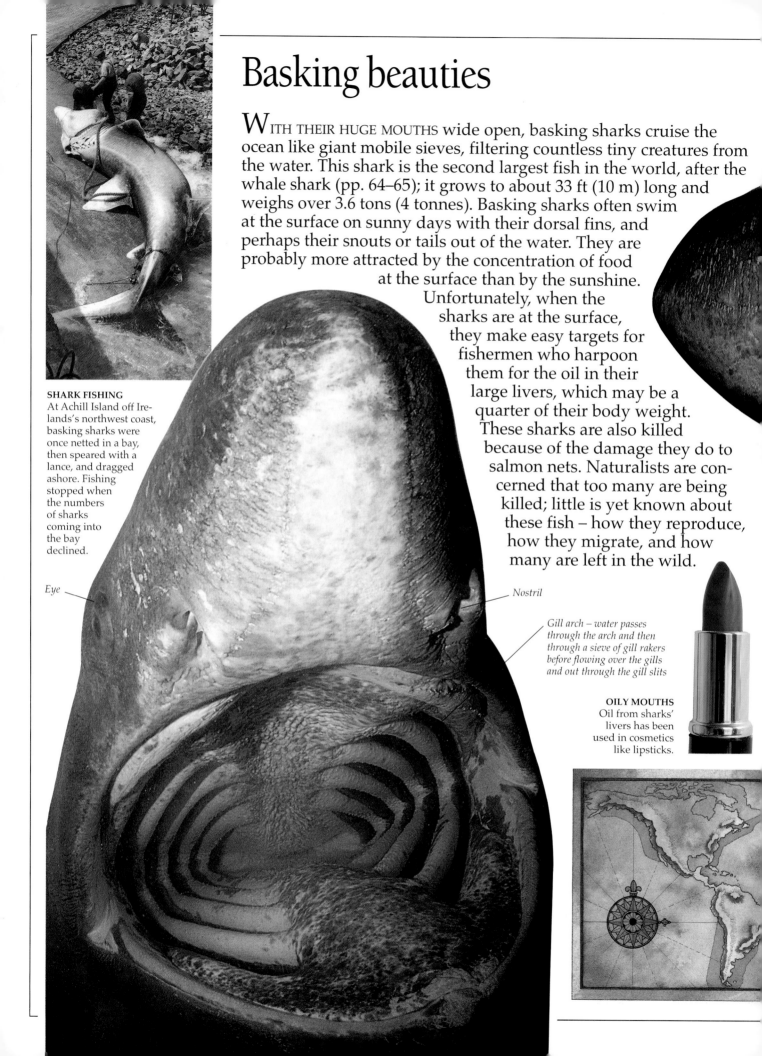

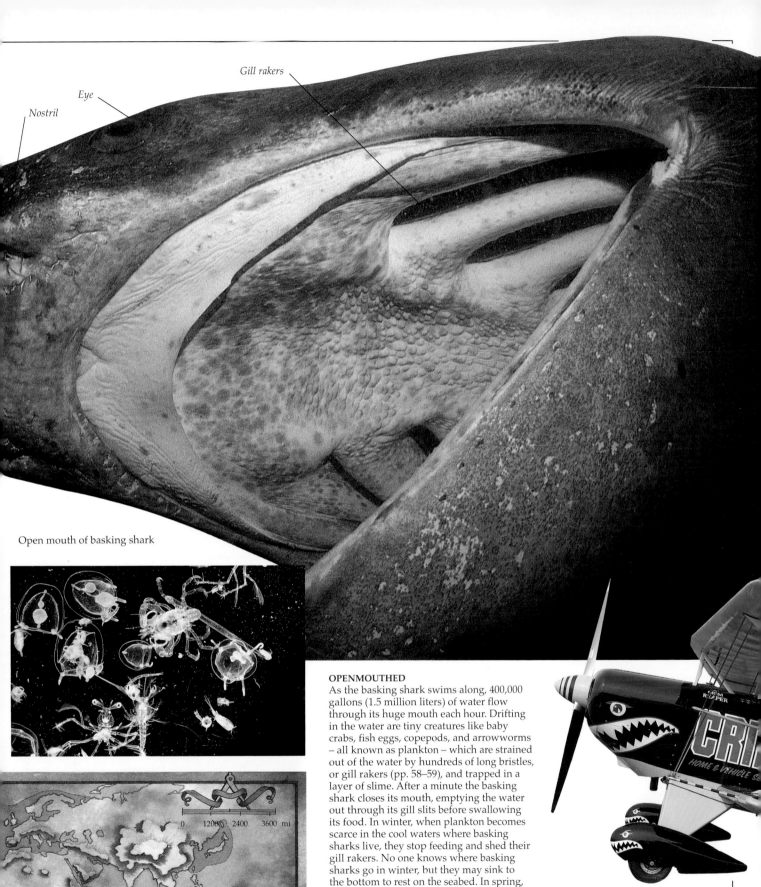

Nostril

Eye

Gill rakers

Open mouth of basking shark

OPENMOUTHED
As the basking shark swims along, 400,000 gallons (1.5 million liters) of water flow through its huge mouth each hour. Drifting in the water are tiny creatures like baby crabs, fish eggs, copepods, and arrowworms – all known as plankton – which are strained out of the water by hundreds of long bristles, or gill rakers (pp. 58–59), and trapped in a layer of slime. After a minute the basking shark closes its mouth, emptying the water out through its gill slits before swallowing its food. In winter, when plankton becomes scarce in the cool waters where basking sharks live, they stop feeding and shed their gill rakers. No one knows where basking sharks go in winter, but they may sink to the bottom to rest on the seabed. In spring, basking sharks appear on the water's surface and start to feed again, having grown a new set of gill rakers.

Distribution of basking sharks

SHARKS AT WAR
In World War II some fighter planes used shark oil to lubricate their instruments. These American planes are decorated with shark jaws to frighten the enemy, but the painted sharks have much bigger teeth than basking sharks do.

Angel sharks

IMAGINE RUNNING A STEAMROLLER over a normal-shaped shark – the result would look very much like an angel shark. These strange, flat sharks have extra-large pectoral fins, which resemble angels' wings. Angel sharks spend much of their lives resting on the seabed or lying in wait for fish or shellfish to move within reach of their snapping, sharp-toothed jaws. They can also swim, using their tails to propel themselves along, just as other kinds of shark do. Angel sharks are most active between dusk and dawn, traveling as far as 5.5 miles (9 km) during the night. There are 13 species of angel shark that live in shallow coastal waters around the world and to depths of over 3,300 ft (1,000 km).

MONK FISH
Ever since the 16th century, angel sharks have been called "monk fish," because the shape of their head looks like the hood on a monk's cloak.

The caudal fin, or lower lobe of the tail, is longer than the upper lobe – a feature unique to angel sharks

Second dorsal fin

0   1200   2400   3600   miles

Distribution of angel sharks

Pelvic fin

First dorsal fin

Eye

Mouth

Spiracle

Gill slit

Pelvic fin

Underside of ray

LOOKALIKES
Rays (pp. 12–13) are flat, just like angel sharks. But unlike angel sharks' pectoral fins, a ray's are completely attached to its head, and its gill slits are located on the underside of its body.

Pectoral fin

Top side of ray

ANGELS
This angel shark grows to nearly 6.5 ft (2 m) long. It is found in the Mediterranean and Baltic seas, the eastern Atlantic Ocean, and the English Channel, down to depths of about 490 ft (150 m). Like all angel sharks, it has eyes on the top of its head so it can see while lying flat on the seabed. For respiration (breathing), it draws in water through its large spiracles, which are also on the top of its head. Water taken in through the spiracles is more likely to be free of silt, which could clog up its gills, than water taken in through its mouth.

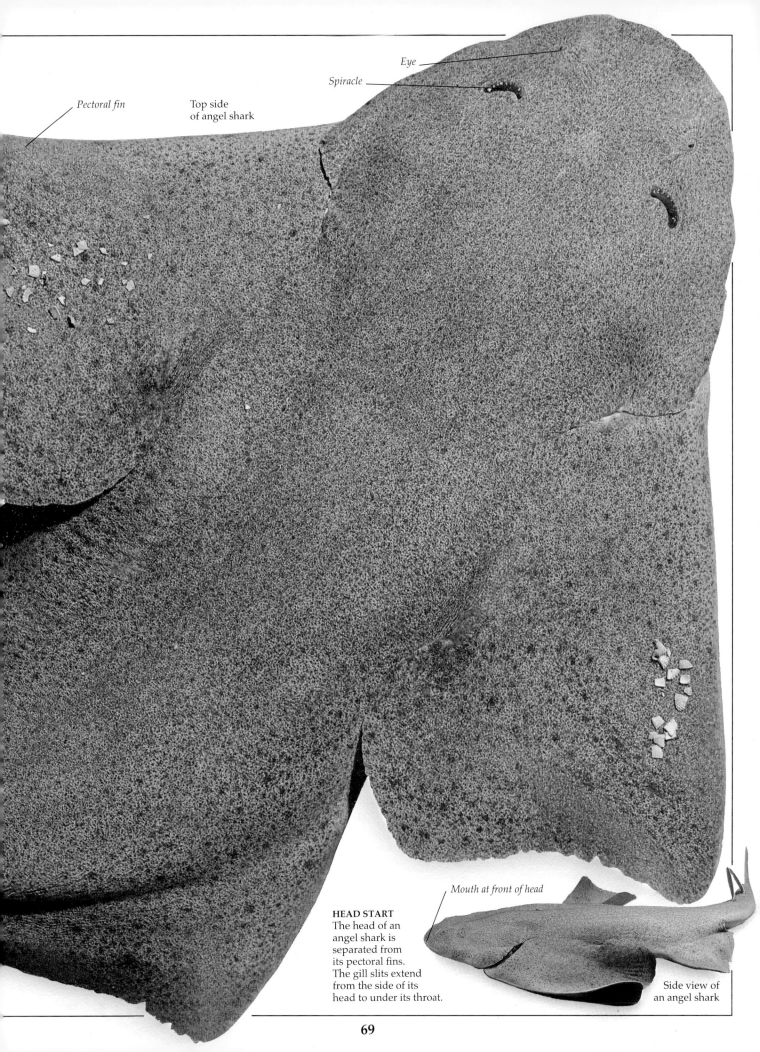

Eye

Spiracle

Pectoral fin

Top side
of angel shark

HEAD START
The head of an
angel shark is
separated from
its pectoral fins.
The gill slits extend
from the side of its
head to under its throat.

Mouth at front of head

Side view of
an angel shark

69

Head like a hammer

OF ALL THE SHARKS, hammerheads have the strangest-shaped heads. There are nine species of hammerhead, including the bonnetheads, which have only small head projections. The winghead shark has by far the widest head; its head can be half as long as its body. Most hammerheads live in warm temperate and tropical coastal waters. The scalloped hammerhead is one of the most common species and is found in warm waters throughout the world. Large schools of scalloped hammerheads often congregate in areas where there are features on the sea floor like undersea peaks, or sea mounts. A hundred of these sharks may form a school, all of them swimming in unison. At dusk they swim off on their own to feed, and then at dawn they regroup in the same place.

Distribution of hammerheads

Bonnetheads
Wingheads

0 1200 2400 3600 mi

HAMMERHEAD SCHOOLS
There are more females in schools than males, but the reason why they group together is unclear. These large predators have few enemies, so it's not likely that they school for protection. The females compete with each other (often butting one another) to stay in the center of the schools. This may give them a better chance to be courted by the males.

DIFFICULT DIET
Stingrays are the favorite food of the great hammerhead even though the rays are armed with one or more venomous spines, or "stingers," on their tails. Hammerheads do not seem to mind being stung – one individual had nearly a hundred spines sticking into its mouth and gullet.

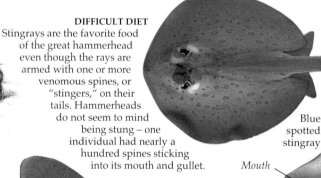

Blue spotted stingray

Mouth

Gill slit

First dorsal fin

TWO DIFFERENT SHARKS
The shape of the hammerhead's head (top) compared to that of other sharks – like the tope (bottom) – fascinated early naturalists.

A FINE BONNET
Bonnetheads are the smallest of the hammerheads, reaching only 5 ft (1.5 m) long. The great hammerhead can grow as long as 19.5 ft (6 m). They usually swim together in small groups, but sometimes huge schools of hundreds of sharks congregate near the surface.

Pectoral fin

WHY A HAMMER?
No one knows why a hammerhead has a hammer-shaped head, but the broad, flat head may give extra lift to the front of the shark's body as it swims. These two hammerheads (right) differ slightly in that the scalloped one (left) has an indentation in the middle of its head, while the smooth, or common, one does not.

Anal fin   Pelvic fin

HEAD ON
Hammerheads swing their heads from side to side as they swim along, which gives them an exellent all-around view, since their eyes are right at the tips of their hammers. Their broad heads bear many ampullae of Lorenzini, which sense tiny electric currents generated by their prey.

Scalloped hammerhead

71

Weird and wonderful

ONE OF THE WORLD'S most extraordinary sharks, the megamouth, was only discovered in 1976. No one had come across this large shark before, though it is over 16 ft (5 m) long and weighs 1,500 lb (680 kg). Since 1976 four more megamouths have been found, including one that was captured alive off the coast of California in 1990. Scientists attached radio tags to this living megamouth so they could follow it. The shark spent the day at 450–500 ft (135-150 m) down, feeding on krill (shrimplike creatures). After sunset it ascended to within 40 ft (12 m) of the surface, following its food source, before its descent into the depths at dawn. Another strange shark, the goblin shark, was found nearly 100 years ago, yet scientists know little about it. Other mysteries have been solved. No one knew what caused disk-shaped bites on seals, whales, and dolphins, but the culprits were found to be cookiecutter sharks. Who knows what other weird and wonderful sharks are still to be found deep in the ocean?

Places where megamouths have been discovered

BIG MOUTH
Megamouth means "big mouth," a good name for a shark with a 3-ft (1-m) grin. This shark may lure krill into its huge mouth with luminous organs around its lips. The first megamouth was brought up dead from 660 ft (200 m), entangled in the sea anchor of a U.S. Navy boat off Hawaii. The second was caught in gill nets (long nets in which fish are trapped) off California; the third was washed up and died on a beach near Perth, Australia; and a fourth was found dead on the coast of Japan. The last one was caught and released off the California coast.

Goblin shark

Long snout with sensory pores for detecting prey

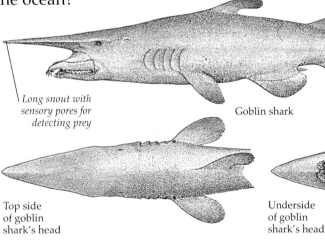

Top side of goblin shark's head

Underside of goblin shark's head

REALLY WEIRD
These ugly sharks (above) were first discovered by scientists off the coast of Japan in 1898. They have flabby bodies and are over 10 ft (3 m) long. Not much is known about these rare sharks that live in deep water at least 530 ft (160 m) down.

Distribution of cookiecutters

GLOWS IN THE DARK
This is one of the lantern sharks, which live in the oceans' dark depths. They are called lantern sharks because they are luminous, or glow in the dark. They are probably the world's smallest sharks, growing to only 8 in (20 cm) long.

BITE SIZED

Cookiecutters have large teeth for sharks only 1.7 ft (0.5 m) long. The common cookiecutter (one of two species) uses its teeth to cut out chunks of flesh from large fish as well as whales, seals, and dolphins. It may wait for such large animals to approach it rather than chasing after them. The cookiecutter forms a suction cup with its lips, bites, then swivels around to take an oval-shaped plug of flesh. Cookiecutters have also taken bites out of the rubber components of submarines and undersea cables.

GODDESS OF LIGHT

The cookiecutters' scientific genus name, *Isistius*, is from Isis, the Egyptian goddess of light. Cookiecutters have many light organs on their bellies and glow in the dark. This may attract prey like whales to come close enough to be bitten.

BORING BITES
The wounds on this seal were made by a cookiecutter shark biting into its flesh.

0   1200   2400   3600 miles

Marine mammals

AT FIRST SIGHT A DOLPHIN looks more like a fish than a person. But like you, the dolphin is a mammal, a warm-blooded animal that feeds its young on mother's milk. It is one of the many kinds of whale, the most successful group of marine mammals. Several other unrelated groups of mammals, including seals and dugongs, also make their homes in salt water. Millions of years ago their ancestors left the land to live in the sea. Over time they evolved to suit their new environment, becoming sleek and streamlined. Unlike fish, which take oxygen from the water, marine mammals must come to the surface regularly to breathe. But taking oxygen from the air is efficient, and most marine mammals are fast swimmers and powerful hunters.

ARISTOTLE
Whales are mammals, not fish. The Greek scientist and philosopher Aristotle recognized this 2,400 years ago. He also noticed that they suckle their young and breathe air, like other mammals.

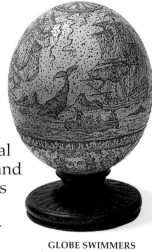

GLOBE SWIMMERS
This globe made from an ostrich egg shows whales swimming all over the world. Marine mammals live in every ocean, from the balmy tropics to the icy polar seas, and in several great rivers. Some migrate vast distances to feed and give birth.

WHALE-SIZED
In every language, the word for 'whale' connotes something large. Even the smallest whales are the size of a person. This pilot whale weighs 2,850 lb (1,300 kg), about 18 times the size of an adult man. The largest whales are bigger than any dinosaur, and the blue whale, the largest of all, weighs 220 tons (200 tonnes) and is as long as a Boeing 737 jet!

Layer of fur protects and keeps animal warm

FIN FOOT
Seals, sea lions, and walruses are pinnipeds, which means "fin-footed." They are powerful swimmers superbly adapted to life in the sea. As their name suggests, they have webbed feet. But unlike whales, they have not lost their back legs and have to come ashore to give birth.

Powerful front flippers used to propel sea lion through water

SEA MONSTER
Whales are mysterious creatures. The biggest species live far out at sea and spend most of their lives under water. Early drawings were based on sailors' stories of sea monsters with huge mouths that huffed and puffed like dragons.

Webbed back flippers

Dorsal fin

Blowhole

WHALES AND DOLPHINS
Of all marine mammals, the best adapted to life in the sea are the cetaceans, or whales. The group gets its name from the Greek word *ketos*, meaning "sea monster". It includes dolphins and porpoises, which are really whales. This bottle-nosed dolphin is a typical whale. It is a powerful swimmer with strong tail flukes, two pectoral (chest) fins, a dorsal (back) fin, and no hind legs. It breathes through a blowhole on the top of its head.

Pectoral fins, used to steer while swimming

Tough, rubbery skin with very few hairs

Swimming muscles that drive the whale through water

Flukes, the correct name for a whale's "tail"

THAR SHE BLOWS!
No group of animals has been hunted as ruthlessly as whales (pp. 124–125). They were once common in all the world's oceans, but by the middle of this century many populations had been virtually wiped out. The industry declined, and a public outcry helped to control the killing. But many whale populations may never recover.

SEA SIRENS
Like whales, manatees and dugongs have no hind legs and spend their entire lives in the water (pp. 106–107). They are gentle vegetarians, and sailors used to mistake them for mermaids. They are known as sirenians, from the Greek word for mermaid, *seiren*.

Light color blends in with snow and ice of Arctic

SEA BEAR
Are polar bears marine mammals? Probably, because they depend on the sea. For much of the year, polar bears live on the floating ice pack, spending hours in the water hunting seals. They are superb swimmers but cannot stay under water very long.

Heavy coat of fur keeps bear warm

SEA OTTER
Most otters are found in rivers, but there are two species that live all the time in salt water. Sea otters entered the oceans relatively recently and are not as well adapted as other marine mammals. They are sleek and streamlined, with dense fur and webbed feet.

Powerful paws used to kill prey such as seals

Seals and sea lions

ALL 34 SPECIES OF SEAL are hunters. Most feed on fish, but some, such as the ferocious leopard seal, eat other seals. There are three families: the true, or earless, seals (18 species), the eared seals (15 species), and the walrus, which is unusual enough to go in a family of its own. Seals are found all over the world, but they are most common in the icy waters of the Arctic and Antarctic. This is probably because food supplies are more reliable in the polar regions than in warmer waters. Many species have been reduced to low numbers by human activities. Sealing was just as ruthless as whaling (pp. 124–125), and millions of animals were killed in the last two centuries. Now other seal populations are seriously threatened by pollution (pp. 124–125). Seals spend much of their lives at sea and so are hard to study. Yet new techniques such as satellite tracking are revealing surprising new information about this remarkable and mysterious group of mammals.

ALL IN THE FAMILY
The largest seal, the male elephant seal, grows to 21 ft (6.5 m) and weighs up to 4.5 tons (4 tonnes). The smallest species, the ringed and Baikal seals, reach 4 ft 6 in (1.37 m) and weigh 140 lb (64 kg).

HAULED OUT
Seals come onto land or ice to give birth. This is called hauling out. Land-breeding seals like the elephant seal gather at a few popular beaches, where competition between bulls (males) can be intense. Bigger, stronger bulls usually triumph, so bulls are usually much larger than cows (females). Ice-breeding seals like this ringed seal are spread out over a larger area, and bulls and cows are closer to the same size.

TRUE SEALS
This common, or harbor, seal is a true seal. It has a round, chubby shape and no obvious earflaps. Like all true seals, it cannot turn its hind flippers under its body, so it cannot climb very well on land. But it moves surprisingly fast on rocky shores. This family includes the world's most common marine mammal, the crabeater seal, and the monk seals, which are among the rarest.

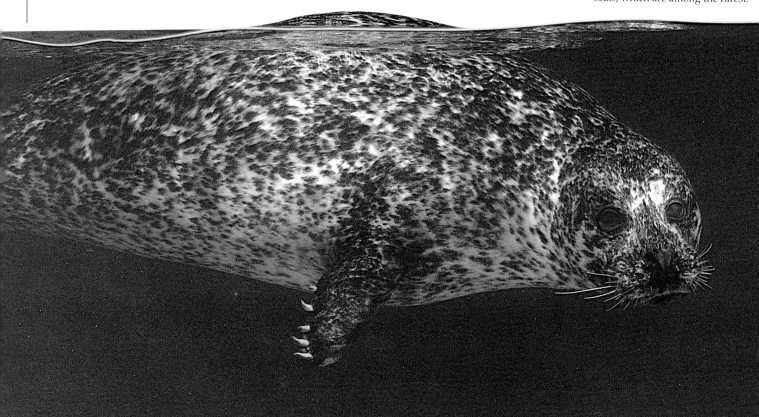

Sensitive whiskers

A COUPLE OF WALRUSES
Walruses live around the moving ice pack of the northern oceans (pp. 104–105). Bulls are about 50 percent heavier than cows. Both sexes are kept warm by a thick blanket of blubber that can make up half of their body weight. Unlike whales, they are quite hairy, with bushy whiskers to help them find their prey in the dark and murky depths.

COLD COMFORT
In the Arctic, the native Inuit people have always hunted the seal for its meat, fur, and hide. They even use the seal's tendons and bones to make tools or rope. This Inuit stone carving of a seal comes from Frobisher Bay in the Canadian Arctic.

Female, or cow, walrus

Thick layer of blubber for warmth and protection

Male, or bull, walrus

Front flippers steer while swimming

Cribbage board carved from a walrus tusk and decorated with seals

WATER HOUNDS
Biologists think seals evolved from doglike carnivores and share the same ancestors as this jackal. But why did they take to the sea 30 million years ago? Probably because changes in ocean currents created rich new food supplies in the oceans.

EARED SEALS
Like all eared seals, this California sea lion is using its long front flippers to swim through the water; true seals and walruses push with their hind flippers instead (pp. 80–81). There are two main groups of eared seals, the sea lions and the fur seals. They have longer limbs than true seals, and are more agile on land. Like most seals, they have large eyes to help them navigate and find underwater prey.

Suited to life in the sea

W‌HALES AND SEALS ARE SUPERBLY SUITED to life in the sea. Because they are supported by the water, they do not need strong legs, and they have evolved a sleek shape that slides easily through the water. Many species can swim as fast as a small boat. Powerful muscles in the tail and flanks drive them forward. Their fins are also streamlined, like a plane's wings. Water is a cold home, and almost all whales and seals have thick layers of blubber which keep them very warm. Many seals also have heavy, oily fur which traps bubbles of air and keeps the animals warm and dry.

DIVING IN
In most of the world, the ocean is cold enough to take your breath away. In polar seas, a human would barely survive a minute. Water is a very good conductor of heat, so an animal loses heat 25 times faster in water than in the air.

Long guard hairs

Fine underfur

A LINED COAT
A close look at a fur seal's coat reveals two kinds of hair. The longer, thicker hairs protect the seal as it scrapes against the rocks. But it is air bubbles caught in the fine, dense underfur that keep the seal warm.

SUNBATHING
Seals and sea lions often bask in the sun to warm up. But they are so well insulated that they can easily get too hot. When this happens, they cool off by waving their front flippers in the air or burying them in the sand. When northern elephant seals overheat, they flip cool sand over their backs (pp. 102–103).

Female California sea lion

Male California sea lion

FAT FOOD
A whale's fat or blubber does not just warm and protect it. It is also a food store. When a right whale is feeding, its blubber may grow to 2 ft (60 cm) thick. The whale can then live off its blubber during the long periods when it does not eat at all.

NOT HALF FAT
Walruses have a lot of fat! As much as half of their body weight is blubber. The rolls of fat keep them warm in the freezing seas and ice floes of the Arctic. Thousands of walruses were once killed (pp. 104–105) for their blubber, which was boiled and turned into oil.

When a walrus is too hot, tiny blood vesssels in the skin fill with blood and the animal seems to blush

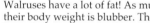

KEEPING YOUR HEAD ABOVE WATER
Humans are poor swimmers. They have no flippers or tail flukes, and get cold because they have hardly any fat. They can barely hold their breath for more than a minute, and have to stick their mouths out of the water to gulp air. Whales have solved all these problems. They have even evolved blowholes that allow them to breathe through the top of the head.

OPEN...
A whale's blowhole is a modified nostril that sits on top of its head. Toothed whales like this orca have only one blowhole. This opens so the whale can snort the old air out of its huge pair of lungs.

Massive, broad pectoral fin

... AND CLOSED
Muscles force the blow-hole shut before the orca submerges.

Coming up to breathe
Taking a breath at sea is a difficult business. Under water, a whale's blow-hole or a seal's nostrils are shut tight. When the whale surfaces, it breathes out very rapidly. The "blow" forms a fine mist of spray up to 13 ft (4 m) high that can be seen miles away. A moment later, the whale breathes in and submerges. Seals breathe out and dive with empty lungs.

DOUBLE-BARRELED
Baleen whales have two blowholes that sit side-by-side. Their blow usually looks like a single spray of mist. Only right whales produce distinctive double blows. This minke whale's blow is almost invisible, except in the very coldest Antarctic waters.

Umbilicus (belly button)

Genital slit

Anus

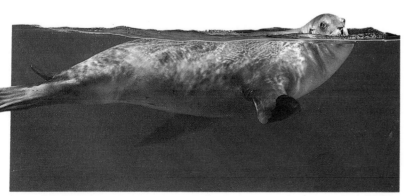

SEAL SOLUTIONS
A seal's eyes and nostrils are at the top of its head, so they stick out of the water while it swims along. Seals and sea lions can even sleep at sea. Some species sleep under water and somehow manage to wake up every few minutes to breathe. Other kinds of seals sleep at the surface with their nostrils poking out of the water like a snorkel. This is called bottling.

TORPEDO-SHAPED
Land animals come in all shapes and sizes. This is because they move in air, which hardly provides any resistance. But swimming through water is hard work, and marine animals all have a similar, stream-lined shape. Even their sexual organs, which would slow them down, are tucked away in a genital slit.

Continued on next page

Long pectoral fin, or flipper

*Throat grooves, a clue that
the humpback is a rorqual*

ON A WING AND A SONG

This leaping humpback is showing off its graceful flippers, much longer than any other whale's. These are much too long for simple steering, and are sometimes used to rub other whales. Humpbacks also slap their flippers on the water, to make loud splashing noises. This is called flippering.

TICKET TO RIDE

Barnacles make their homes on the skin of slow-moving whales such as right and gray whales. Rorquals such as the blue whale are too fast for most hangers-on. Sperm whales are slow, but they regularly shed huge sheets of dead skin. This makes it hard for other animals to hitch a free ride for long.

Finding their way around

Whales and seals live in a world that is very different from our own. Even in the clearest ocean water visibility is rarely more than 100 ft (30 m), and they have to hunt at night or in murky water. Seals rely on sensitive whiskers. Toothed whales have developed a system of echolocation, using sounds to find food and their way around (pp. 88–89). How whales navigate when they migrate thousands of miles is another question. They may have a special magnetic sense and a built-in compass.

Earflap

Nose like a dog's

Large eyes

Long whiskers, specialized hairs used in close quarters

EYEBALL TO EYEBALL

In the murky ocean, eyes are less useful than they are on land. This gray whale's eyes are not much larger than a cow's. They must be pretty useless while the whale is feeding on the muddy ocean bottom. But gray whales spy hop – stick their heads out of the water to have a look around.

HEAD FULL OF SENSES

For their size, seals have much bigger eyes than whales. Their senses are similar to a dog's. Apart from the walrus (pp. 104–105), seals can all see well in and out of the water. This California sea lion has large eyes and good vision even in dim light. Its nose is very doglike. The long whiskers are especially useful in dark or murky waters.

These muscles contract to pull tail up

Upstroke begins

Upstroke

Downstroke begins

FISHY TAIL

A fish's tail is vertical, not horizontal like a whale's. It moves its tail from side to side to swim.

These muscles contract to pull tail down

Swimming power

Whales are incredible swimmers. Underneath their blubber are huge muscle blocks. The killer whale has been clocked at 34 mph (56 km/h), faster than any other sea mammal. Other species travel thousands of miles in their seasonal migrations. The gray whale makes the longest journey, from Mexico to its feeding grounds off Alaska and back again, a round trip of more than 12,000 miles (20,000 km).

A whale's tail has many tiny blood vessels and works like a car radiator to cool the animal down

DRIVING FORCE
Like a boat's propeller, a whale's tail drives it through the water. Its flukes – the propeller's blades – are flat and rigid. The whale pulls its flukes up and down with large muscles connected to the top and bottom of the spine . The whole back third of a killer whale is solid swimming muscle.

Skin covered in a film of oil that helps whale slide through water

Skin feels smooth and rubbery, like a hard-boiled egg

MOSTLY MUSCLE
Do not be fooled by their blubbery appearance. Seals are powerful swimmers, though they cannot compete with whales. Under the fat, this gray seal is mostly muscle.

Open to brake

Closed for cruising

REAR FLIPPER DRIVE
True seals (pp. 76–77) swim by moving their back flippers and tail from side to side. Young seals sometimes swim by moving both back flippers together. But adult seals usually move them one at a time. True seals of all ages steer with their front flippers.

FRONT FLIPPER DRIVE
Like all eared seals (pp. 76–77), fur seals swim with their large front flippers. The rear flippers help to steer. On land, the fur seal can tuck them under its body, so it can waddle around. Like dolphins, some seals "porpoise" – that is, leap out of the water when they are swimming fast.

Upstroke begins again

Downstroke ends

THE GREAT SWIMMER
Dolphins are fast and graceful swimmers. People have always admired the apparent ease with which they glide through the water. Dolphins swim by moving their strong tails up and down. Both the upstroke and the downstroke generate power. But dolphins can swim really fast only in short bursts. A close look at a dolphin's skin shows rows of microscopic ridges. It is not clear how these corrugations help the dolphin; they may reduce turbulence at high speed.

Downstroke

Front flippers used only for steering

81

Ocean giants

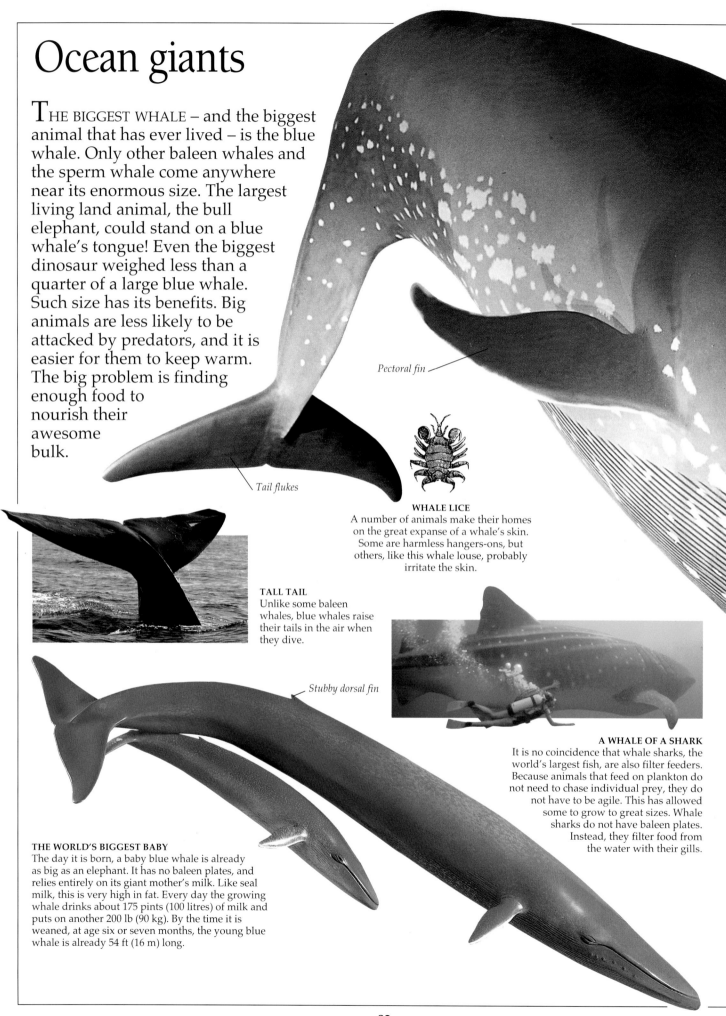

THE BIGGEST WHALE – and the biggest animal that has ever lived – is the blue whale. Only other baleen whales and the sperm whale come anywhere near its enormous size. The largest living land animal, the bull elephant, could stand on a blue whale's tongue! Even the biggest dinosaur weighed less than a quarter of a large blue whale. Such size has its benefits. Big animals are less likely to be attacked by predators, and it is easier for them to keep warm. The big problem is finding enough food to nourish their awesome bulk.

Pectoral fin

Tail flukes

WHALE LICE
A number of animals make their homes on the great expanse of a whale's skin. Some are harmless hangers-on, but others, like this whale louse, probably irritate the skin.

TALL TAIL
Unlike some baleen whales, blue whales raise their tails in the air when they dive.

Stubby dorsal fin

A WHALE OF A SHARK
It is no coincidence that whale sharks, the world's largest fish, are also filter feeders. Because animals that feed on plankton do not need to chase individual prey, they do not have to be agile. This has allowed some to grow to great sizes. Whale sharks do not have baleen plates. Instead, they filter food from the water with their gills.

THE WORLD'S BIGGEST BABY
The day it is born, a baby blue whale is already as big as an elephant. It has no baleen plates, and relies entirely on its giant mother's milk. Like seal milk, this is very high in fat. Every day the growing whale drinks about 175 pints (100 litres) of milk and puts on another 200 lb (90 kg). By the time it is weaned, at age six or seven months, the young blue whale is already 54 ft (16 m) long.

WHALE OUT OF WATER
Whales can reach such incredible sizes only because their weight is supported by the water. When a large whale such as this sperm whale (pp. 100–101) is stranded, it cannot support its own weight and its internal organs are crushed.

BLUE SPLASH
No one knows why whales leap out of the water, or breach. Adults often breach in the company of other whales. This suggests that the big splash is a way of communicating (pp. 88–89). Young animals such as this baby blue may start breaching when they are only a few weeks old. Perhaps by playing they are learning skills which will be important to them as adults.

Paired blowholes

THE BIG BLUE
Blue whales grow to more than 100 ft (32 m) and weigh up to 220 tons (200 tonnes). But we cannot be sure of the exact size of the biggest individuals. Blue whales were hunted mercilessly in the southern oceans, and most of the information on them comes from the whaling industry. Weights were estimated by measuring chopped-off chunks and adding a few tons to make up for lost blood. Even the lengths may be incorrect, as the whales could have been stretched by towing. Blue whales received complete protection from whalers in 1966. But there are no signs that numbers have increased, and there may be only a few hundred left in the entire southern oceans.

Throat grooves, which allow baleen whales to gulp huge amounts of water

PILOT STUDY
Measuring a stranded whale is easy. But how do you measure a live whale at sea? One way is to take a series of photos as the whale surfaces. By lining them end to end, scientists can piece together the animal's entire length.

Teeth for grasping…

MOST WHALES AND SEALS are hunters that catch their slippery prey with rows of sharp teeth. Like most meat-eating mammals (including people), seals and sea lions have a range of different teeth. They grasp their food with powerful canines and incisors and then chew it up with premolars and molars. But toothed whales have simple, peglike teeth that are all the same shape. Teeth are also used for fighting. One of the most amazing teeth of all, the male narwhal's tusk, is probably used to establish dominance over other males (pp. 98–99). Some beaked whales have teeth that are so strangely shaped that it is hard to imagine what they are for! Perhaps the simple sight of the male's huge teeth makes him irresistible to female whales.

MYSTERY TOOTH
Only mature male sperm whales have teeth. These are huge, up to 10 in (25 cm) long. How females and young males manage to feed and what males use their teeth for are mysteries.

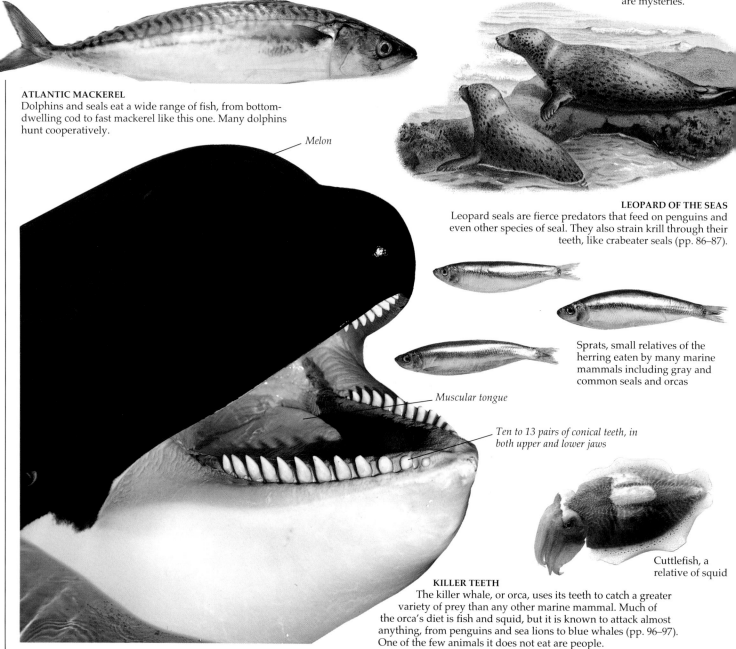

ATLANTIC MACKEREL
Dolphins and seals eat a wide range of fish, from bottom-dwelling cod to fast mackerel like this one. Many dolphins hunt cooperatively.

LEOPARD OF THE SEAS
Leopard seals are fierce predators that feed on penguins and even other species of seal. They also strain krill through their teeth, like crabeater seals (pp. 86–87).

Melon

Sprats, small relatives of the herring eaten by many marine mammals including gray and common seals and orcas

Muscular tongue

Ten to 13 pairs of conical teeth, in both upper and lower jaws

Cuttlefish, a relative of squid

KILLER TEETH
The killer whale, or orca, uses its teeth to catch a greater variety of prey than any other marine mammal. Much of the orca's diet is fish and squid, but it is known to attack almost anything, from penguins and sea lions to blue whales (pp. 96–97). One of the few animals it does not eat are people.

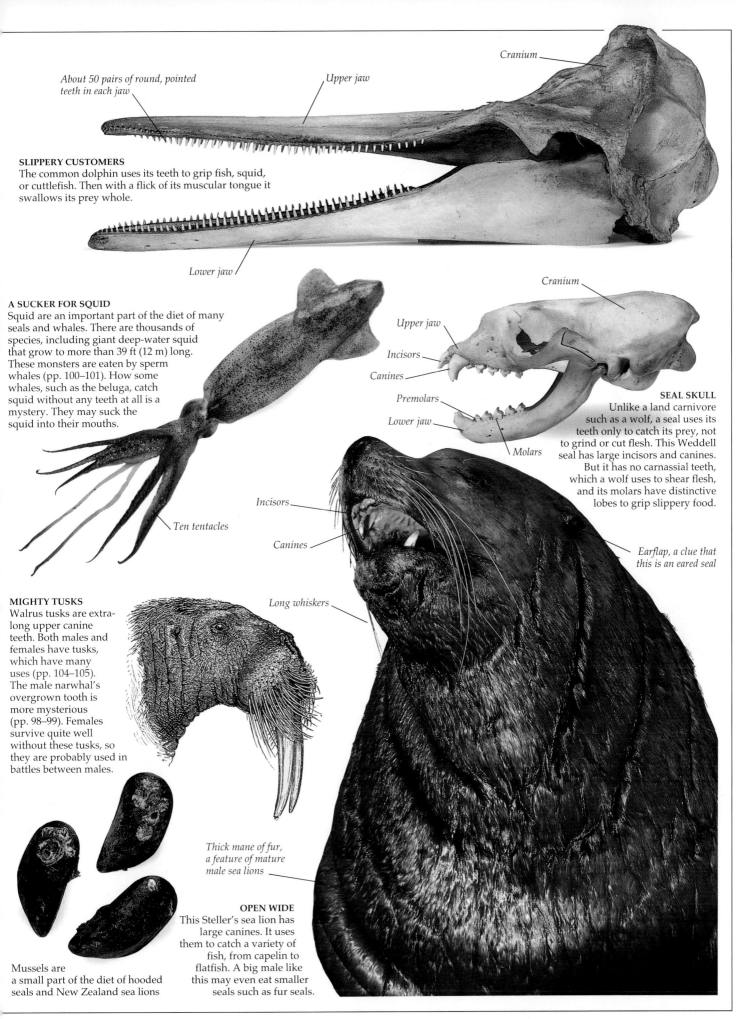

Cranium

About 50 pairs of round, pointed
teeth in each jaw

Upper jaw

SLIPPERY CUSTOMERS
The common dolphin uses its teeth to grip fish, squid,
or cuttlefish. Then with a flick of its muscular tongue it
swallows its prey whole.

Lower jaw

Cranium

A SUCKER FOR SQUID
Squid are an important part of the diet of many
seals and whales. There are thousands of
species, including giant deep-water squid
that grow to more than 39 ft (12 m) long.
These monsters are eaten by sperm
whales (pp. 100–101). How some
whales, such as the beluga, catch
squid without any teeth at all is a
mystery. They may suck the
squid into their mouths.

Upper jaw

Incisors

Canines

Premolars

Lower jaw

Molars

SEAL SKULL
Unlike a land carnivore
such as a wolf, a seal uses its
teeth only to catch its prey, not
to grind or cut flesh. This Weddell
seal has large incisors and canines.
But it has no carnassial teeth,
which a wolf uses to shear flesh,
and its molars have distinctive
lobes to grip slippery food.

Incisors

Canines

Ten tentacles

Earflap, a clue that
this is an eared seal

Long whiskers

MIGHTY TUSKS
Walrus tusks are extra-
long upper canine
teeth. Both males and
females have tusks,
which have many
uses (pp. 104–105).
The male narwhal's
overgrown tooth is
more mysterious
(pp. 98–99). Females
survive quite well
without these tusks, so
they are probably used in
battles between males.

Thick mane of fur,
a feature of mature
male sea lions

OPEN WIDE
This Steller's sea lion has
large canines. It uses
them to catch a variety of
fish, from capelin to
flatfish. A big male like
this may even eat smaller
seals such as fur seals.

Mussels are
a small part of the diet of hooded
seals and New Zealand sea lions

… and baleen for filtering

SOME OF THE BIGGEST WHALES feed by filtering. Their filters are baleen plates, huge fringed brushes that hang inside their mouths like giant sieves. The three families of baleen whales have evolved different filtering techniques. But they all draw seawater into their mouths and spit it back out through the baleen, trapping any tasty morsels on the inside. Some feed mainly on krill, small shrimplike animals found in huge numbers in the southern oceans. Others gulp down entire schools of fish. Most baleen whales pack a whole year's feeding into four or five summer months. In this time their weight may increase by 40 percent. Much of the energy is stored as fat in preparation for the long migrations to winter breeding grounds (pp.80–81).

ANOTHER FILTERER
Like whales, flamingos are filter feeders. They have fringed beaks similar to baleen plates which they skim through the mud upside down.

BIG GULP
Rorquals have throat grooves which allow them to expand their mouths to engulf huge quantities of water. A blue whale can take in 66 tons (60 tonnes) of water in one gulp. Then the whale forces the water out by closing its mouth and contracting the grooves. Anything too large to pass through the baleen filter is trapped on the inside and swallowed.

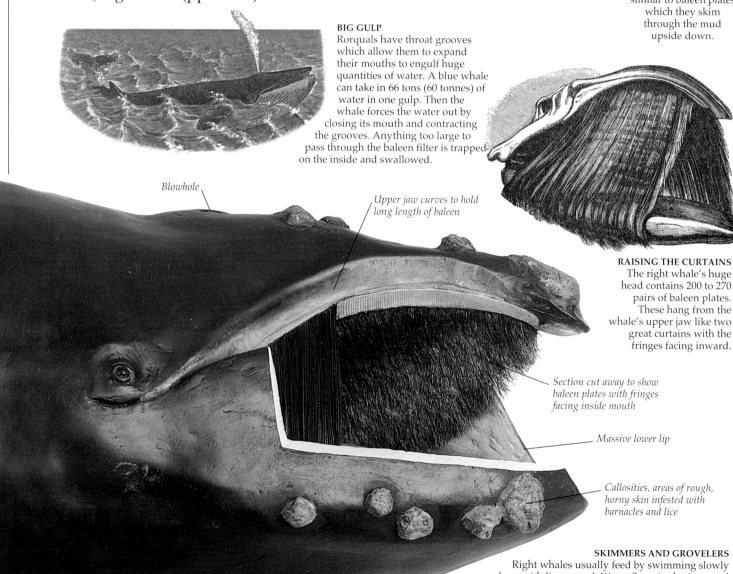

Blowhole

Upper jaw curves to hold long length of baleen

RAISING THE CURTAINS
The right whale's huge head contains 200 to 270 pairs of baleen plates. These hang from the whale's upper jaw like two great curtains with the fringes facing inward.

Section cut away to show baleen plates with fringes facing inside mouth

Massive lower lip

Callosities, areas of rough, horny skin infested with barnacles and lice

SKIMMERS AND GROVELERS
Right whales usually feed by swimming slowly along with lips parted. Water flows in the front and out the sides of the mouth. Unlike rorquals, they do not open their mouth very wide, but their high, curved lips can hold much longer baleen plates. These are protected by huge lower lips, up to 16 ft (5 m) high in large individuals. The gray whale, the other kind of baleen whale, swims along the bottom making troughs in the mud like a bulldozer. Bowhead whales, a kind of right whale, have been seen feeding in both ways.

The right whale's head can make up a quarter of its body length

Hard outer edge

Inner fringe

FIN WHALE BALEEN
Like your hair and fingernails, baleen is made of a substance called keratin. It grows continually, replacing the fringe as it is worn away.

FINE FILTER
A right whale's baleen grows to 14 ft (4.3 m), much longer than that of any other whale. The extremely fine hairs can trap very small animals.

Top attaches to whale's upper jaw

FITTING TOGETHER
Baleen plates grow from ridges like the ones you can feel on the roof of your mouth. They fit together like cards in a deck.

Baleen plate decorated by 19th-century whaler

KRILL
Krill are shrimplike creatures no longer than your finger. In the summer they occur in enormous swarms that can cover miles of the southern oceans, where they are the main food for most baleen whales.

Fine fringe where prey is trapped

Incisors

Canines

Cheek teeth with three lobes trap krill in mouth

SIEVING SEAL
Despite its name, the crabeater seal does not eat crabs! Instead it uses its strangely shaped teeth to filter krill from the water. This unusual tactic must be successful, because there are more crabeater seals in the world than any other species of seal.

Upper jaw of first whale

Upper jaw of second whale

Baleen plate

BLOWING BUBBLES
In some parts of the world, humpback whales use bubbles to herd fish together. This is known as bubble netting. The whale swims in a spiral under the fish, blowing bubbles all the time. Then with its mouth wide open it surfaces in the middle and gulps down the whole school. Humpbacks feed alone or in groups of up to 25 animals. These two are fishing together in the cold waters of the Antarctic.

Lower jaw of first whale, bulging with water and fish

Clicks, barks, and songs

SOUND TRAVELS WELL in water, and the seas are noisy places. Whales and seals live in a world dominated by sound. Dolphins coordinate their hunts with whistles and clicks, and male humpbacks sing to attract females. Most large whales make sounds by slapping the surface or breaching – leaping out of the water and coming down with a splash. These splashes can be heard for miles and are probably a kind of communication. The most sophisticated use of sound is in echolocation. Only toothed whales and bats have perfected this skill. By sending out a pulse of sound and listening to the returning echo, whales can find their way around and locate fish and squid in the dark water. The biggest toothed whale, the sperm whale, may even stun squid with loud clicks (pp. 100–101). Baleen whales also make loud sounds. Early sailors were terrified when they heard strange rumbles and groans through the hulls of their wooden ships. We are just beginning to understand these low-frequency calls, which may travel hundreds of miles through the seas.

EAR BONE
From the outside, a small pinprick is the only sign of a whale's ear. This dense bone is part of a baleen whale's inner ear.

SIGNATURE WHISTLE
Every dolphin makes its own, unique whistle. Scientists listen to these "signature whistles" to identify individuals. Mothers and their calves have similar-sounding whistles.

WHISTLING WALRUS
Seals that mate in the water make elaborate underwater sounds. Among the noisiest of all are male walruses courting females. Their songs include loud gongs, like underwater bells. They also rise out of the water to bark, whistle, growl, and clack their teeth.

HUMPBACK HITS
Humpback whales are the only nonhumans to make it into the music charts. Many people enjoy listening to the soothing sounds of humpbacks, belugas, and killer whales. A recording of humpback songs was put aboard the *Voyager* space probe as a greeting from Planet Earth.

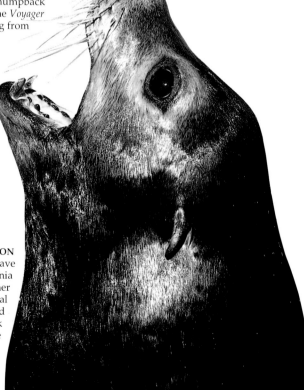

LOVE SONG
The male humpback whale sings a beautiful, haunting song for hours on end. All alone, he sings floating motionless in the water with his head hanging down. Like a lot of male birds, humpbacks sing to attract females. The song consists of a number of phrases repeated over and over again. Each individual sings his own song, slightly different from any other, which evolves slowly from year to year. Whales from different areas sing distinctive themes, so scientists can tell which population a whale comes from by its song.

BARKING SEA LION
The bark of a seal or sea lion can have many meanings. Male California sea lions bark to frighten off other males. If a female elephant seal (pp. 102–103) is about to be mated by a small male, she will bark to attract the attention of the dominant male, who rushes over and chases away the small male. Seal mothers and pups bark to find each other on the crowded beach (pp. 92–93).

MOBY CLICK
When sperm whales get together, they often repeat slow patterns of clicks, called codas. When one whale produces a particular coda, another will repeat it in turn. Sperm whales have huge brains (pp. 100–101). But it is hard to imagine that they can say anything very complicated with such simple clicks.

Two-ton killer whale, or orca

WAILING IT OUT
When famous Italian opera singer Luciano Pavarotti sings, he is forcing air past vocal cords that vibrate in his throat. The air leaves through his mouth, so he has to pause every few seconds to breathe in. But whales have no vocal cords, and humpbacks can warble for half an hour between breaths. To do this they must be able to recycle air. Some dolphins can even whistle and echolocate at the same time.

OUT OF THE WATER...
Why do whales breach? The loud splashes can be heard many miles away, and are probably a way of communicating. Whales probably slap the water with their tails (lobtailing, pp. 100–101) or flippers (pp. 80–81) for the same reason.

...AND DOWN WITH A SPLASH!
Whales are more likely to breach when they are with other whales, and humpbacks breach more in rough weather than calm. This may be the only way to make themselves heard above the water noise.

Melon, a waxy bulge in the forehead, which may be a lens to focus sounds

Blowhole

Clicks produced in nasal sacks, bulges in nasal tubes below blowhole

Lower jaw may be used to receive echo

Echoes "heard" through inner ear, where lower jaw meets skull

SOUND SENSATION
Dolphins produce trains of clicks for echolocation. These can sound like buzzes or doors creaking. But don't be fooled by this open mouth; dolphins produce sounds in nasal sacks beneath their blowholes. Echolocation is an incredibly precise sense. Blindfolded, dolphins can still find objects or distinguish between two balls of slightly different sizes. They may also make loud bangs to stun fish.

Courtship and birth

THE URGE TO REPRODUCE is strong, and takes up a lot of a whale's or a seal's time and energy. Seals risk the danger of coming ashore to find a mate and give birth. In many species of whale and seal, the males compete for females, with the winning (dominant) males mating with many females. In these species, the males are usually bigger than the females. The most amazing example of this is the elephant seal, where big males are 10 times bigger than females (pp. 102–103). Whales and seals usually mate and give birth in the spring, so their pregnancies last a year. Most seals have a pup every year, but many species of whale raise only one calf every 3 or even 10 years.

THE RIGHT STUFF
In winter, southern right whales gather in shallow bays to mate. Several males mate with each female, one after another. The only way a female can escape is by plunging her head under water and sticking her tail in the air. The males just wait, because they know that sooner or later she will have to take a breath.

ICE BREEDER
A seal's link with land may be brief. Common seals are born at low tide and swim off before the tide is high again. This hooded seal has a huge choice of ice floes to haul out on, so females are not crowded into a small area. Males are usually seen with only one female at a time. But each female is probably mated by several males, one after another.

TUSK, TUSK!
There is usually a lot of bluffing and counterbluffing when males compete. In most species, full-blown fights are rare. These male walruses are fighting for a spot in the water close to a herd of females. A lot is at stake. The winner may mate with more than a dozen females; the loser may never mate at all.

Female walrus, identified by her smaller size and darker color

The walrus's pregnancy lasts 15 to 16 months, longer than any other seal's

LOVE IN A COLD CLIMATE
Walruses have a long and intimate courtship. Males seduce females with barks, growls, and haunting whistles (pp. 88–89). A female who is impressed by his love song will slip off with a male. This female (left) and male (right) are rubbing mustaches. Each female mates with only one male. Mating takes place in the water.

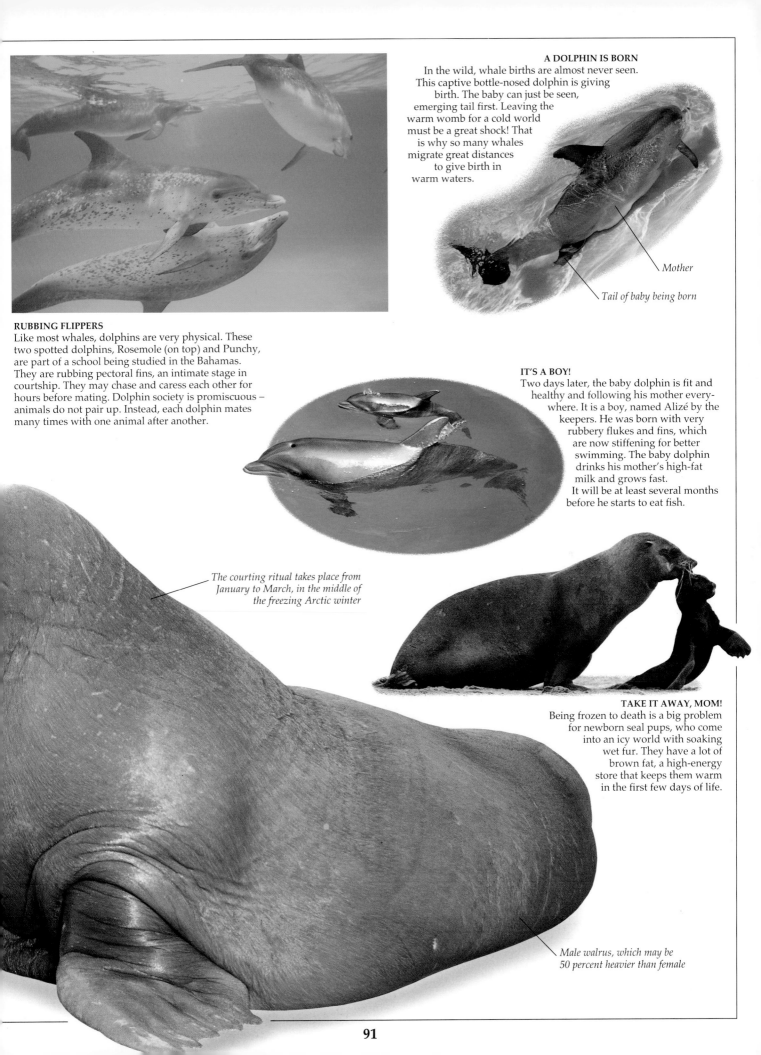

A DOLPHIN IS BORN

In the wild, whale births are almost never seen. This captive bottle-nosed dolphin is giving birth. The baby can just be seen, emerging tail first. Leaving the warm womb for a cold world must be a great shock! That is why so many whales migrate great distances to give birth in warm waters.

Mother

Tail of baby being born

RUBBING FLIPPERS

Like most whales, dolphins are very physical. These two spotted dolphins, Rosemole (on top) and Punchy, are part of a school being studied in the Bahamas. They are rubbing pectoral fins, an intimate stage in courtship. They may chase and caress each other for hours before mating. Dolphin society is promiscuous – animals do not pair up. Instead, each dolphin mates many times with one animal after another.

IT'S A BOY!

Two days later, the baby dolphin is fit and healthy and following his mother everywhere. It is a boy, named Alizé by the keepers. He was born with very rubbery flukes and fins, which are now stiffening for better swimming. The baby dolphin drinks his mother's high-fat milk and grows fast. It will be at least several months before he starts to eat fish.

The courting ritual takes place from January to March, in the middle of the freezing Arctic winter

TAKE IT AWAY, MOM!

Being frozen to death is a big problem for newborn seal pups, who come into an icy world with soaking wet fur. They have a lot of brown fat, a high-energy store that keeps them warm in the first few days of life.

Male walrus, which may be 50 percent heavier than female

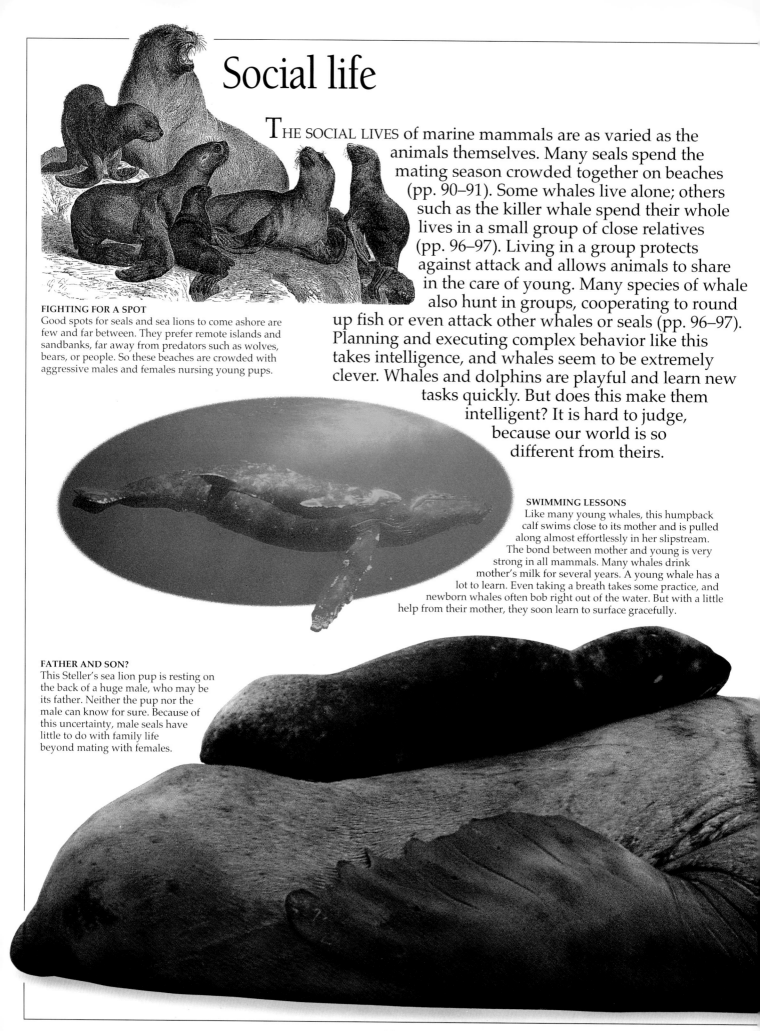

Social life

THE SOCIAL LIVES of marine mammals are as varied as the animals themselves. Many seals spend the mating season crowded together on beaches (pp. 90–91). Some whales live alone; others such as the killer whale spend their whole lives in a small group of close relatives (pp. 96–97). Living in a group protects against attack and allows animals to share in the care of young. Many species of whale also hunt in groups, cooperating to round up fish or even attack other whales or seals (pp. 96–97). Planning and executing complex behavior like this takes intelligence, and whales seem to be extremely clever. Whales and dolphins are playful and learn new tasks quickly. But does this make them intelligent? It is hard to judge, because our world is so different from theirs.

FIGHTING FOR A SPOT
Good spots for seals and sea lions to come ashore are few and far between. They prefer remote islands and sandbanks, far away from predators such as wolves, bears, or people. So these beaches are crowded with aggressive males and females nursing young pups.

SWIMMING LESSONS
Like many young whales, this humpback calf swims close to its mother and is pulled along almost effortlessly in her slipstream. The bond between mother and young is very strong in all mammals. Many whales drink mother's milk for several years. A young whale has a lot to learn. Even taking a breath takes some practice, and newborn whales often bob right out of the water. But with a little help from their mother, they soon learn to surface gracefully.

FATHER AND SON?
This Steller's sea lion pup is resting on the back of a huge male, who may be its father. Neither the pup nor the male can know for sure. Because of this uncertainty, male seals have little to do with family life beyond mating with females.

DANCE OF THE DOLPHINS
Dolphin societies are complex and difficult for people to observe. The warm, shallow waters of the Bahamas are one of the few places in the world where schools can be studied over long periods. These spotted dolphins live in schools of 50 or more. Like other social animals, dolphins have disagreements and conflicts. They often confront each other head to head, squawking with open mouths. These conflicts rarely end in physical injury.

SUCKLING SEA LION
This female Steller's sea lion is many times smaller than the male below. She is suckling a young pup. The breeding beaches are so crowded that pups are often crushed when the huge males rush over to mate with females. A female leaves her pup regularly to go fishing. So how does she tell her pup from the hundreds of others on the beach when she gets back? She starts by making a warbling call which attracts any nearby pups. Then she smells and touches any likely-looking youngsters until she is sure she has found hers.

THE DAILY STRUGGLE
These Steller's sea lions are fighting over a fish. During the day, groups of about 50 sea lions have been seen heading out to sea. They work together to find and herd schools of fish or squid.
At night, the sea lions usually hunt alone.

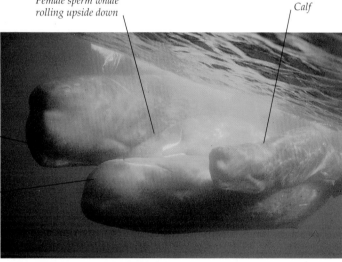

Female sperm whale rolling upside down

Calf

Female sperm whale

Female rolling upside-down

COMMUNAL BABY-SITTING
Because whales live so long, studying their family lives takes decades. Such studies have only just begun, and little is known about most species. We know that female sperm whales live together in big groups with their young calves (pp. 100–101). Males spend only a few hours with each family group every year. One of the females in this group is probably the mother of the small calf. The other females may be sisters or aunts. When the mother dives deep under water to feed, another female will baby-sit the calf, protecting it from sharks or killer whales.

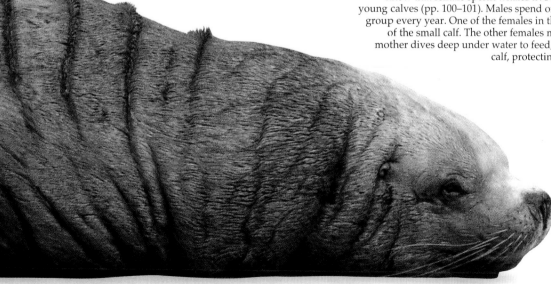

Dolphins and porpoises

PEOPLE HAVE LONG been fascinated by the graceful dolphin. Imagine the magical sight of a school of dolphins leaping for the sheer fun of it, or bow-wave riding, cruising effortlessly on the pressure waves of a boat. The oceangoing dolphins and their close relatives the porpoises are common in all the world's oceans (except for the coldest polar seas). There is still discussion about how the 60 or more species are related. Some species number in the millions and are found all over the world. Others are limited to tiny areas, which makes them more vulnerable. A few species have been reduced to very low numbers by human activity (pp. 124–125). So far, no species has become extinct, and there may just be time to save the two most at risk, the Gulf of California porpoise (vaquita) and the Chinese river dolphin.

PORPOISING
Leaping into the air while swimming along is called porpoising. Strangely enough, most porpoises never do it! The one exception is Dall's porpoise.

LE DAUPHIN
The eldest son of the king of France was given the title *Le Dauphin*, French for "The Dolphin". The title was first adopted by the lords of Viennois, France, who had three dolphins on their coat of arms. When his father died, *Le Dauphin* became king. What happened to the last *Dauphin*, the son of Louis XVI, is still a mystery. His father was executed in 1793, during the French Revolution.

Tail flukes with a central nick, like virtually all whales

WITH TIME ON HIS SIDE
Almost nothing is known about the hourglass dolphin, which gets its name from the pretty black-and-white pattern on its sides. Though these dolphins are not shy and often bow-wave ride, they are usually found far out to sea in the remote waters of the southern oceans.

FISHY TAILS
The ancient Minoans and Greeks were fascinated by dolphins, which were more common in the Mediterranean Sea at the time those civilizations flourished. Many Greek myths and legends feature dolphins. Like most seafarers, Greek sailors were happy to see dolphins playing near their boats. These animals come from the great palace of Knossos on the island of Crete. They are about 3,500 years old. The painter has given the dolphins vertical tails, so they look more like fish.

ACROBAT
Dusky dolphins are great leapers. They are coastal animals that live off New Zealand, southern Africa, and South America. Off Peru they are hunted in large numbers for their meat.

Hump instead of dorsal fin

BOTTLE-NOSED DOLPHIN
Different populations of the same species can look very distinct. The bottle-nosed dolphin is one of the biggest and most common dolphins, found in all kinds of habitats from shallow coastal waters to the deep ocean. Coastal dolphins are smaller and often stay in a particular area. Oceanic animals grow over 13 ft (4 m) long and wander widely.

Small eyes (some species of river dolphin are completely blind)

Long beak

Big flippers for steering

RIVER DOLPHIN
Some dolphins have pink patches, but only the Amazon River dolphin is pink all over. Like the four other species of river dolphin, it has a long beak studded with many teeth. In the murky rivers where these dolphins live, eyes are virtually useless. The dolphins rely instead on echolocation to find fish to eat. It is still unclear if the five river dolphins are closely related. They may have just evolved similar solutions to the problems of river life.

Coin from Tarentum showing Taras, son of Poseidon, the Greek god of the sea, on a dolphin, 331–302 B.C.

Distinctive beak, a feature of dolphins but not of porpoises

Broad, curving flippers

JUMP FOR JOY
Porpoising is an efficient way to take a breath without slowing down. One way of calculating how fast a dolphin swims is to measure how high it leaps. To jump 18 ft (5.5 m) high, a dolphin would have to break the surface at 22 mph (36 km/h). But dolphins do not just leap for practical reasons. They also seem to jump for the sheer fun of it!

SPOTTED SCHOOL
Spotted dolphins have long, slender bodies and pronounced beaks. They are very similar to their close relatives the striped and spinner dolphins. Like most species, they live in schools and have complex social lives that we are barely beginning to understand (pp. 92–93).

Tall, sickle-shaped dorsal fin

BITTEN AND SCARRED
Risso's dolphins are squid eaters. They are found in all but the coldest waters of the Indian, Pacific, and Atlantic oceans. Risso's is the only species of dolphin that has no beak. They live in big groups and are constantly biting each other in fights and in play. Old animals are almost white with thousands of crisscross scars.

Scars from bites

Long, curving flippers

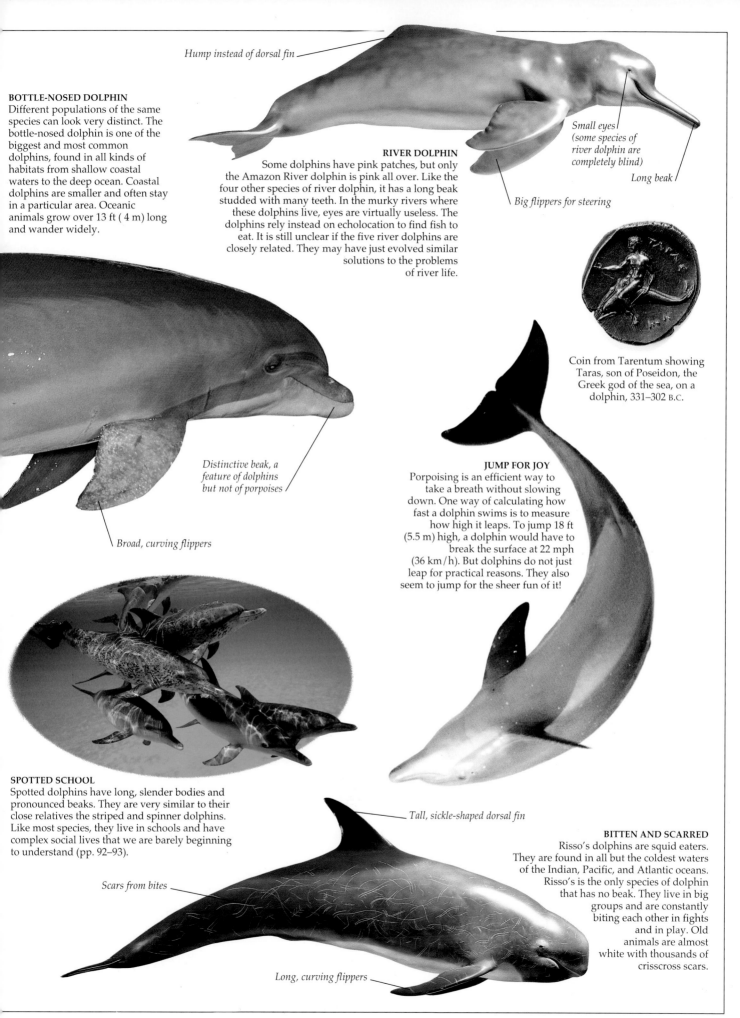

The killer whale

THERE IS NO MISTAKING an orca, or killer whale, with its tall dorsal fin, rounded head and startling black-and-white pattern. An adult male can be 30 ft (9 m) long and weigh 11 tons (10 tonnes). Most of this is muscle, for the orca is the fastest mammal in the seas (pp. 80–81), sprinting at up to 34 mph (56 km/h). This awesome hunter eats almost everything, from small fish to great whales 10 times its size. Because of its ferocious appetite, the orca's common name is killer whale. Orcas have no natural predators. Until the 1960s, they were feared and sometimes shot. But opinions have changed, partly because orcas do not seem to eat humans. Orcas live long lives – a female may reach 90 years old. But they reproduce slowly, with a calf about every eight years. They live in tight social groups called pods, hunt cooperatively, and seem to be highly intelligent. Pods of orcas have been seen working together to herd salmon or tip a seal off an ice floe.

GIANT KILLERS
Imagine the struggle between a great whale and a pod of killers. Even a huge blue whale has no chance against such an attack. Orcas have been seen organizing attacks on all sorts of whales, including a whole pod of sperm whales.

FALSE KILLER
Like the two kinds of pilot whale, this false killer whale is a close relative of the orca. False killers are black all over. They swim with a slow, lazy action. They are the largest whales to bow-wave ride, hitching a free swim from the waves made by boats (pp.94–95). False killers occasionally eat other marine mammals.

Eye

White patch, not eye!

Stiff dorsal fin

Rounded flippers are black top and bottom

White belly

WHY ARE THEY BLACK AND WHITE?
The jet black and shocking white may help to camouflage a killer whale by breaking up its outline. This makes it hard to see as it flits through the water.

SURPRISE!
Orcas are one of the few whales that come onto shore, on purpose. On the Valdés Peninsula in Argentina and the Crozet Islands in the Indian Ocean, orcas swim up onto the beach to grab baby sea lions. Then they use their front flippers to turn around and wiggle back into the surf while they hold the sea lion firmly in their jaws.

LIKE A CAT WITH A MOUSE
All is not yet over for the sea lion. The orca plays with the limp animal like a cat with a mouse. It will fling its prey high into the air with a quick flick of the tail. Young orcas have to learn how to do this, and often join their parents in the game. Finally the terrified sea lion is eaten.

PEA IN A POD
This female killer
is only seven years old and already weighs 2.2 tons
(2 tonnes). Both males and females remain in the same
pod as their mother for life. An older female seems to be
in charge of the pod. Orcas never mate within a pod, but
only when two pods meet. They breach and lobtail a lot
during these exciting encounters.

IT'S A FAMILY AFFAIR
This orca pod lives in British Columbia, Canada. They belong to
the best-studied population of whales anywhere in the world.
The 200-plus individuals are easily recognized by the nicks in
their dorsal fins (p. 60) and the shapes of their "saddles," the
gray patches behind the fins. The mature male in this pod has a
huge dorsal fin. These fins can grow to be 6 ft (2 m) tall.

SHOULD I STAY OR SHOULD I GO?
Orcas live in every ocean of the world. Researchers in
British Columbia have found two types. Resident
orcas stay in one area, where they eat fish
and squid and make a lot of under-water
sounds. In contrast, transients
(wanderers) roam widely. They
move stealthily and silently
and tackle larger prey
like seals and other
whales.

Melon

Blowhole

BIG SUCKERS
Fishermen and orcas are often in
conflict. In many areas, the fishermen feel that orcas eat valuable
salmon and herring. The whales
are clever. In Alaska, orcas follow
fishing boats and gently suck the
fish from the lines as they are
hauled in. The fishermen pull
up nothing but are the
fishes' lips.

The amazing narwhal

THE MYTHICAL UNICORN, a white horse with a horn growing out of its forehead, was really a whale – the "unicorn-whale" or narwhal. Narwhal tusks were sold in Europe long before the real animal was widely known, so it was easy for imaginative traders to claim that the tusks came from unicorns. Even today the narwhal is a mysterious animal. We are still not certain what its strange overgrown tooth is for, though people have offered many ideas. Like its close relative the beluga, the narwhal lives in the remote, icy waters of the Arctic and so is hard to study. Both narwhals and belugas migrate with the seasons, following the receding ice north in the summer and south in the winter. As the sea freezes over, they are sometimes trapped in the ice. They can usually keep breathing holes open, but many narwhals and belugas probably drown when the ice catches them far from open water.

THE UNICORN
In the Middle Ages, narwhal tusks were sold as unicorn horns, which were thought to have magical properties. Cups made from them were supposed to neutralize any poison. The tusks were also ground into a medicinal powder. This was still sold in Japan in the 1950s under the name *ikkaku*.

Fan-shaped tail, more marked in older narwhals

Row of low bumps instead of dorsal fin

Right tooth, which usually does not grow beyond the gums

Pectoral flipper

Left tooth, or tusk, grows in a counterclockwise spiral

WHAT'S IT FOR?
People have suggested all kinds of uses for the narwhal's tusk. Some guess that the giant tooth is used to spear fish or to break holes in the ice. Others say the narwhal may use it as a hoe to root out animals on the ocean floor. But all these ideas are probably wrong, because they do not explain why males have tusks, while females survive very well without them!

LONG IN THE TOOTH
A bottom view of a male narwhal's skull shows the roots of its mighty tooth. All narwhals have two teeth, though in females they almost never grow beyond the gums. The same is usually true for a male's right tooth, while the left grows out to become the tusk. In adults, the tusk can be 10 ft (3 m), more than half as long as the whale's body. Every now and then a female grows a tusk, or a male grows two. Two-tusked skulls were especially prized, and many are displayed in museums.

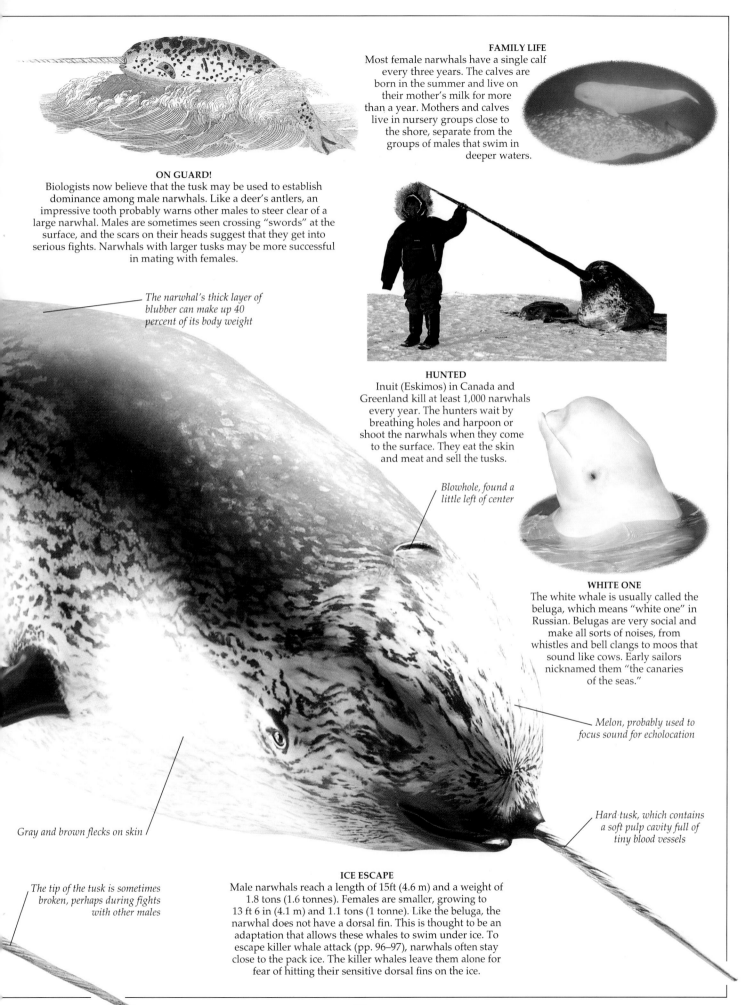

ON GUARD!
Biologists now believe that the tusk may be used to establish dominance among male narwhals. Like a deer's antlers, an impressive tooth probably warns other males to steer clear of a large narwhal. Males are sometimes seen crossing "swords" at the surface, and the scars on their heads suggest that they get into serious fights. Narwhals with larger tusks may be more successful in mating with females.

FAMILY LIFE
Most female narwhals have a single calf every three years. The calves are born in the summer and live on their mother's milk for more than a year. Mothers and calves live in nursery groups close to the shore, separate from the groups of males that swim in deeper waters.

The narwhal's thick layer of blubber can make up 40 percent of its body weight

HUNTED
Inuit (Eskimos) in Canada and Greenland kill at least 1,000 narwhals every year. The hunters wait by breathing holes and harpoon or shoot the narwhals when they come to the surface. They eat the skin and meat and sell the tusks.

Blowhole, found a little left of center

WHITE ONE
The white whale is usually called the beluga, which means "white one" in Russian. Belugas are very social and make all sorts of noises, from whistles and bell clangs to moos that sound like cows. Early sailors nicknamed them "the canaries of the seas."

Melon, probably used to focus sound for echolocation

Gray and brown flecks on skin

Hard tusk, which contains a soft pulp cavity full of tiny blood vessels

The tip of the tusk is sometimes broken, perhaps during fights with other males

ICE ESCAPE
Male narwhals reach a length of 15ft (4.6 m) and a weight of 1.8 tons (1.6 tonnes). Females are smaller, growing to 13 ft 6 in (4.1 m) and 1.1 tons (1 tonne). Like the beluga, the narwhal does not have a dorsal fin. This is thought to be an adaptation that allows these whales to swim under ice. To escape killer whale attack (pp. 96–97), narwhals often stay close to the pack ice. The killer whales leave them alone for fear of hitting their sensitive dorsal fins on the ice.

The sperm whale

SPERM WHALES HAVE THE LARGEST brains that have ever existed and a range that spans the globe. They are creatures of the open ocean that dive to incredible depths to feed on squid, a food resource that is out of reach of most other predators. A male sperm whale eats more than a ton of squid a day, and every year sperm whales eat more food than the total amount caught by all the world's fishermen. We still know little about how the whale hunts in its dark underwater world. The function of its huge square forehead is also unclear. It may help the sperm whale dive to such amazing depths. The whale may even use its head to produce powerful clicks to stun its prey.

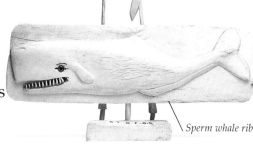
Sperm whale rib

MADEIRA SPERM WHALE
Catching sperm whales from open boats was a dangerous occupation. Until a few years ago, whales were still killed in this way off Madeira and the Azores Islands in the Atlantic Ocean. The Azores population is still healthy, but there are few sperm whales left off Madeira.

THE WHITE WHALE
The most famous sperm whale is Moby Dick, the hero of Herman Melville's novel. It is the story of Captain Ahab, who has lost a leg in a battle with the huge white whale. He becomes obsessed with killing the whale and hunts it all over the globe. In the end, Moby Dick sinks the ship and the captain goes down with it. Albino (white) sperm whales do occur, but they are very rare.

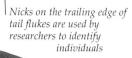

Nicks on the trailing edge of tail flukes are used by researchers to identify individuals

PYGMY SPERM
Almost nothing is known about the pygmy and dwarf sperm whales, the other members of the family. Both are relatively small, less than 10 ft (3 m) long. Like the sperm whale, they are deep divers that live in the open ocean.

FOUL-SMELLING PEARL
Once worth its weight in gold, ambergris is a foul-smelling wax that was used to make perfumes. It is occasionally secreted in the sperm whale's guts, perhaps around squid beaks. Whalers who found a lump of ambergris considered it a valuable prize. It sometimes washes ashore in places such as the Maldive Islands, to the delight of the local people.

GIANT SQUID
Only one man, a whaler by the name of Frank Bullen, has ever seen a battle between a giant squid and a sperm whale. The largest squid ever found in a whale's stomach was 39 ft (12 m) long! But the average size is much smaller, and even monster squid must have little chance against a sperm whale. The famous "battles" are probably just the squids wriggling to try and get out of the whale's jaws.

MAKING A SPLASH
This sperm whale is lobtailing – lifting its muscular tail flukes into the air and slamming them down on the water. Like breaching (pp. 88–89), this is probably a way of communicating. It is usually females that lobtail, often in the presence of males. The big splashes made by lobtailing and breaching can be heard a long distance under water.

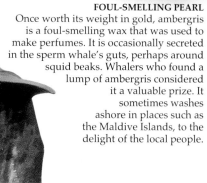

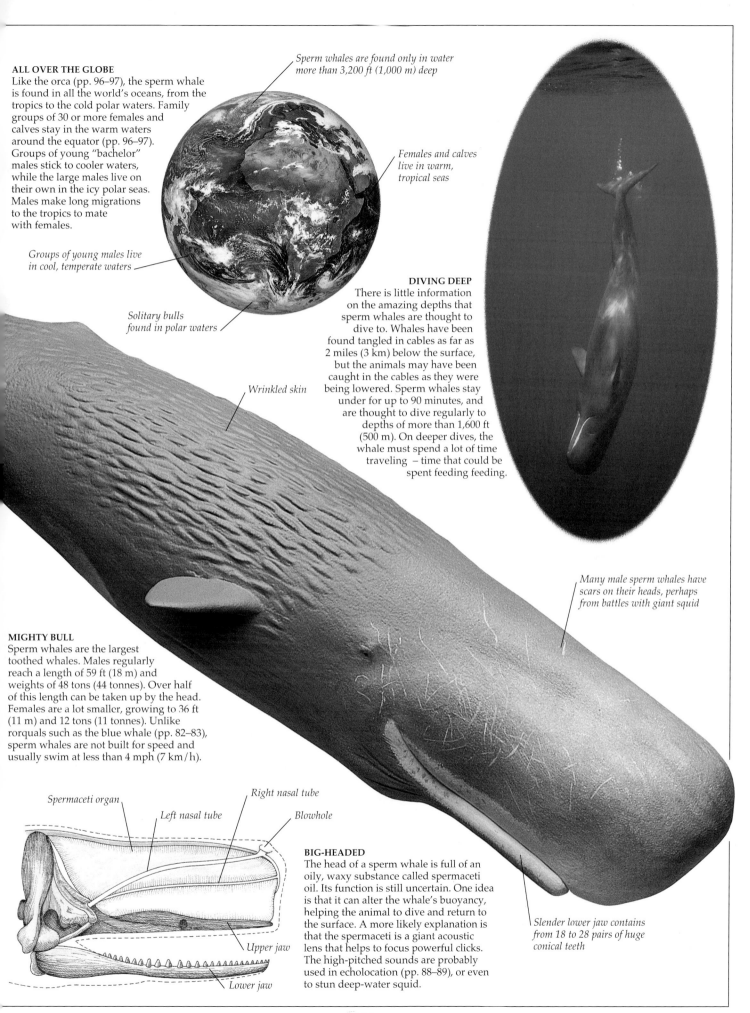

ALL OVER THE GLOBE
Like the orca (pp. 96–97), the sperm whale is found in all the world's oceans, from the tropics to the cold polar waters. Family groups of 30 or more females and calves stay in the warm waters around the equator (pp. 96–97). Groups of young "bachelor" males stick to cooler waters, while the large males live on their own in the icy polar seas. Males make long migrations to the tropics to mate with females.

Sperm whales are found only in water more than 3,200 ft (1,000 m) deep

Females and calves live in warm, tropical seas

Groups of young males live in cool, temperate waters

Solitary bulls found in polar waters

Wrinkled skin

DIVING DEEP
There is little information on the amazing depths that sperm whales are thought to dive to. Whales have been found tangled in cables as far as 2 miles (3 km) below the surface, but the animals may have been caught in the cables as they were being lowered. Sperm whales stay under for up to 90 minutes, and are thought to dive regularly to depths of more than 1,600 ft (500 m). On deeper dives, the whale must spend a lot of time traveling – time that could be spent feeding feeding.

Many male sperm whales have scars on their heads, perhaps from battles with giant squid

MIGHTY BULL
Sperm whales are the largest toothed whales. Males regularly reach a length of 59 ft (18 m) and weights of 48 tons (44 tonnes). Over half of this length can be taken up by the head. Females are a lot smaller, growing to 36 ft (11 m) and 12 tons (11 tonnes). Unlike rorquals such as the blue whale (pp. 82–83), sperm whales are not built for speed and usually swim at less than 4 mph (7 km/h).

Spermaceti organ

Left nasal tube

Right nasal tube

Blowhole

BIG-HEADED
The head of a sperm whale is full of an oily, waxy substance called spermaceti oil. Its function is still uncertain. One idea is that it can alter the whale's buoyancy, helping the animal to dive and return to the surface. A more likely explanation is that the spermaceti is a giant acoustic lens that helps to focus powerful clicks. The high-pitched sounds are probably used in echolocation (pp. 88–89), or even to stun deep-water squid.

Upper jaw

Lower jaw

Slender lower jaw contains from 18 to 28 pairs of huge conical teeth

The elephant seal

WHAT A SCHNOZZ!
Male elephants seals are up to 10 times heavier than females (which do not have such large noses). Every male tries to control a harem (group) of females and keep other males away. He scares off rivals by bellowing, rearing up on his belly, and filling his nose with air. He hopes that other males will think he is huge and leave him in peace.

BATTLE OF THE GIANTS
These two males are fighting for control of a beach crowded with females. These battles start with a lot of huffing and puffing and showing off of noses. Usually the smaller male then sneaks away and avoids a fight. But two big males may have a violent showdown. Most large males are covered with scars and bite marks.

THE ELEPHANT seal gets its name from the male's huge, swollen nose, which plays an important role in the seal's mating ritual. Elephant seals are enormous, weighing up to 3.3 tons (three tonnes). They come ashore in large groups to mate, give birth, and suckle their young. There is constant activity on the crowded beaches as the biggest, strongest males battle for places among the females, while less dominant males hang around the edges. The pups and females grunt and groan, and the males roar. These beaches are dangerous places for people, who could be attacked by an aggressive male. There are two species of elephant seal, southern and northern. Although they live thousands of miles apart, they are thought to be closely related. Northern elephant seals are found off the west coast of North America, where they haul out (come ashore) on isolated islands from San Francisco to Baja, Mexico. Southern elephant seals are found all around the Antarctic.

NOSE JOB
Most animals just use their noses to smell. But the elephant's trunk is like an arm, good for picking up objects, even spraying water like a hose. The sperm whale has the largest nose of all. It probably uses this to focus sounds (pp. 100-101).

The elephant seal is a true seal and cannot tuck its hind flippers under its body

BLUBBERING ABOUT
Elephant seals are deep divers. They are known to reach depths of more than a half-mile below the surface. At such depths the pressure is enormous. A fur coat would not keep the animal warm, because the bubbles trapped between the hairs would be compressed to almost nothing (p. 78). Instead, elephant seals stay warm with thick layers of blubber.

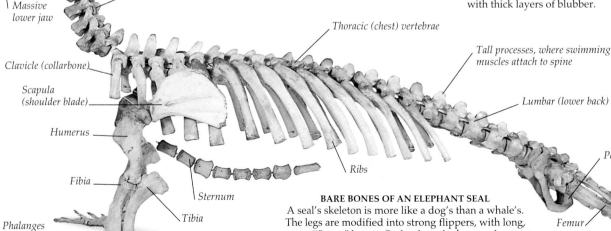

Cranium (brain case)

Processes where strong neck muscles attach to spine

Neck vertebrae, not fused like a whale's

Massive lower jaw

Thoracic (chest) vertebrae

Tall processes, where swimming muscles attach to spine

Clavicle (collarbone)

Scapula (shoulder blade)

Lumbar (lower back) vertebrae

Humerus

Fibia

Sternum

Tibia

Ribs

Pelvic girdle (hips)

Phalanges (finger bones)

Wristbones

Femur

BARE BONES OF AN ELEPHANT SEAL
A seal's skeleton is more like a dog's than a whale's. The legs are modified into strong flippers, with long, strong "finger" bones. On land an elephant seal cannot lift its whole weight with its flippers, but keeps its belly on the ground and moves by flexing its back.

Phalanges (toe bones)

TRUE LOVE?
The female elephant seal (on the left) cannot really say no when it comes to mating. The huge male pins her down and may bite her neck to keep her still. As soon as he finishes, he moves on to the next female.

MILK LIKE MAYONNAISE
Seal milk looks like mayonnaise. Southern elephant seal milk contains up to 43 percent fat. The mother does not eat at all for the whole three to four weeks of suckling. She loses a lot of weight, while the pup puts it on fast. Some northern elephant seal pups grow even faster by sneaking milk from several females.

POLLUTED BEACH
A big threat to elephant seals these days is pollution. Most of this ugly rubbish is harmless. But seals often get tangled in packing straps and nets. As the seal grows, its neck or flipper is cut by the hard plastic. This is a slow and painful way to die.

WE ARE FAMILY
The northern elephant seal was hunted almost to extinction at the end of the 19th century. When the killing stopped, there were less than 100 seals left. This small band of survivors made an incredible recovery, and all the animals of this species that are alive today are descended from them. The population has reached 120,000. But all these seals are closely related, and people are worried that they may suffer from inbreeding.

Half of body weight may be blubber

Large front flippers, used to steer while swimming

Hind flippers, the seal's driving force

I am the walrus

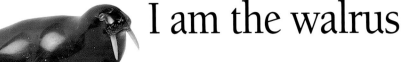

WITH ITS HUGE TUSKS, bushy mustache, and thick rolls of blubber, the walrus is unlike any other seal. For this reason it is put in a family all its own. There are about 250,000 walruses left, all found in the cold waters of the North Pacific and Atlantic oceans. They live in large groups which huddle together for warmth. The life cycle of the walrus follows the seasonal ebb and flow of the Arctic ice. Females give birth in spring. Then they migrate as far as 1,800 miles (3,000 km) north following the melting ice. Despite their huge size, walruses have two formidable enemies: polar bears (pp. 74–75) and killer whales. In the Canadian Arctic, bears are seen chasing or sneaking up on walruses. In Russia, polar bears have even been seen throwing chunks of ice at them! A pod of killer whales (pp. 96–97) hunts together, rounding up the walruses and taking turns swimming through the middle of the herd with their jaws open wide. They may also ram ice floes to try to tip walruses into the sea.

TRADITIONAL FOOD SOURCE
The Inuit still kill walruses, as they always have. But in the last three centuries, Europeans hunted large numbers commercially. The herds suffered greatly, and only the North Pacific population has completely recovered.

TOOTH WALK
The German artist Albrecht Dürer drew a walrus pulling itself onto an ice floe with its tusks. This explains the Latin name, *Odobenus rosmarus*, which means "tooth-walking seahorse." Tusks are also useful for enlarging breathing holes in the ice.

THE TIME HAS COME, THE WALRUS SAID...
Lewis Carroll's famous story *Through the Looking-Glass* stars a walrus and a carpenter. They invite some oysters to take a walk with them. As you might have guessed, the oysters end up being eaten! In real life, walruses do eat shellfish, but they stick to bivalves like clams that live in the mud (p. 85). They spit jets of water into the murky sea floor to help root out their food.

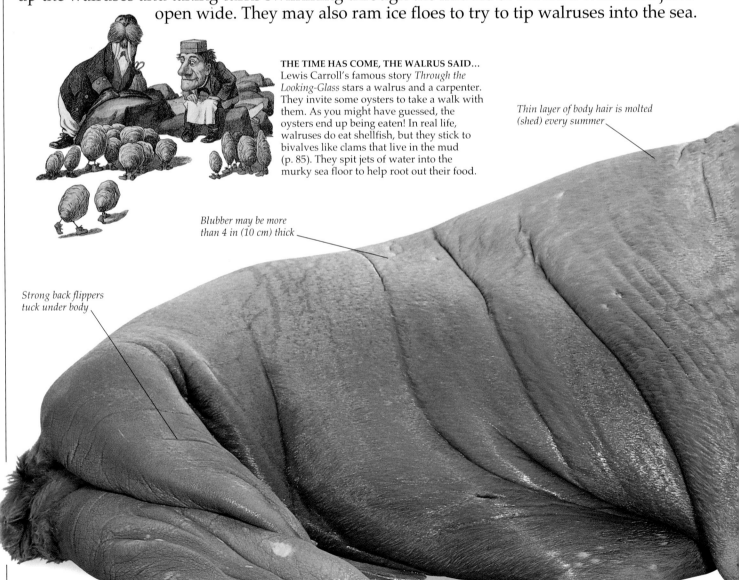

Thin layer of body hair is molted (shed) every summer

Blubber may be more than 4 in (10 cm) thick

Strong back flippers tuck under body

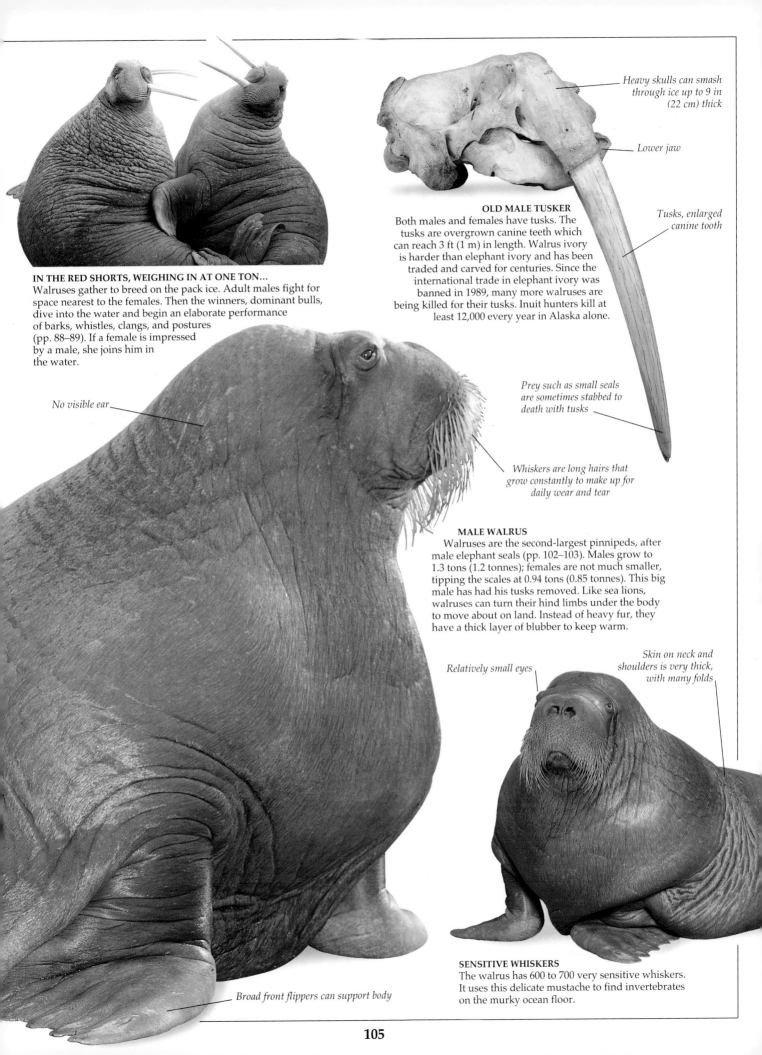

IN THE RED SHORTS, WEIGHING IN AT ONE TON...
Walruses gather to breed on the pack ice. Adult males fight for space nearest to the females. Then the winners, dominant bulls, dive into the water and begin an elaborate performance of barks, whistles, clangs, and postures (pp. 88–89). If a female is impressed by a male, she joins him in the water.

Heavy skulls can smash through ice up to 9 in (22 cm) thick

Lower jaw

OLD MALE TUSKER
Both males and females have tusks. The tusks are overgrown canine teeth which can reach 3 ft (1 m) in length. Walrus ivory is harder than elephant ivory and has been traded and carved for centuries. Since the international trade in elephant ivory was banned in 1989, many more walruses are being killed for their tusks. Inuit hunters kill at least 12,000 every year in Alaska alone.

Tusks, enlarged canine tooth

Prey such as small seals are sometimes stabbed to death with tusks

No visible ear

Whiskers are long hairs that grow constantly to make up for daily wear and tear

MALE WALRUS
Walruses are the second-largest pinnipeds, after male elephant seals (pp. 102–103). Males grow to 1.3 tons (1.2 tonnes); females are not much smaller, tipping the scales at 0.94 tons (0.85 tonnes). This big male has had his tusks removed. Like sea lions, walruses can turn their hind limbs under the body to move about on land. Instead of heavy fur, they have a thick layer of blubber to keep warm.

Relatively small eyes

Skin on neck and shoulders is very thick, with many folds

Broad front flippers can support body

SENSITIVE WHISKERS
The walrus has 600 to 700 very sensitive whiskers. It uses this delicate mustache to find invertebrates on the murky ocean floor.

Sea cows

WITH THEIR FLESHY SNOUTS, chubby bodies, and gentle ways, dugongs and manatees are, not surprisingly, often called sea cows. The three species of manatee and the single species of dugong all live in warm waters. They are slow-moving vegetarians, grazing on sea grass, water hyacinths, and occasionally seaweed. Manatees stay in rivers or salty estuaries and rarely venture into the open sea. This makes the dugong the only vegetarian marine (sea-going) mammal. Like whales, manatees and dugongs have lost their back legs and spend their entire lives in the water. Also like whales, they reproduce slowly, giving birth to one calf every three years. Therefore they are very vulnerable to extinction. Wherever they occur, dugongs are hunted for their tasty meat. Many manatees and dugongs are also killed in collisions with boats.

MERMAID
Since ancient times, sailors have told stories of mermaids, beautiful women with fishes' tails. The legends are probably based on sightings of dugongs or manatees. But you would have to spend a long time at sea to imagine a dugong was a beautiful woman! Mermaids were bad omens and were said to lure ships onto rocks.

WHERE THEY LIVE
Of the three species of manatee, one never leaves the Amazon River, and the other two live in estuaries as well as rivers. The dugong is entirely marine.

West Indian manatee
Brazilian manatee
African manatee
Dugong

WEST INDIAN MANATEE
The West Indian manatee has been studied more than its relatives. Weighing up to 1.7 tons (1.6 tonnes), this fat vegetarian lives in coastal waters, estuaries, and rivers in parts of the Caribbean and Atlantic. Adult males travel widely and often gather in large groups around females that are ready to mate. Manatees can stay under water for 10 to 15 minutes and digest their food slowly in their long guts.

NOISY EATERS
Manatees and dugongs are specialized eaters, the only mammals that feed on underwater vegetation. Manatees are noisy eaters. When they feed at the surface, the chomping of their teeth and flapping of their lips are easy to hear. Semi-captive manatees have even been used as underwater lawn mowers, to clear waterways and dams choked with water hyacinths. In the sea, they eat varieties of sea grass.

POWER HUNGRY
This manatee has algae growing all over its back. If manatees get too cold, they become constipated and die. So in winter, they seek out warm waters such as hot springs. In Florida, manatees gather around the warm water outlets of power stations and factories. This may endanger their long-term health.

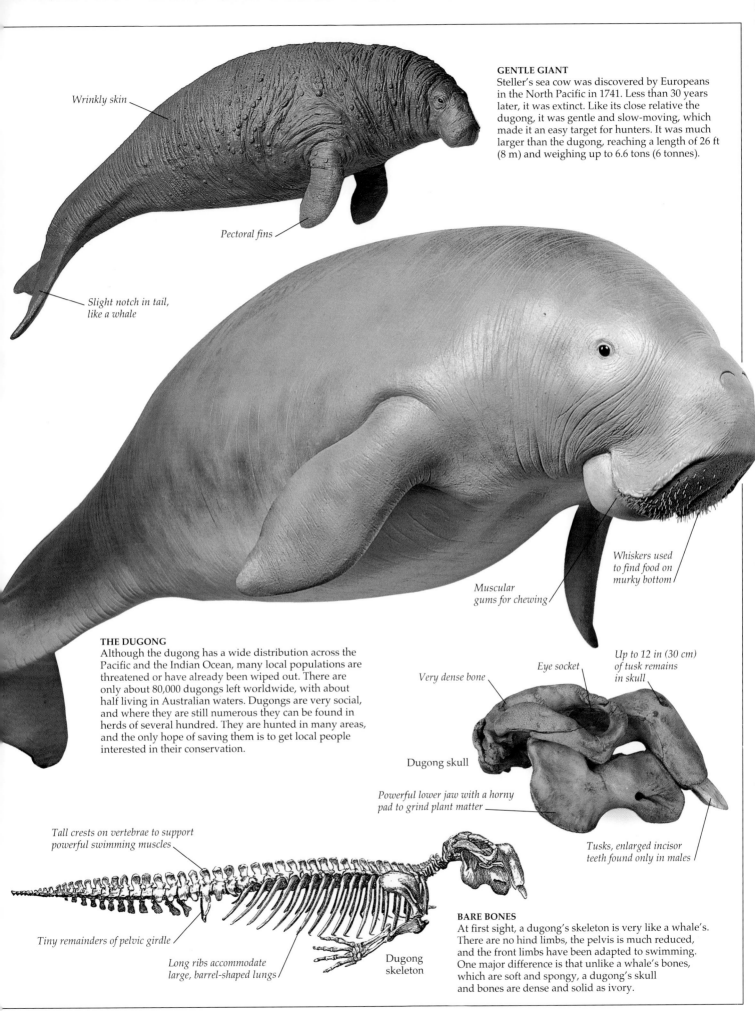

Wrinkly skin

Pectoral fins

Slight notch in tail, like a whale

GENTLE GIANT
Steller's sea cow was discovered by Europeans in the North Pacific in 1741. Less than 30 years later, it was extinct. Like its close relative the dugong, it was gentle and slow-moving, which made it an easy target for hunters. It was much larger than the dugong, reaching a length of 26 ft (8 m) and weighing up to 6.6 tons (6 tonnes).

Whiskers used to find food on murky bottom

Muscular gums for chewing

THE DUGONG
Although the dugong has a wide distribution across the Pacific and the Indian Ocean, many local populations are threatened or have already been wiped out. There are only about 80,000 dugongs left worldwide, with about half living in Australian waters. Dugongs are very social, and where they are still numerous they can be found in herds of several hundred. They are hunted in many areas, and the only hope of saving them is to get local people interested in their conservation.

Very dense bone

Eye socket

Up to 12 in (30 cm) of tusk remains in skull

Dugong skull

Powerful lower jaw with a horny pad to grind plant matter

Tusks, enlarged incisor teeth found only in males

Tall crests on vertebrae to support powerful swimming muscles

Tiny remainders of pelvic girdle

Long ribs accommodate large, barrel-shaped lungs

Dugong skeleton

BARE BONES
At first sight, a dugong's skeleton is very like a whale's. There are no hind limbs, the pelvis is much reduced, and the front limbs have been adapted to swimming. One major difference is that unlike a whale's bones, which are soft and spongy, a dugong's skull and bones are dense and solid as ivory.

Waves and weather

SEAWATER IS CONSTANTLY moving, and waves can be 50-ft (15-m) troughs. Major surface currents are driven by the earth's winds, including trade winds, which blow toward the equator. Both surface and deep-water currents affect the world's climate by taking cold water from the polar regions toward the tropics, and vice versa. Shifts in this flow can also affect ocean life. In an El Niño (climate change), trade winds diminish and warm water flows down western South America. This stops nutrient-rich, cold water from rising up and cause plankton and fisheries to fail. Heat from oceans creates air movement, like swirling hurricanes. Daytime onshore breezes form when the ocean heats up more slowly than the land in the day. Cool air above the water blows in, replacing warm air above the land. At night, offshore breezes occur when the reverse happens.

DOWN THE SPOUT
Water spouts (spinning sprays sucked up from the surface) begin when whirling air drops down from a storm cloud to the ocean.

RIVERS OF THE SEA
Currents are huge masses of water moving through the oceans. The course currents follow is not precisely the same as the trade winds and westerlies, because currents are deflected off land and the Coriolis force produced by the earth's rotation. The latter causes currents to shift to the right in the Northern Hemisphere and to the left in the Southern. There are also currents that flow due to differences in density of seawater.

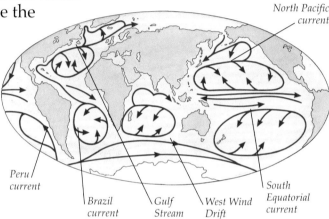

North Pacific current

Peru current

Brazil current

Gulf Stream

West Wind Drift

South Equatorial current

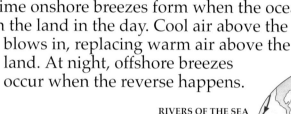

Day 2: Thunderstorms as swirling cloud mass

Day 4: Winds have increased in intensity

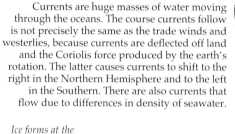

Day 7: Strong winds

A HURRICANE IS BORN
These satellite photographs show a hurricane developing. On day 2 a swirling cloud mass is formed. By day 4 fierce winds develop at the center. By day 7 winds are the strongest.

Ice forms at the very top of the clouds

Hurricanes are enormous – some may be 500 miles (800 km) across

Warm, moist air spirals up around the eye inside the hurricane

Torrential rains fall from clouds

Energy to drive storm comes from warm ocean at 80°F (27°C) or more

Strongest winds of up to 220 mph (360 kph) occur just outside the eye

HEART OF A HURRICANE
Hurricanes (also called typhoons) are the most destructive forces created by oceans. They develop in the tropics, where warm, moist air rises up from the ocean's surface and creates storm clouds. As more air spirals upward, energy is released, fueling stronger winds that whirl around the "eye" (a calm area of extreme low pressure). Hurricanes move onto land, causing terrible devastation. Away from the ocean, hurricanes die out.

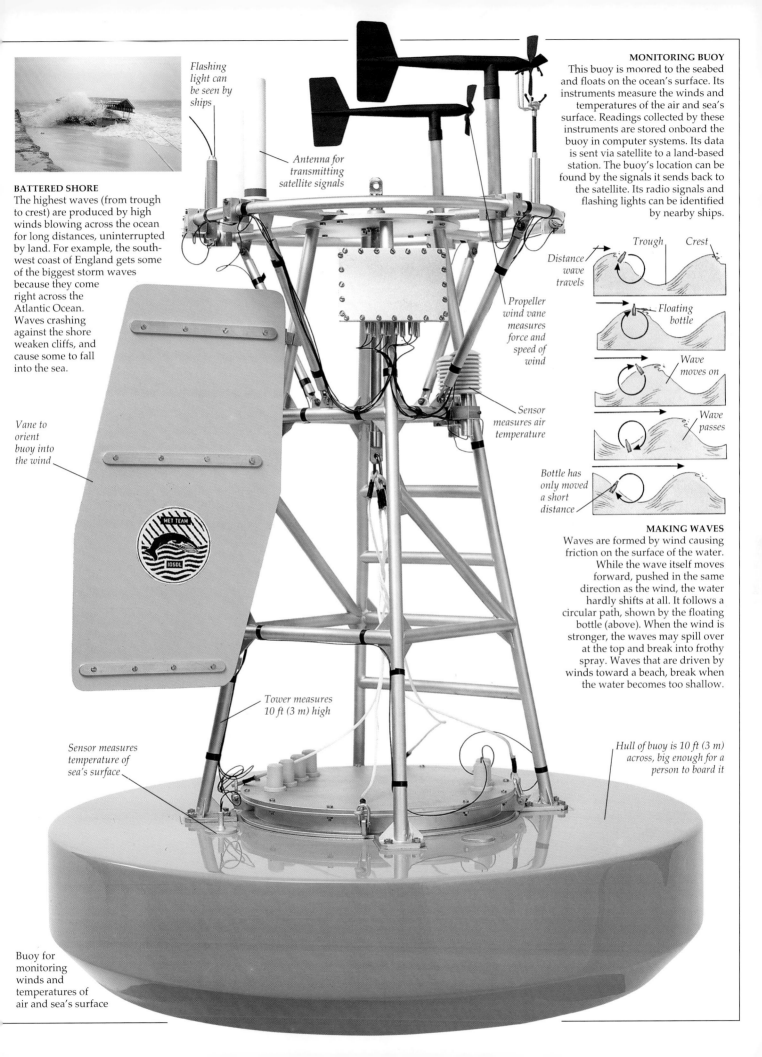

Flashing light can be seen by ships

Antenna for transmitting satellite signals

MONITORING BUOY

This buoy is moored to the seabed and floats on the ocean's surface. Its instruments measure the winds and temperatures of the air and sea's surface. Readings collected by these instruments are stored onboard the buoy in computer systems. Its data is sent via satellite to a land-based station. The buoy's location can be found by the signals it sends back to the satellite. Its radio signals and flashing lights can be identified by nearby ships.

BATTERED SHORE

The highest waves (from trough to crest) are produced by high winds blowing across the ocean for long distances, uninterrupted by land. For example, the south-west coast of England gets some of the biggest storm waves because they come right across the Atlantic Ocean. Waves crashing against the shore weaken cliffs, and cause some to fall into the sea.

Propeller wind vane measures force and speed of wind

Sensor measures air temperature

Distance wave travels — *Trough* *Crest*

Floating bottle

Wave moves on

Wave passes

Bottle has only moved a short distance

Vane to orient buoy into the wind

MET TEAM
IOSDL

MAKING WAVES

Waves are formed by wind causing friction on the surface of the water. While the wave itself moves forward, pushed in the same direction as the wind, the water hardly shifts at all. It follows a circular path, shown by the floating bottle (above). When the wind is stronger, the waves may spill over at the top and break into frothy spray. Waves that are driven by winds toward a beach, break when the water becomes too shallow.

Tower measures 10 ft (3 m) high

Hull of buoy is 10 ft (3 m) across, big enough for a person to board it

Sensor measures temperature of sea's surface

Buoy for monitoring winds and temperatures of air and sea's surface

Diverse divers

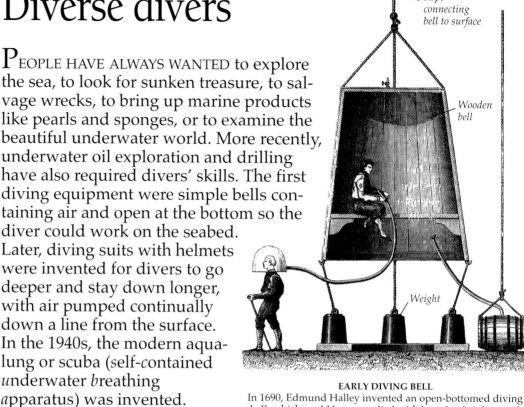

P EOPLE HAVE ALWAYS WANTED to explore the sea, to look for sunken treasure, to salvage wrecks, to bring up marine products like pearls and sponges, or to examine the beautiful underwater world. More recently, underwater oil exploration and drilling have also required divers' skills. The first diving equipment were simple bells containing air and open at the bottom so the diver could work on the seabed. Later, diving suits with helmets were invented for divers to go deeper and stay down longer, with air pumped continually down a line from the surface. In the 1940s, the modern aqualung or scuba (*s*elf-*c*ontained *u*nderwater *b*reathing *a*pparatus) was invented. Divers could carry their own supply of compressed air in tanks on their backs.

Umbilical supplies air, as well as electricity for light

Weight belt

UNDERWATER WORKER
This diver, wearing a wet suit for warmth, has air pumped into the helmet via a line linked to the surface. A harness around the diver's middle carries tools. Flexible boots help the diver clamber around beneath an oil rig.

Rope connecting bell to surface

Wooden bell

Weight

EARLY DIVING BELL
In 1690, Edmund Halley invented an open-bottomed diving bell, which could be resupplied with barrels of air lowered from the surface. Heavy weights anchored the bell to the seabed, and a leather tube connected the lead-lined air barrel to the wooden bell. Used at depths of 60 ft (18 m), the bell could house several divers at a time.

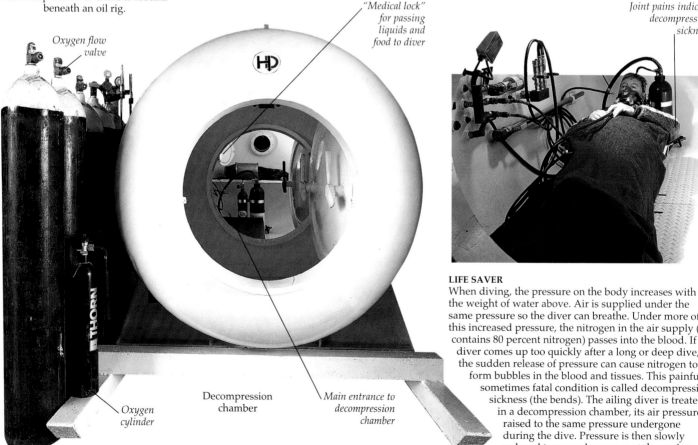

Oxygen flow valve

"Medical lock" for passing liquids and food to diver

Joint pains indicate decompression sickness

Oxygen cylinder

Decompression chamber

Main entrance to decompression chamber

LIFE SAVER
When diving, the pressure on the body increases with the weight of water above. Air is supplied under the same pressure so the diver can breathe. Under more of this increased pressure, the nitrogen in the air supply (air contains 80 percent nitrogen) passes into the blood. If a diver comes up too quickly after a long or deep dive, the sudden release of pressure can cause nitrogen to form bubbles in the blood and tissues. This painful, sometimes fatal condition is called decompression sickness (the bends). The ailing diver is treated in a decompression chamber, its air pressure raised to the same pressure undergone during the dive. Pressure is then slowly reduced to normal pressure at the surface.

Example of an early diving suit

Helmet equipped with two-way communication system so diver can talk to someone on the surface

Helmet made of copper and brass

Face plate

Weight is about 30 lb (13 kg)

Wrench for tightening bolts on breastplate

A CLASSIC DIVING SUIT

The "Standard" diving suit was invented by Augustus Siebe in the 1830s. Modified versions of this classic, hard-helmeted suit are still in use today. The tunic was made of layers of canvas and rubber so that it was hardwearing and waterproof. The copper and brass helmet fit onto a heavy corselet (breastplate) bolted onto the tunic. The diver wore leather boots with heavy lead bottoms and two additional weights. It would take about half an hour to get outfitted in all this gear. Then the diver would sink down to the bottom to work at depths of about 200 ft (60 m).

Diver has two weights – one at the front, a second at the back

Bolt screws corselet to tunic – number of bolts can be six, eight, or twelve

Long johns made from wool for greater warmth and insulation

Complete "Standard" diving suit

Rubber cuff for extra waterproofing

Ribbed cuff helps trap warm air

Suit made of a layer of rubber between two layers of canvas

Each boot weighs 18 lb (8 kg)

Leather boot with lead base to help weigh down diver in water

Underwater machines

THE FIRST SUBMARINES had simple designs. They allowed travel underwater and were useful in war. More modern submarines were powered by diesel or gasoline on the surface and used batteries underwater. In 1955, the first sub to run on nuclear fuel traversed the oceans. Nuclear power allowed submarines to travel great distances before needing to refuel. Today, submarines have sophisticated sonar systems for navigating underwater and pinpointing other vessels. They can carry high-powered torpedoes to fire at enemy craft or nuclear missiles. Submersibles (miniature submarines), used to explore the deep-sea floor, cannot travel long distances. They need to be lowered from a support vessel on the surface.

Snort mast renews and expels air with help of bellows

Augur for drilling into enemy ship to attach mine on rope

Delayed action mine

Vertical propeller

Side propeller powered by foot pedals

"TURTLE" HERO
A one-man wooden submarine, the *Turtle*, was used during the Revolutionary War in 1776 to attach a delayed-action mine to an English ship blockading New York Harbor. The operator became disoriented when carbon dioxide built up inside the *Turtle*, and the mine struck metal instead of the ship's wooden hull. Both the ship and operator survived, but the mine was jettisoned.

UNDERWATER ADVENTURE
Inspired by the recent invention of modern submarines, this 1900 engraving depicted a scene in the year 2000 with people enjoying a journey in a submarine liner. In a way, the prediction has come true, as tourists can now take trips in small submarines to view marine life in places such as the Red Sea. However, most people explore the underwater world by learning to scuba-dive or snorkel.

External steering bar operated by diver

Internal steering position

Hand pump for pressurizing air reservoir and emptying ballast tanks

Front wheels smaller than back ones for easier turning

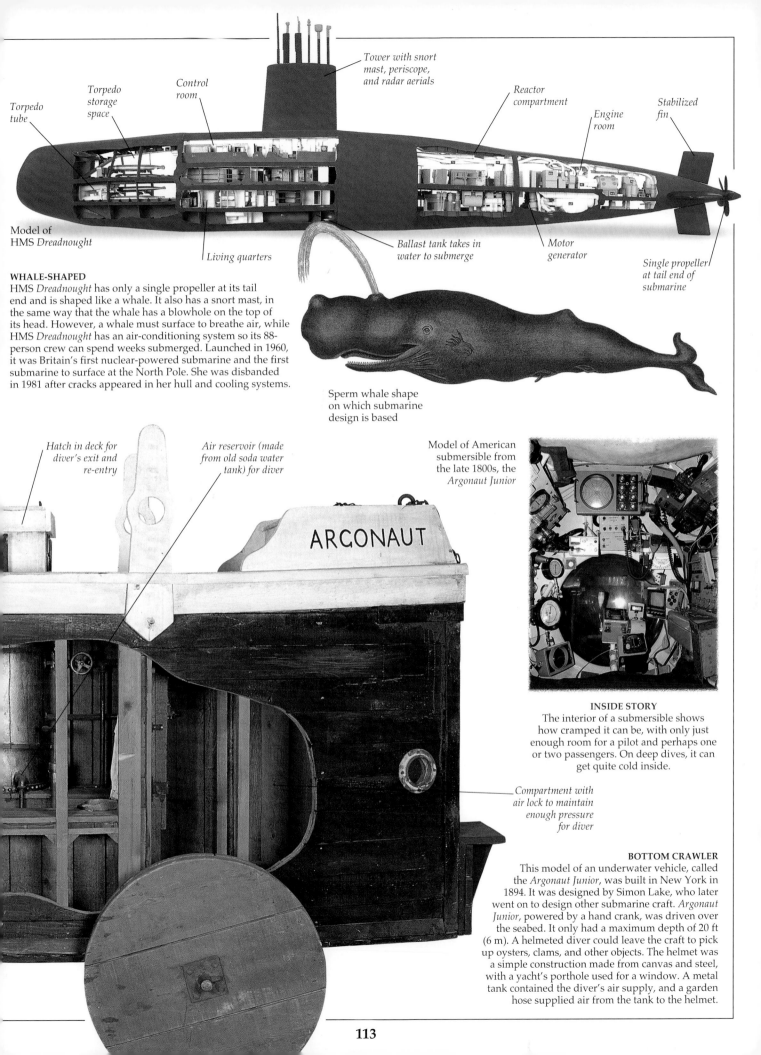

Tower with snort
mast, periscope,
and radar aerials

Control
room

Torpedo
storage
space

Torpedo
tube

Reactor
compartment

Engine
room

Stabilized
fin

Model of
HMS *Dreadnought*

Living quarters

Ballast tank takes in
water to submerge

Motor
generator

Single propeller
at tail end of
submarine

WHALE-SHAPED
HMS *Dreadnought* has only a single propeller at its tail
end and is shaped like a whale. It also has a snort mast, in
the same way that the whale has a blowhole on the top of
its head. However, a whale must surface to breathe air, while
HMS *Dreadnought* has an air-conditioning system so its 88-
person crew can spend weeks submerged. Launched in 1960,
it was Britain's first nuclear-powered submarine and the first
submarine to surface at the North Pole. She was disbanded
in 1981 after cracks appeared in her hull and cooling systems.

Sperm whale shape
on which submarine
design is based

Hatch in deck for
diver's exit and
re-entry

Air reservoir (made
from old soda water
tank) for diver

Model of American
submersible from
the late 1800s, the
Argonaut Junior

ARGONAUT

INSIDE STORY
The interior of a submersible shows
how cramped it can be, with only just
enough room for a pilot and perhaps one
or two passengers. On deep dives, it can
get quite cold inside.

Compartment with
air lock to maintain
enough pressure
for diver

BOTTOM CRAWLER
This model of an underwater vehicle, called
the *Argonaut Junior*, was built in New York in
1894. It was designed by Simon Lake, who later
went on to design other submarine craft. *Argonaut
Junior*, powered by a hand crank, was driven over
the seabed. It only had a maximum depth of 20 ft
(6 m). A helmeted diver could leave the craft to pick
up oysters, clams, and other objects. The helmet was
a simple construction made from canvas and steel,
with a yacht's porthole used for a window. A metal
tank contained the diver's air supply, and a garden
hose supplied air from the tank to the helmet.

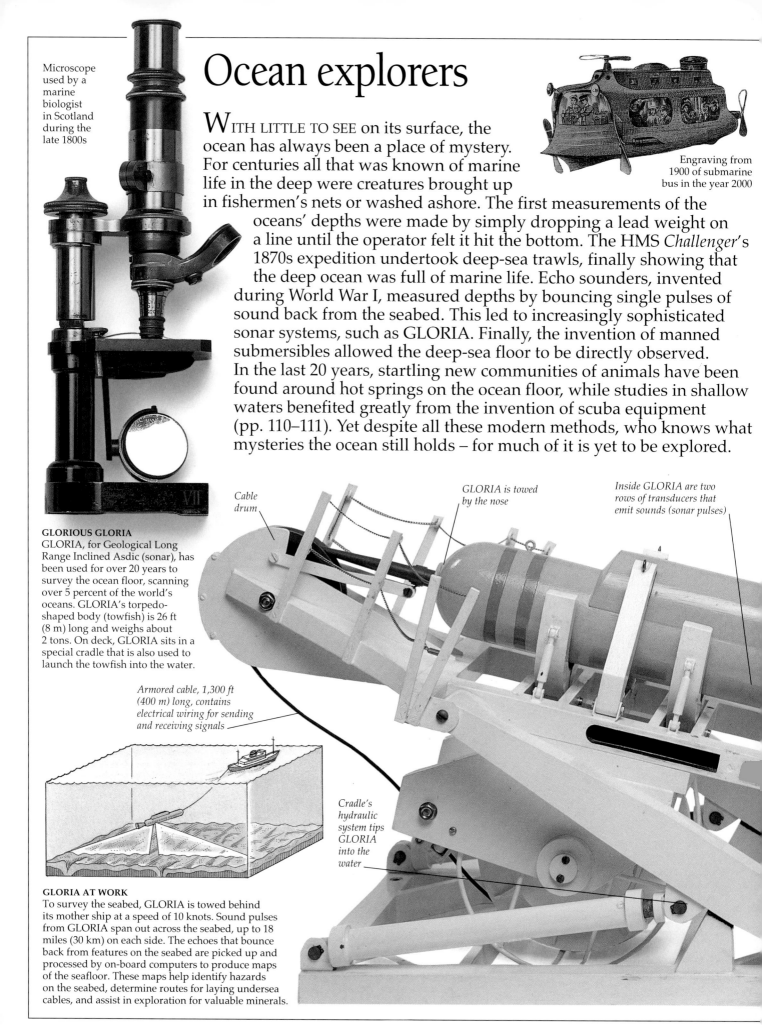

Microscope used by a marine biologist in Scotland during the late 1800s

Ocean explorers

With LITTLE TO SEE on its surface, the ocean has always been a place of mystery. For centuries all that was known of marine life in the deep were creatures brought up in fishermen's nets or washed ashore. The first measurements of the oceans' depths were made by simply dropping a lead weight on a line until the operator felt it hit the bottom. The HMS *Challenger*'s 1870s expedition undertook deep-sea trawls, finally showing that the deep ocean was full of marine life. Echo sounders, invented during World War I, measured depths by bouncing single pulses of sound back from the seabed. This led to increasingly sophisticated sonar systems, such as GLORIA. Finally, the invention of manned submersibles allowed the deep-sea floor to be directly observed. In the last 20 years, startling new communities of animals have been found around hot springs on the ocean floor, while studies in shallow waters benefited greatly from the invention of scuba equipment (pp. 110–111). Yet despite all these modern methods, who knows what mysteries the ocean still holds – for much of it is yet to be explored.

Engraving from 1900 of submarine bus in the year 2000

GLORIOUS GLORIA
GLORIA, for Geological Long Range Inclined Asdic (sonar), has been used for over 20 years to survey the ocean floor, scanning over 5 percent of the world's oceans. GLORIA's torpedo-shaped body (towfish) is 26 ft (8 m) long and weighs about 2 tons. On deck, GLORIA sits in a special cradle that is also used to launch the towfish into the water.

Cable drum

GLORIA is towed by the nose

Inside GLORIA are two rows of transducers that emit sounds (sonar pulses)

Armored cable, 1,300 ft (400 m) long, contains electrical wiring for sending and receiving signals

Cradle's hydraulic system tips GLORIA into the water

GLORIA AT WORK
To survey the seabed, GLORIA is towed behind its mother ship at a speed of 10 knots. Sound pulses from GLORIA span out across the seabed, up to 18 miles (30 km) on each side. The echoes that bounce back from features on the seabed are picked up and processed by on-board computers to produce maps of the seafloor. These maps help identify hazards on the seabed, determine routes for laying undersea cables, and assist in exploration for valuable minerals.

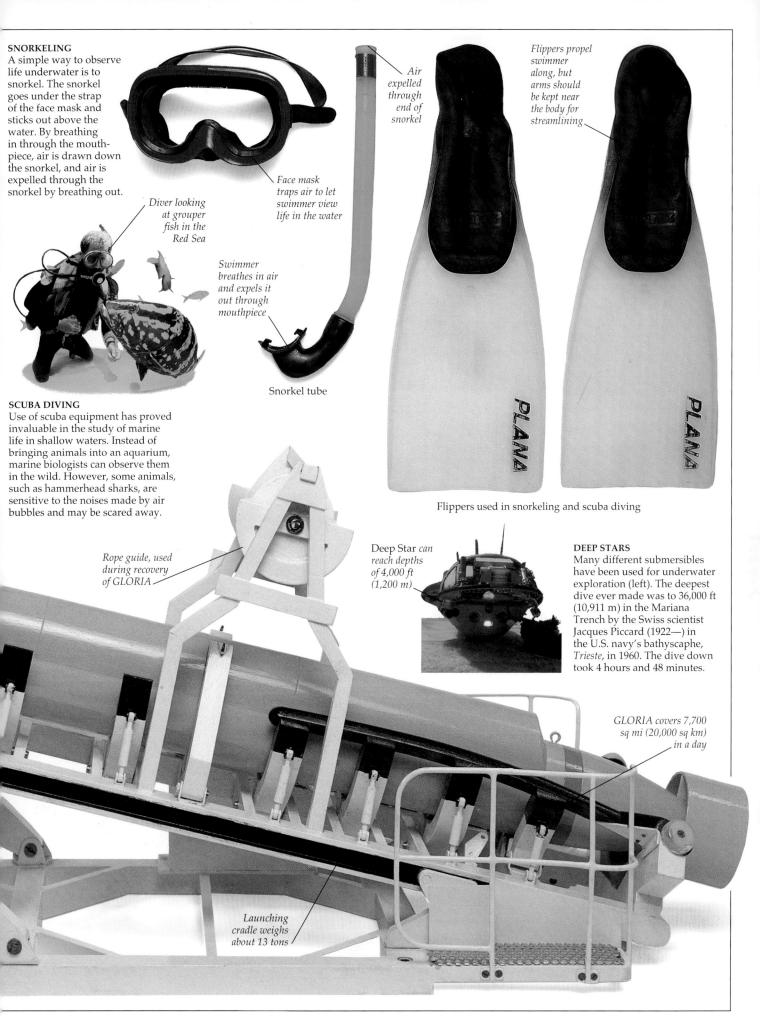

SNORKELING

A simple way to observe life underwater is to snorkel. The snorkel goes under the strap of the face mask and sticks out above the water. By breathing in through the mouthpiece, air is drawn down the snorkel, and air is expelled through the snorkel by breathing out.

Diver looking at grouper fish in the Red Sea

Air expelled through end of snorkel

Face mask traps air to let swimmer view life in the water

Flippers propel swimmer along, but arms should be kept near the body for streamlining

Swimmer breathes in air and expels it out through mouthpiece

Snorkel tube

SCUBA DIVING

Use of scuba equipment has proved invaluable in the study of marine life in shallow waters. Instead of bringing animals into an aquarium, marine biologists can observe them in the wild. However, some animals, such as hammerhead sharks, are sensitive to the noises made by air bubbles and may be scared away.

Flippers used in snorkeling and scuba diving

Rope guide, used during recovery of GLORIA

Deep Star can reach depths of 4,000 ft (1,200 m)

DEEP STARS

Many different submersibles have been used for underwater exploration (left). The deepest dive ever made was to 36,000 ft (10,911 m) in the Mariana Trench by the Swiss scientist Jacques Piccard (1922—) in the U.S. navy's bathyscaphe, *Trieste*, in 1960. The dive down took 4 hours and 48 minutes.

GLORIA covers 7,700 sq mi (20,000 sq km) in a day

Launching cradle weighs about 13 tons

Wrecks on the seabed

Ever since people took to the sea in boats, there have been wrecks on the seabed. Drifts of mud and sand cover them, preserving wooden boats for centuries. This sediment protects the timbers from wood-boring animals by keeping out the oxygen they need. Seawater, however, badly corrodes metal-hulled ships. The *Titanic*'s steel hull could disintegrate within a hundred years. Wrecks in shallow water get covered by plant and animal life and turn into living reefs. Animals such as corals and sponges grow on the outside of the ship, while fish use the inside as an underwater cave to shelter in. Wrecks and their contents tell much about life in the past, but first archeologists must survey them carefully. Objects brought up must be washed clean of salt or preserved with chemicals. Treasure seekers, unfortunately, can do much damage.

Less valuable silver coin

GLITTERING GOLD
Gold is among the most sought-after treasure. These Spanish coins, much in demand by pirates, sometimes ended up on the seabed when a ship sunk.

Sonar equipment

Titanium sphere protects passengers

IFREN
DCN CEF

SUPER SUB
The French submersible *Nautile* recovered objects from the seabed surrounding the wreck of the *Titanic*. When the ship went down, it broke in two, scattering objects far and wide. Only a submersible could dive deep enough to reach the *Titanic*, 2.3 mi (3,780 m) down. A sphere made of titanium metal to withstand the immense pressure at these depths, the *Nautile* has space for only three – a pilot, a co-pilot, and an observer. Extra-thick, curved Plexiglas portholes flatten on the dive due to pressure. The journey to the wreck takes about an hour and a half, and *Nautile* can stay down for eight hours.

VALUABLE PROPERTY
In 1892, divers worked on the wreck of the tug *L'Abeille*, which sank off Le Havre, France. For centuries, people have salvaged wrecks to bring up items of value.

Lights for video camera

Manipulator arm for picking objects off seabed

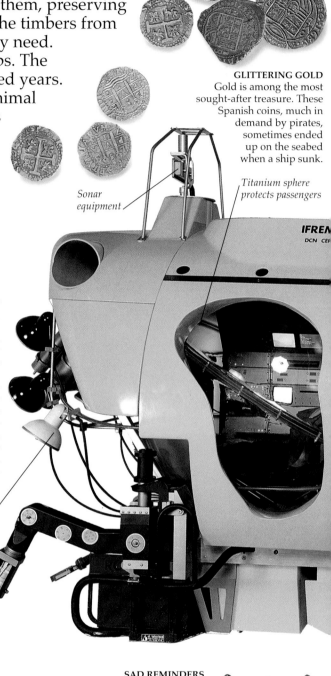

SAD REMINDERS
Many items recovered from the *Titanic* wreck were not valuable but everyday items used by those aboard. Personal effects, such as buttons or just cutlery, remind us of those who died.

THE UNSINKABLE SHIP
In 1912, the *Titanic* sailed from England to New York on her maiden voyage. Because of her hull's water-tight compartments, she was thought unsinkable, but hit an iceberg four days into the voyage. She took two hours and forty minutes to sink, with only 705 people saved of 2,228. She was discovered in 1985 by a French-U.S. team using remote-controlled video equipment. Submersibles *Alvin* (United States) and *Mir* (Russia) have also dived to the wreck since then.

PLANE WRECK
Airplanes sometimes crash into the sea and sink to the bottom, like this Japanese biplane discovered off Papua New Guinea in the Pacific. The Bermuda Triangle, an area in the Atlantic, is famous for the many planes and ships that mysteriously disappeared there.

SUNKEN TREASURE
These precious jewels are among many valuable items salvaged from the wreck of a Spanish galleon, the *Tolossa*, in the 1970s. Bound for Mexico in 1724, a hurricane blew up and it foundered on a massive coral reef. Many luxury goods were recovered from the wreck, which show that the Spanish were exporting fine things to their New World colonies during the 1700s. Other items from the wreck include brass guns, iron grenades, and hundreds of pearls.

Gold, diamonds, and pearls salvaged from the wreck of the Tolossa *off Hispaniola*

Nautile measures 26 ft 3 in (8 m) in length

Thruster provides the power for the 3.7 mi (6 km) dive

NAUTILE

IFREMER

Encrusted Roman jar

Barnacle

Mollusk

MISSING LAND
This poster advertises a film about the lost continent of Atlantis, which supposedly sank beneath the sea. This myth may be true, since a Greek island sank beneath the waves after an earthquake in 1450 B.C.

HOME, SWEET HOME
Hard barnacle shells and tubes of worms grew on this Roman jar while it rested for hundreds of years on the seabed. Animals that normally live on rocks are just as happy to settle on any hard objects left in the sea, such as shipwrecks, but some animal growths are hard to remove without damaging objects.

Worm tube

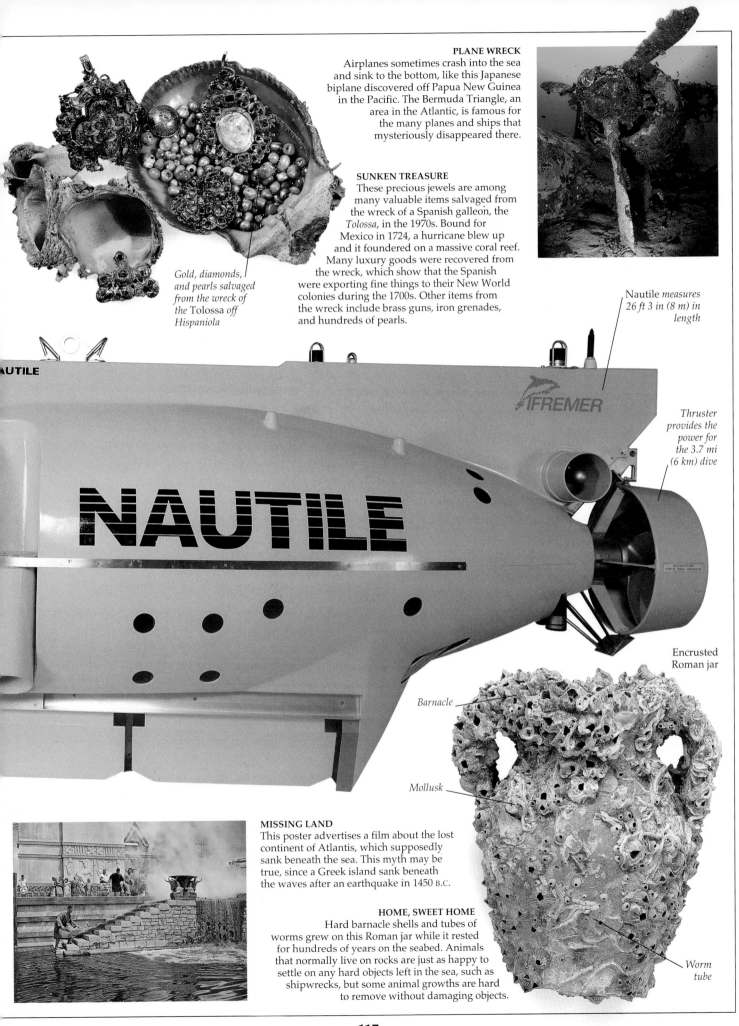

Harvesting fish

FISH ARE THE MOST popular kind of seafood, with some 70 million tons caught around the world each year. Some fish are caught by hand-thrown nets and traps in local waters, but far more are caught at sea by modern fishing vessels using the latest technology. Some fish are caught on long lines with many hooks or ensnared when they swim into long walls of drift nets. Bottom-dwelling fish are trawled or whole schools are gathered up in huge nets set in midwater. The use of sonar to detect schools leaves few places where fish can escape notice. Even fish living in deep waters, such as orange roughy at depths of 3,300 ft (1,000 m), can be brought up in numbers. Many people are concerned that too many fish are being caught and numbers will take a long time to recover. Competition for fish stocks is fierce and it is difficult for fishermen to make a living. But some fish, like salmon, are grown in farms to help meet demands.

1 HATCHING OUT
Salmon begin life in rivers and streams, where they hatch from eggs laid in a shallow hollow among gravel. First the fry (alevins) grow, using the contents of their egg sac attached to their bellies as food.

2 YOUNG SALMON
At a few weeks old, the egg sac disappears, so young salmon must feed on tiny insects in the river. Soon dark spots appear on the parr (young salmon). The parr stay in the river for a year or more before turning into silvery smolt that head for the sea.

3 AT SEA
Atlantic salmon spend up to four years at sea, feeding on other fish. They grow rapidly, putting on several pounds (or kilos) annually. Then the mature salmon return to their home rivers and streams, where they hatch. They recognize their home stream by a number of clues, including its "smell" – combinations of tiny quantities of substances in the water.

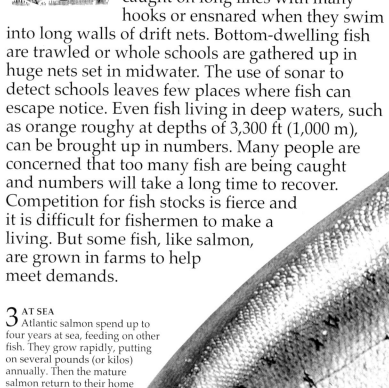

Fin rays are well developed

Large, first dorsal fin

Pelvic fin

Pectoral fin

Operculum (flap covering gills)

Mouth for feeding and taking in water to "breathe"

FISH FARMING
Salmon are among the few kinds of sea fish to be farmed successfully. Young salmon are reared in fresh water. When they are large enough, they are released into floating pens in the sea. These are located in relatively calm waters so the fish are not washed away. To help them grow quickly, the salmon are fed regularly with dried fish pellets. Like any farmed animals, care must be taken to keep the salmon from developing diseases.

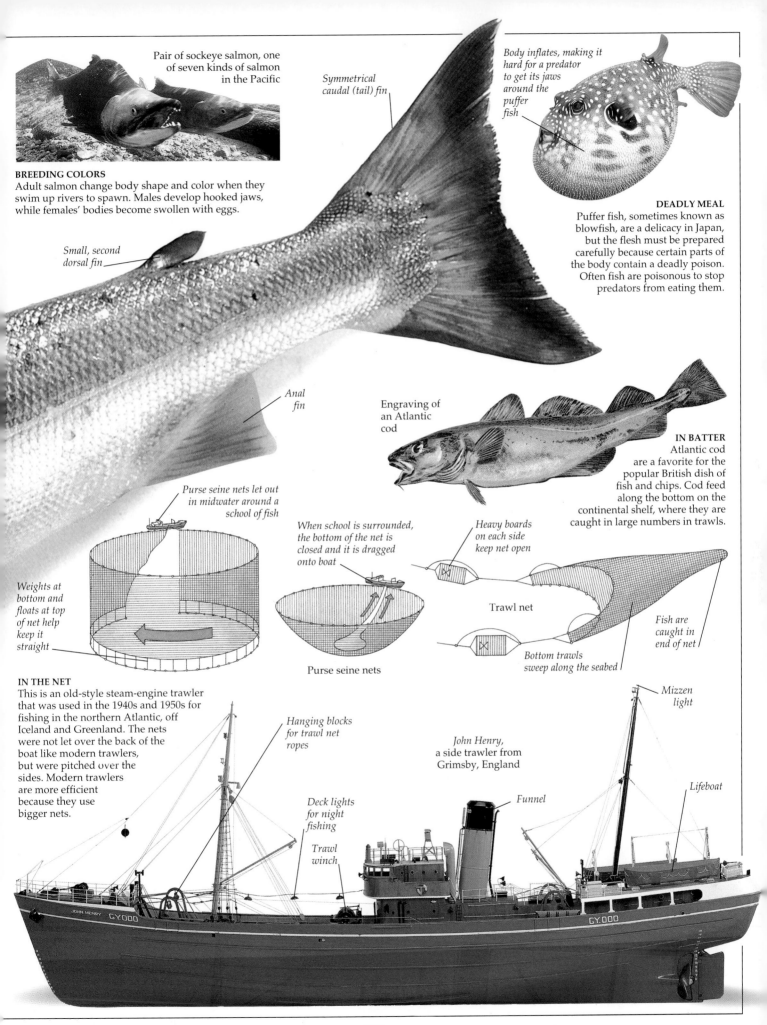

Pair of sockeye salmon, one of seven kinds of salmon in the Pacific

BREEDING COLORS
Adult salmon change body shape and color when they swim up rivers to spawn. Males develop hooked jaws, while females' bodies become swollen with eggs.

Symmetrical caudal (tail) fin

Body inflates, making it hard for a predator to get its jaws around the puffer fish

DEADLY MEAL
Puffer fish, sometimes known as blowfish, are a delicacy in Japan, but the flesh must be prepared carefully because certain parts of the body contain a deadly poison. Often fish are poisonous to stop predators from eating them.

Small, second dorsal fin

Anal fin

Engraving of an Atlantic cod

IN BATTER
Atlantic cod are a favorite for the popular British dish of fish and chips. Cod feed along the bottom on the continental shelf, where they are caught in large numbers in trawls.

Purse seine nets let out in midwater around a school of fish

When school is surrounded, the bottom of the net is closed and it is dragged onto boat

Heavy boards on each side keep net open

Trawl net

Weights at bottom and floats at top of net help keep it straight

Fish are caught in end of net

Purse seine nets

Bottom trawls sweep along the seabed

IN THE NET
This is an old-style steam-engine trawler that was used in the 1940s and 1950s for fishing in the northern Atlantic, off Iceland and Greenland. The nets were not let over the back of the boat like modern trawlers, but were pitched over the sides. Modern trawlers are more efficient because they use bigger nets.

Hanging blocks for trawl net ropes

Mizzen light

John Henry, a side trawler from Grimsby, England

Funnel

Lifeboat

Deck lights for night fishing

Trawl winch

Ocean products

PEOPLE HAVE ALWAYS HARVESTED plants and animals from the ocean. Many different kinds are collected for food, from fish, crustaceans (shrimp, lobsters), mollusks (clams, squid) to more unusual foods such as sea cucumbers, barnacles, and jellyfish. Seaweeds also are eaten, either in a recognizable state or as an ingredient of ice cream and other processed foods. The products made from sea creatures are amazing, although many (such as mother-of-pearl buttons and sponges) are now made with synthetic materials. Yet the appeal of natural ocean products is so great that some animals and seaweeds are grown in farms. Among the sea creatures cultivated today are sponges, giant clams (for their pretty shells), mussels (for food), and pearl oysters. Farming is one way to meet product demand, and to avoid over-harvesting the ocean's wildlife.

Yarn dyed purple from pigment of sea snails

ROYAL PURPLE
Sea snails were used to make purple dye for clothes worn by kings in ancient times. Making dye was a smelly business, as huge quantities of salted snails were left in vats gouged out of rocks. The purple liquid was collected and heated to concentrate the dye. These sea snails (from Florida and the Caribbean) are used to make purple dye.

Slate-pencil sea urchin from tropical coral reefs in the Indo-Pacific

Short, blunt spines surround mouth

Long, very strong spines help protect urchin from predators

Five strong white teeth protrude from urchin's mouth (viewed from underneath)

Soft skeleton is all that is left after processing living sponge

USEFUL SPINES
The spines of this urchin were once used as pencils to write on slate boards. Slate-pencil urchins are still collected, their spines used for wind chimes. The spines, hung from threads, clink together when the wind blows through them. Urchins use their big spines to help them walk across the seabed when they emerge from crevices to feed at night.

Spines help urchin move and stay in place

SOFT SKELETON
Bath sponges grow among sea grasses in reef lagoons. When harvested from the bottom, the sponges are covered with slimy, living tissues. Collected from the Mediterranean, Caribbean, and Pacific, natural sponges are prone to diseases and over-collecting.

SEAWEED FARM
In Japan, seaweeds are used in crackers or to wrap up bites of raw fish. Nori, a red seaweed, is grown in the sea on bamboo poles, collected, and dried. Laver, another red seaweed, is eaten in Wales, in the U.K. Agar, a jelly-like substance, is made from red seaweeds and used in foods and in medical research. Seaweeds are also used in fertilizers.

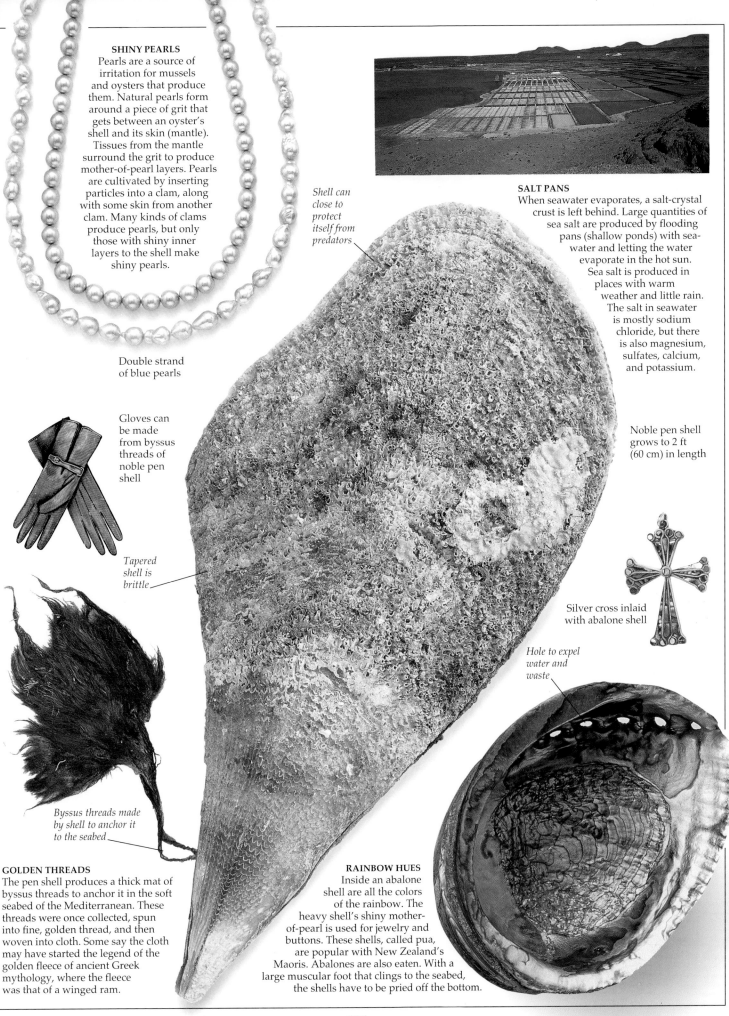

SHINY PEARLS
Pearls are a source of irritation for mussels and oysters that produce them. Natural pearls form around a piece of grit that gets between an oyster's shell and its skin (mantle). Tissues from the mantle surround the grit to produce mother-of-pearl layers. Pearls are cultivated by inserting particles into a clam, along with some skin from another clam. Many kinds of clams produce pearls, but only those with shiny inner layers to the shell make shiny pearls.

Double strand of blue pearls

Shell can close to protect itself from predators

SALT PANS
When seawater evaporates, a salt-crystal crust is left behind. Large quantities of sea salt are produced by flooding pans (shallow ponds) with seawater and letting the water evaporate in the hot sun. Sea salt is produced in places with warm weather and little rain. The salt in seawater is mostly sodium chloride, but there is also magnesium, sulfates, calcium, and potassium.

Gloves can be made from byssus threads of noble pen shell

Noble pen shell grows to 2 ft (60 cm) in length

Tapered shell is brittle

Silver cross inlaid with abalone shell

Hole to expel water and waste

Byssus threads made by shell to anchor it to the seabed

GOLDEN THREADS
The pen shell produces a thick mat of byssus threads to anchor it in the soft seabed of the Mediterranean. These threads were once collected, spun into fine, golden thread, and then woven into cloth. Some say the cloth may have started the legend of the golden fleece of ancient Greek mythology, where the fleece was that of a winged ram.

RAINBOW HUES
Inside an abalone shell are all the colors of the rainbow. The heavy shell's shiny mother-of-pearl is used for jewelry and buttons. These shells, called pua, are popular with New Zealand's Maoris. Abalones are also eaten. With a large muscular foot that clings to the seabed, the shells have to be pried off the bottom.

121

Oil and gas exploration

VALUABLE RESERVOIRS OF OIL AND GAS lie hidden in rocks on the seabed. They are tapped by drilling into the rock, but first geologists must know where to drill. Only certain kinds of rocks hold oil and gas, and must be in shallow enough water to be reached by drilling. Geologists use underwater air guns and explosions on the surface to send shock waves through the seabed and distinguish between rock layers by returning signals. After a source is pin-pointed, temporary rigs are set up to see if the oil is the right quality and quantity. If it is, a more permanent oil platform is built and firmly anchored to the seabed. As the oil or gas is extracted, it is off-loaded from the platform's storage tanks into larger tankers or sent ashore via pipelines. There is a great demand for oil and gas, but the earth's supplies are limited. As reservoirs dry up, new sources have to be found. Today's main offshore oil fields are in the North Sea, Gulf of Mexico, Persian Gulf, and the coasts of South America and Asia.

ON FIRE
Oil and gas are highly flammable. Despite precautions, accidents do happen, like the North Sea's Piper Alpha disaster in 1988 when 167 people died. Since then safety measures have been improved.

MILK ROUND
Helicopters deliver supplies to oil platforms far out at sea. Up to 400 people can live and work on an oil platform, but fly by helicopter for breaks onshore every few weeks.

OIL PLATFORM
One of the smaller oil platforms in the North Sea has concrete legs. Platforms are built in sections on shore. The largest section is towed out to sea and tipped upright onto the seabed, then living quarters are added. A tall derrick holds drilling equipment – several pipes tipped with strong drill bits for grinding the rocks. Special mud is sent down the pipes to cool the drill bit, wash out ground-up rock, and keep oil from gushing out. Oil platforms extract oil or gas, but rigs drill wells during exploration.

Tallest structure on this platform is flare stack, for safety reasons

Flare stack for burning off any gas that rises with the oil and cannot be used

Fireproof lifeboat gives better chance of survival

Derrick (a steel tower) holds drilling equipment

Crane hoists supplies up to platform from ship

Hand rail to protect personnel

Helicopter brings fresh food and milk to the platform

Living quarters

Helicopter pad

DEATH AND DECAY
Plant and bacteria remains from ancient seas fell to the seafloor and were covered by mud layers. Heat and pressure turned them into oil, then gas, which moved up through porous rocks, to be trapped by impermeable rocks.

Impermeable rock prevents oil from traveling farther

Oil is trapped in porous reservoir rock

Porous rock that oil can pass through

Formation of fossil fuels

AT WORK
On an oil platform, some people work on deck operating the drill, while others work inside with computers. Geologists examine rock, oil, and gas samples. Mechanics keep the machinery going. There are also cooks and cleaners to look after the crew.

ON THE BOTTOM
Divers (minus Newt suits) doing repairs underwater work longer if they return to a pressurized chamber, then back into the sea, without having to decompress after each dive.

Strong structure to withstand buffeting by wind and waves

Oxygen carried in cylinders on the back

NEWT SUIT
Thick-walled suits, like the one above, resist pressure. When underwater, the diver breathes air at normal pressure, as if inside a submersible. This means a diver can go deeper without having to undergo decompression. Newt suits (above) are used in oil exploration to depths of 1,200 ft (365 m). Joints in the arms and legs allow the diver to move.

Oceans in peril

Jewelry made of teeth of great white shark, now protected in some areas

THE OCEANS AND THE LIFE THEY SUPPORT are under threat. Sewage and industrial waste are dumped and poured from pipelines into the oceans. Carrying chemicals and metals, waste creates a dangerous buildup in the food chain. Oil spills, which smother marine life, do obvious damage. Garbage dumped at sea also kills. Turtles mistake plastic bags for jellyfish, and abandoned fishing nets entangle both seabirds and sea mammals. Over-harvesting has depleted many ocean animals, from whales to fishes. Even the souvenir trade threatens coral reefs. The situation is improving, however. New laws stop ocean pollution, regulations protect marine life, and in underwater parks people can look at ocean life without disturbing it.

Opening carved like a helmet

HAVE A HEART
Many people collect sea shells because of their beauty, but most shells sold in shops have been taken as living animals. If too many shelled creatures are collected from one place, such as a coral reef, the pattern of life can be disrupted. Shells should only be bought if the harvest is properly managed. It is better to go beachcombing and collect shells of already dead creatures. Always check before taking even empty shells, as some nature reserves do not permit this.

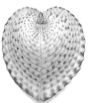

Heart cockle shells

OIL SPILL
Oil is needed for industry and motor vehicles. Huge quantities are transported at sea in tankers, sent along pipelines, and brought up from the seabed. Accidents happen and massive amounts of oil are spilled. Sea birds and sea mammals die of the cold, because their feathers or fur no longer contain pockets of air to keep them warm. Trying to clean themselves, animals die from consuming the oil, which also blocks their airways. Some are rescued, cleaned, and released back into the wild.

SAVING BEAUTY
No one can help but admire this beautiful 17th-century chambered nautilus shell. There are six kinds of nautilus living in the Pacific and Indian oceans, where they are all at risk from over-collecting. Live nautili are easily hunted at night when they rise to the surface, though dead shells can also be collected because they too float at the surface. Chambered nautili grow slowly, reaching maturity in six or more years. If too many are collected, the populations can take a long time to recover.

WORSE FOR WHALES

For centuries, whales have been hunted for their meat, oil, and bones. Whale oil was used in foods, as lubricants, and in soap and candles, and the broad baleen plates were made into household items such as brushes. The wholesale slaughter by commercial whalers drastically reduced the number of whales. Now most whales are protected, but scientists doubt whether some populations will ever recover their former numbers. Some kinds of whales are still caught for food, mainly by local people.

Japanese painting showing early whalers in small boats, risking their lives in pursuit of whales

Oily whale meat extract used to make margarine

Ground-up whale meal used in animal feed and pet food

Whale liver oil was a source of vitamin A

Sperm oil was a high-grade lubricant for motors and cars

Cameo panels set into engraved nautilus shell

Intricate floral pattern engraved in two colors

Sponges settled on scrap iron in a Red Sea harbor

OCEAN LITTER

Basket sponges can grow large enough for a diver to fit inside, but no one should do this because of possible damage to the sponge. One this size could be 100 years old. Many kinds of sea life are more fragile than they look. Corals can be damaged by being held or kicked by divers. All kinds of junk end up on the seabed (top right), even in the deep ocean. In the past, no one cared about dumping garbage at sea, but now there are laws to prevent this. Litter is still thrown from ships and dumped off coasts. Some disintegrates or is covered by marine life, but some plastics are virtually indestructible.

Index

Acknowledgments

DK would like to thank:

For their invaluable assistance during photography, providing specimens and species information:
The University Marine Biological Station, Scotland, especially Prof. John Davenport, David Murden, Bobbie Wilkie, Donald Patrick, Phil Lonsdale, Ken Cameron, Dr. Jason Hall-Spencer, Simon Thurston, Steve Parker, Geordie Campbell, and Helen Thirlwall.
The staff of Sea Life Centres (UK), especially Robin James, David Copp, Patrick van der Merwe, Ian Shaw, and Ed Speight (Weymouth); Rod Haynes (Blackpool); and Marcus Goodsir (Portsmouth).
David Bird at the Poole Aquarium.
The staff of the Natural History Museum, London, especially Oliver Crimmen of the Fish Department, Tim Parmenter, Simon Caslaw, Paul Ruddock, and Harry Taylor.
Jon Kershaw and the staff of Marineland, Antibes, France.
Ron Kastelein and the staff of Harderwijk Marine Mammal Park, Holland.
Adrian Friday and Ray Symonds at the University Museum of Zoology, Cambridge for the skeletons (pp. 85, 87, 98, 102, 105).
Bob Headland at the Scott Polar Institute, Cambridge, for the Inuit sculptures (pp. 77 and 104).
John Ward at the British Antarctic Survey for the krill (p. 87).

For their invaluable research help:
Colin Pelton, Peter Hunter, Dr. Brian Bett, and Mike Conquer of the Institute of Oceanographic Sciences.
Margaret Bidmead of the Royal Navy Submarine Museum, Gosport.
The Marine Biological Association (UK). The Marine Conservation Society (UK). Sarah Fowler of the Nature Conservation Bureau (UK).
Dr. Peter Klimley (University of California), Rolf Williams (UK), and Jocelyn Steedman (Vancouver, Canada).
IFREMER for their kind permission to photograph the model of *Nautile*.
David Fowler of Deep Sea Adventure.
Mark Graham, Andrew and Richard Pierson of Otterferry Salmon Ltd.
Bob Donaldson of Angus Modelmakers.
Sally Rose for additional research.
Kathy Lockley for providing props.

Helena Spiteri, Djinn von Noorden, David Pickering, Peter Bailey, Ivan Finnegan, Mark Haygarth, Chris Howson, Joe Hoyle, Jabu Mahlangu, Earl Neish, Manisha Patel, Sharon Spencer, and Susan St. Louis, for their editorial and design assistance.

Vassili Papastavrou would like to dedicate the marine mammals section of this book (pp. 74–107) to Catherine, and to thank Mel Brooks, Nigel & Jennifer Bonner, Tom Arnbom, Bill Amos, Denise Herzing, Graham Leach, Gill Hartley, Simon Hay, and Nick Davies.

Additional photography: Harry Taylor, Natural History Museum, London; Ivor Curzlake, British Museum, London (p. 95); Steve Gorton; Dave King (pp. 74, 94–95); Ray Möller; and Jerry Young (p. 75).

Model makers: Peter Griffiths and David Donkin
Maps: Sallie Alane Reason
Artwork: John Woodcock
Indexers: Marion Dent, Hilary Bird, Céline Carez, and Jane Parker

Editorial Coordinator: Marion Dent
Editors: Julie Ferris & Nicola Waine
Designer: Emma Bowden

Picture credits
(l =left r=right t=top b=below c=center a=above)

American Museum of Natural History (New York): 9tl (no. 419(2)), 82-83.
Ancient Art & Architecture: 74tl, 98tl.
Heather Angel: 34bc. ·
Ardea/F. Gohier: 80tl; D. Parer & E. Parer-Cook: 53tc; Ron & Valerie Taylor: 45br, 52cl, 53tl, 59bc; Val Taylor: 53bl, 124tl.
Tom Arnbom: 103tl, 103tr.
Auscape International/D. Parer & E. Parer-Cook: 96cr, 96br.
Aviation Picture Library/Austin J. Brown: 67br.
Tracey Bowden/Pedro Borrell: 117tc.
Bridgeman Art Library/Giraudon: 94tl; The Prado, Madrid: 7tr; *The Tooth Extractor* by Theodor Rombouts (1597-1637) 64bl; Private Collection: *The Little Mermaid* by E.S. Hardy 55tl; Uffizi Gallery, Florence: 12tr.
British Museum (London): 104tr, 116tr.
Cable & Wireless Archive: 40tr.
J. Allan Cash: 61br.
Bruce Coleman Ltd/Atlantide SDF: 121tr; Jane Burton: 34bl; Dr. I. Everson: 103cl; Jeff Foott: 24tr, 75bl, 97tr, 118tr; Charles & Sandra Hood: 23tc; F. Lanting: 97cr; Orion Service & Trading Co.: 120br; Dr. E. Potts: 99cr; H. Reinhard: 105tl; Carl Roessler: 18c; Michael Roggo: 119tl; Frieder Sauer: 22tr; Nancy Sefton: 125br.
Neville Coleman's Underwater Geographic Photo Agency: 54cr.
Steven J. Cooling: 123tr.
Dorling Kindersley/Colin Keates: 59tr, 64bl; Kim Taylor: 55tl; Jerry Young: 70cr.
Richard Ellis (US): 51r.
Mary Evans Picture Library: 9tr, 15tl, 16tl, 24tl, 29tr, 30tr, 36cl, 41tr, 46t, 68t, 94tr, 96tl, 98bl, 99tl, 104cl, 108tr, 110tr, 111tl, 112bl, 114tr, 116c, 122tl.
Peter Goadby (Australia): 62t.
Ronald Grant Archive: 38cl, 117bl.
T. Britt Griswold: 72b.
Tom Haight (USA): 73t.
Robert Harding Picture Library: 21tl, 28tr, 28bc, 35br, 52tr, 119tr, 125tl.
Michael Holford: 94bl.
The Hulton Picture Company: 66tl, 70cl.
I.F.A.W.: 93cr.
Institute of Oceanographic Sciences: 42lc.
Intervideo Television Clip Entertainment Group Ltd: 44t.
Jacana/F. Gohier: 82cl, 83cr.
© Japanese Meteorological Agency/Meteorological Office: 108l.
Frank Lane Photo Agency/Peter Lugårch: 102cl; M. Newman: 9br.
Eric Le Feuvre (USA): 54br.
William MacQuitty: 73bc.
Marineland/J. Foudraz: 91tr, 91c.
Minden Pictures/© F. Nicklin: 101tr.
N.H.P.A./Agence Natur: 40c; Joe B. Blossom: 57cr; P. Johnson: 92crb; T. Nakuniara: 92cl; John Shaw: 57tl.
National Marine Fisheries Service/Charles Stillwell: 57tc, 57tr.
Natural History Museum (London): 82b, 98-99.
Ocean Images/Rosemary Chastney: 62b, 63b, 63c; Walt Clayton: 49br; Al Giddings: 49cr, 73br; Charles Nicklin: 63br; Doc White: 54cl, 54bcl.
O.S.F./D. Allan: 80cl, 87b, 99tr, 99cra; D. Fleetham: 88bl; L.E. Lauber: 90cl.Oxford Scientific Films/Fred Bavendam: 39tl, 59cl; Tony Crabtree: 66b, 67t; Jack Dermid: 59cr; Max Gibbs: 61cbr; Rudie Kuiter: 71bl; Godfrey Merlen: 71br; Peter Parks 67c; Toi de Roy: 25tr; Norbert Wu 73cr.
V. Papastavrou: 100br.
Planet Earth Pictures/Steve Bloom: 33c; Gary Bell: 19br, 117tr; Neville Coleman: 29cr; Mark Conlin: 21c, 32br; Walter Deas: 58bc; Georgette Doowma: 125cr; Robert A. Jureit: 56c, 56cr, 57c, 57cl; A. Kerstitch: 55cr, 55bc, 55b; J. King: 100bl; Ken Lucas: 26tl, 54tr, 58cr; Larry Madin: 39br; Krov Menuhin 25tc, 61bl, 80tr; Andrew Mounter: 34br; D. Murrel 64t; Doug Perrine: 56cl, 57br, 59t, 60bc; Christian Petron: 70br; Brian Pitkin: 58tl; Peter Scoones: 7tl; Marty Snyderman: 54bl, 61t, 70t, 71t, 82cr, 95clb; Ken Vaughan: 113cr; James P. Watt: 64t, 64b, 65t, 65b; J. D. Watt: 74cl; Norbert Wu: 8–9c, 16cl, 36tr, 36tl, 37tl, 38tr, 60c.
Rex Features Limited/E. Thorburn: 89tr.
Roger-Viollet: 83tr.
Science Photo Library/Ron Church: 115cr; European Space Agency: 101tl; Dr. G. Feldman: 22bl; Simon Fraser: 124bl.
Sea Life Cruises/R. Fairbairns 79c.
Service Historique de la Marine, Vincennes/Gallimard Jeunesse 74bl.
Frank Spooner Pictures: 43tr, 43cr, 116br, 116bl, 122tr, 122cr.
Tony Stone Images/Jeff Rotman: 115lc.
Stolt Comex Seaway Ltd.: 123l.
Texas A & M University at Galveston/Dr. B. Würsig: 94br.
Town Docks Museum, Hull: 125tr.
Wild Dolphin Project Inc./D. Herzing 91tl, 93tl.
Rolf Williams: 50tl, 52cr (in block of six).
ZEFA: 32cl, 118ct.

Every effort has been made to trace the copyright holders of photographs. The publishers apologize for any omissions and will amend future editions.